Washed By The Water

Galveston Crime Scene Book 3

Leigh Jones

Galveston Crime Scene Press

Cover art by Elizabeth Mackey.

ISBN:

979-8-9896913-1-9 (paperback)

979-8-9896913-0-2 (hardback)

978-1-7334900-9-2 (ebook)

For Lynn

Thanks for celebrating each week's word count with me!
Your constant encouragement is a blessing.

He sent from on high, he took me;
he drew me out of many waters.
He rescued me from my strong enemy
and from those who hated me,
for they were too mighty for me.
They confronted me in the day of my calamity,
but the LORD was my support.
He brought me out into a broad place;
he rescued me, because he delighted in me.

Psalm 18:16-19

Chapter 1

"Bennett! What are you waiting for? Get in here."

Kate cringed as Managing Editor Kenton Mattingly's voice boomed through the newsroom. It seemed to rattle the storm-proof windows. Indignation swelled in her chest.

"I was waiting for you to tell me you were ready," she muttered under her breath.

But that wasn't quite true, as the twinge in her conscience reminded her. She'd been waiting with an illogical hope she could somehow avoid the meeting she'd been dreading for days.

Kate stood from her desk slowly and picked up a notebook out of habit. She wouldn't be asking the questions this morning. She would be answering them.

Mattingly stood behind his desk as she trudged into his office. A scowl of impatience twisted his perpetual look of annoyance into something much more fearsome. In one of the wing-backed chairs facing the desk sat the newspaper's lawyer. The slight smirk on his face suggested he was both amused and familiar with the managing editor's bark. He stood as Kate came around the other chair and held out his hand.

"Ms. Bennett, it's good to see you again." He smiled without conviction and dropped the hand she gave him almost as quickly as he'd grasped it.

Kate took a deep breath and focused on hiding her contempt behind a neutral expression. Carl Zimmerman had only one goal: keeping the newspaper out of legal trouble. And he had no interest in flexing the journalistic muscle necessary to defend the truth, no matter the cost. His aversion to legal risks hobbled all their work.

"We have five days until this trial begins," Mattingly said. "Mr. Zimmerman just wants to go over a few additional details with you to make sure you're ready."

To make sure I don't say anything that could get the newspaper in trouble, you mean, Kate grumbled to herself. But she nodded as she took her seat, clasping her hands tightly on top of the notebook in her lap. Her nerves stretched as tight as they had the first time she'd sat in that same chair, getting her first assignment for the Galveston Gazette two and a half years ago. Ironic, since that assignment had led to today's meeting.

"The district attorney has assured me he has no intention of raising any issues that could be problematic for us," Zimmerman said. "It's the defense I'm most concerned about."

No kidding. Kate forced herself to nod her agreement.

"Rhett Townsend is going to do everything he can to make you look bad, especially when it comes to your relationship with Detective Johnson."

Heat rushed into Kate's cheeks. She clenched her teeth in frustration. She'd known exactly where this conversation was headed and she still couldn't control her reaction at even the mention of Peter's name.

"I know that," she said, a little too sharply. She took a deep breath to slow her racing heart. "But we've been over this. It was my first day on the job, and I'd only known Detective Johnson for a few hours. That had absolutely no bearing on anything that happened that day."

Mattingly grunted. Zimmerman nodded slowly. "Unfortunately, that is irrelevant. All Townsend wants to do is make the jury think something other than duty influenced Detective Johnson. That alone will give his client a fighting chance at a lesser sentence."

The two cups of coffee she'd had for breakfast swirled in her stomach. Kate swallowed back a wave of nausea. Her desire for justice always burned like hot coals in her heart. But with Tommy Gage, it raged like an out-of-control forest fire. He deserved every minute of the two life sentences the district attorney would ask jurors to give him. Knowing anything she said or did could thwart that punishment made Kate sick.

For her first assignment at the Gazette, Mattingly had sent her to cover a suicide. A man had apparently jumped from the top of an abandoned downtown building. But it turned out he'd had help to hurtle to his death. Kate discovered the truth by accident when she went to interview the grieving widow. Instead, she found the couple's teenaged son. Tommy Gage had seemed slightly unbalanced when he invited her into the family home, but she chalked it up to shock. It was a nearly fatal mistake. Gage, who had murdered both his parents, took her hostage and tried to use her as a bargaining chip to negotiate his way out of a police standoff. Peter had saved her by crashing through the back door with a SWAT team and shooting Gage in the shoulder.

Two and a half years later, Gage was finally going to trial. And Kate was the star witness.

"You can bet your trip to Cuba will come up," Mattingly growled. He'd almost quit needling her about the Cuba trip, until it became obvious Gage's defense attorney would use it to his advantage during the trial. That had raised her boss's ire all over again.

Kate squeezed her hands together so hard her fingers turned red.

"I know that," she said again, more calmly this time. "I'm prepared to answer questions about that, even though it has nothing to do with what happened with Gage."

Zimmerman waved his hand impatiently. "The truth is irrelevant. It's all about the power of suggestion. And Townsend will suggest that his client is somehow the victim of a too-cozy relationship between you and Detective Johnson. Your best weapon against that attack is your reaction. Tell the truth, of course. But don't get tricked into believing it will save you—or condemn Gage. Only your demeanor on the stand can do that."

Kate suppressed a smile at the thought of how Peter would react to Zimmerman's cavalier take on the truth. They'd had many discussions about truth since their return from Cuba. Kate still struggled to believe Peter's explanation for its source, but she had always embraced its existence. Zimmerman's utilitarian view grated like nails on a chalkboard.

"The truth is reality," Kate said. "I have a better chance convincing the jury of what is real than Townsend does of persuading them to believe a lie."

"Don't bet on it," Mattingly huffed.

"Just remember, Townsend's goal isn't to make jurors believe his client is innocent. It's just to generate some sympathy in the hope they'll go easy on him."

Gage had pleaded not guilty by reason of insanity. Kate's testimony about what she'd heard and seen during the few hours he'd held her captive could torpedo that defense.

"You need to spend the next five days imagining every possible question Townsend could ask," Zimmerman continued. "Picture him asking them. Imagine how they will make you feel. His goal is to provoke an angry reaction that will make it look like you're hiding something. Get mad in your mind, by all means. But practice hiding it so no one, not even Detective Johnson, has any idea how you really feel."

Kate mashed her lips together. That shouldn't be too hard. She'd been doing that for the past year.

Detective Peter Johnson slapped the file down on the conference room table with a sigh. Its momentum carried it so far across the shiny surface that it almost slid into District Attorney Nathan Mahoney's lap. He looked up from his own notes with a raised eyebrow.

"That was a pretty cursory review," he said, disapproval creasing his forehead.

"I've read this report so many times in the last five months I could recite it by heart," Peter said.

"I hope so. I'll go through it with you on the stand in as much detail as possible. Hopefully that's what will stick in jurors' minds. But if you need to refer to it at any point when Townsend starts his questioning, don't hesitate to ask."

Peter nodded.

"He's going to come at you with everything he's got, anything he can find to make you look bad," the district attorney continued.

Peter nodded again. This wouldn't be the first time he'd gone toe-to-toe with a defense attorney.

"Even before your police career."

Peter's nodding stilled. He felt like he'd been hit by the Taser hanging innocuously at his hip. Alarm bells sounded in his head as anxiety crackled up his spine.

"That's never been an issue before," he said, barely forcing the words out through clenched teeth.

"You've never had to testify in a case that hinged on your character," Mahoney shot back. "I know you grew up overseas, but that's about all. Anything you need to tell me?"

Peter put every ounce of his concentration behind the withering look he gave as his reply.

Mahoney returned his look with narrowed eyes for several seconds before nodding curtly.

"Fine," he said. "I wasn't really worried about it, but I don't want him to catch you off guard if he asks about what you did before you got your badge. I'll object if he gets too far off track, but his primary goal will be to get you flustered. Try not to let anything surprise you. And if you start to get uncomfortable, don't let it show."

Uncomfortable wouldn't be the half of it if Townsend started asking about his childhood in Africa and his reasons for coming home. He'd never been more grateful that he'd kept that part of his life a secret from everyone. Even Kate. There was no way Tommy Gage's lawyer could dig those skeletons out of his closet.

"My biggest concern is Kate Bennett," Mahoney continued. "Your little tet-a-tet in Cuba did more than ruin my case against Aaron Newhouse. It put this one in jeopardy as well."

Peter bit back a caustic reply. Never mind that he and Kate had saved the district attorney from prosecuting an unwinnable case. In an election year, no less.

"That was eighteen months after Tommy Gage's arrest. It had absolutely nothing to do with it," he said calmly.

"Doesn't matter, and you know it," Mahoney said, pointing at Peter accusingly. "If Townsend can prove you have a relationship now, he stands a chance of convincing the jury that played a role in the way you handled the standoff with Gage."

"That's ridiculous. I'd only met her once!"

"The truth doesn't matter in this case, only doubt."

Peter shook his head. The pursuit of justice in an imperfect world sometimes required a strange mix of moral gymnastics and intellectual dishonesty.

"The truth is the only thing that matters," he said softly.

"Out there, maybe," Mahoney snapped, pointing toward the window. "But in the courtroom"—he jerked a thumb over his shoulder—"unfortunately, it's not."

Unwilling to scatter pearls before a professional arguer, Peter stood to go.

"Don't worry, I'll be ready when the trial starts on Monday."

"Good. And listen, Johnson, I know the chief is already breathing down your neck about Bennett, so this probably goes without saying. But stay away from her until this trial is over. I know you want to see Gage convicted. She does, too. Don't do anything to mess that up."

Peter felt like he was walking down the beach at high tide as he made for the door. His boss had warned him away from Kate for the last year. He'd done everything but threaten his job. But Peter sensed that ultimatum was right around the corner. He hoped he'd have more clarity from Kate before then. Walking away from his career was one thing. But could he do it without some assurance that he'd gain a far greater treasure in return? He'd spent his life living by faith. But this felt more like jumping off a cliff.

"Cheer up, this trial won't last forever." Delilah Peters, the Gazette's most senior reporter, stood in front of Kate's desk and flashed her a wicked grin. "It'll be instructive to experience it from the other side. Think of it as professional development."

Kate rolled her eyes, and Delilah laughed.

"And besides, you'll get tons of interesting material. You can write a book, retire from journalism, and live happily ever after with a certain law enforcement officer you're currently forbidden from seeing."

Kate scowled as Delilah's barb landed too close to her mark. "I have no intention of writing a book or retiring," she snapped.

Delilah leaned over so that her face was about a foot from Kate's. "What about the happily ever after part?"

"Argh, Delilah!" Kate snatched a notebook off her desk and threw it at her co-worker's hastily retreating back. The older woman's laugh sounded more like a cackle as the notebook missed her by a wide margin and landed harmlessly in the middle of the newsroom floor.

Kate caught a snicker to her left and glanced over in time to see business reporter Jessica Linton smirking at her. Kate resisted the urge to stick out her tongue. Jessica always brought out her inner second-grader.

Kate forced herself to look back at the city council agenda she'd been studying before Delilah's interruption. She'd already stared blindly at it for twenty minutes, but couldn't recall a single item. She put her elbow on her desk and rested her chin on her upturned hand. In a perverse reaction to what she knew she shouldn't do, all she could think about was calling Peter.

She felt like they'd been circling each other since the day they met—the day Tommy Gage tried to kill her. But for the last year, their circles had gotten tighter and tighter, developing a gravitational pull. Some days she fought it. Other days, she let herself slide, surrendering to the inevitability of the eventual collision. But next week's trial had knocked her out of orbit. And now that she had to step back and look at it from the outside, she saw how impossible the situation was.

She could no longer pretend she didn't have to make a decision.

The grating scrape of the newsroom door startled her out of her brooding. Ben Denison, the Gazette's police reporter, strode into the room, brandishing his cell phone.

"Heads up, kids," he said. "There's a storm brewing."

Tropical wave curls off African coast

Forecasters keeping an eye on storm's projected path | By Kate Bennett

A tropical disturbance formed in the Atlantic Ocean on Wednesday. If it spins into a hurricane, as forecasters expect, it will become the tenth named storm of this season.

None of the storms so far have threatened the Texas coast.

But the origins of this weather pattern have local officials worried. The unnamed storm that devastated Galveston in 1900 began in about the same spot.

"This storm—really potential storm—is a long way off," said Liam Arnold with the National Weather Service office in League City. "It's far too early to tell where it might end up. It could be the Yucatan Peninsula or central Florida."

Still, local officials encouraged Galveston residents to review their family emergency plans and stock up on batteries, bottled water, and non-perishable pantry items.

"It never hurts to be prepared," said Stephen Rush, the city's emergency management coordinator. "It's way too early to talk about evacuations, but it's always a good idea to know where you would go if you had to leave in a hurry."

Galveston has a long history of storms and recovery. Longtime residents, especially those who grew up on the island, have plenty of storm stories. Few include leaving.

"You won't catch me turning tail to run from a little bad weather," said Preston Hart, who was mowing the grass outside his home on 16th Street Thursday evening. "Aint never done it yet. Don't plan to start now."

When asked about an emergency plan or provisions, he shrugged.

"A flashlight and a cooler full of beer should just about do it, I reckon."

Gregory West, president of the Galveston Chamber of Commerce, said his biggest concern now was that bad weather might interrupt one of the last weekends of the summer season.

"We want to end this summer on a high note," he said. "Our beaches have been full, and so have our hotels. It's been a great year so far, and I expect that to continue."

Tracking models show the storm strengthening over the next few days as it moves toward the Caribbean. It could gain hurricane strength by Saturday, when forecasters will have a better idea of where it might make landfall.

Chapter 2

The next morning, Kate smacked her alarm clock with more force than usual and rolled over. Bright sunlight streamed through the nearly floor to ceiling windows of her downtown loft apartment. From where she lay, she could see cerulean skies overhead. She groaned and pulled the covers up over her head.

For the last week, Tommy Gage had haunted her dreams. His shadowy presence loomed large and menacing over everything. She spent all night trying to escape. He never caught her, but she never got away either. And every morning she woke up overwrought and exhausted.

She dragged herself to the kitchen and fumbled in the cabinet above the coffeepot. When her hand grasped air, instead of the comforting crunch of her favorite dark roast, she brought her fist down on the counter. With yesterday's drama over the trial and the late-breaking news about the storm, she'd forgotten she needed to stop at the store.

To make up for her lack of caffeine, she took a long, hot shower, letting the water loosen the knots in her neck and shoulders. When it ran cold, she turned it off and wrapped herself in a towel. She stood staring into her closet for several minutes, time she rarely bothered wasting. But yesterday, she'd dressed up for her meeting with Zimmerman. Today, she wanted to be comfortable, especially if Mattingly sent her out to do any more man-on-the-street storm prep interviews. She pulled on a cotton skirt and a T-shirt nice enough to pass for office casual on a Friday and ran a wide-toothed comb through her hair. After applying a little eyeliner, mascara, and light pink lip gloss, she was ready. She grabbed her laptop bag and car keys and headed out the door.

The late August morning had already reached a simmer by the time she opened the door to her building and stepped onto the sidewalk. She glanced up. Not a cloud in sight.

It took her less than five minutes to walk to her favorite coffee shop, where the usual group of locals already filled the outside tables. She waved in greeting and smiled when she saw they were reading the hurricane story that topped the front page.

"I don't like the look of this one," called an older man sitting with several friends in the middle of the patio. He waved the paper in her direction and pointed to her byline.

"Don't be ridiculous," scoffed one of his table mates. "A little rain, that's all. We could all use a break from this miserable heat."

The worrier grunted. "I hope you're right. But we're due, you know."

Kate shook her head as she stepped inside the shop and walked up to the counter. That tug of war between fear and apathy shaped the island's approach to storms. It had been decades since anything terrible had blown ashore, but islanders lived with the constant threat hanging over their heads. The only way to endure that tension was to pretend the big one would never come.

Kate ordered a triple-shot Americano and moved to the end of the counter to wait. She closed her eyes and tried to block out the conversation between the two teenagers at the nearest table.

"I hope it comes into the Gulf at least," the girl said.

"Why? Then I'll have to spend hours helping my dad board up our windows."

"Yeah, but maybe they'll delay the start of school, and we'll get a few more days of summer!"

Kate grabbed her coffee as soon as the barista set it down on the counter and bolted for the door. The teen's prattle grated on her nerves, but as she took her first scalding sip, a kernel of anticipation took root. If this storm did end up heading for Galveston, maybe it would interrupt the Gage trial and give her a few more days of peace. She grimaced. Scratch that. She wanted this nightmare over as soon as possible.

Before heading out to the newspaper office, Kate stopped by city hall. She ducked past the main suite on the first floor, where the mayor and city manager had their offices, and headed to the second floor. She wound her way down the labyrinthine back hallways until she reached the closet-sized space occupied by the city's communications director. Ashleigh Tarver had only held the job for six months, and Kate had worked hard to turn her into an ally. She'd mostly succeeded in preventing her from becoming an adversary.

Kate tapped lightly on the open door.

"Hey, Kate," the fresh-faced young woman said, looking up with a smile from the thick three-ring binder spread open on her desk. "Thanks to your story in today's paper, I'm spending my morning brushing up on the city's hurricane plan."

"Anything interesting?" Kate asked, perching on the edge of the chair that barely fit into the narrow space between the door and the desk.

Ashleigh waved her hand vaguely. "Not especially. Just protocols for calling evacuations and organizing the initial cleanup efforts."

"Based on what I heard this morning when I was getting my coffee, I think evacuation's going to be a tough sell."

Ashleigh nodded gravely. "I can't imagine the mayor would call for anything more than a voluntary evacuation, unless it looked really bad."

"He certainly won't do anything unpopular," Kate sneered.

Ashleigh kept her eyes locked on the binder, studying the open page as though she'd just discovered something she hadn't seen before. Kate bit her lip. She tried to squash her disdain for Mayor Matthew Hines in public, but sometimes it evaded her best efforts. Most people didn't know the truth about his involvement in a sex trafficking scandal Kate had covered during her first year in Galveston. She'd never gotten over his complicity and willingness to cover for his friend, the ring's mastermind.

"This will be your first storm, right?" she asked, returning to safer subjects. "I mean, if it comes ashore anywhere near us."

Ashleigh nodded. "I remember a few pretty intense tropical storms growing up, but no hurricanes."

"People seem to think we're due for a bad one, whatever that means."

A spark of fear ignited in the young woman's blue eyes before she blinked it away and plastered a confident smile on her face.

"I'm sure no matter what happens, we'll be ready. It's not like we don't have plenty of time to prepare."

Kate nodded absently but couldn't help think of the coverage she'd seen last year of the storm that struck the Florida panhandle. They'd had plenty of time to prepare, too, but there's only so much you can do against 150-mile-an-hour winds. The damage was catastrophic.

"Well, keep me posted if the mayor or city manager calls any news conferences," she said, standing up and inching her way around the chair.

"You'll be the first one I call!" Ashleigh said in a sing-song voice. Kate knew for sure that wasn't true. Hanes would want the Houston television crews to be the first ones to know about anything he had to say. The *Gazette* was the least of his concerns. Ashleigh was only doing her job, but Kate wished she felt a little less loyalty to her undeserving boss.

Kate started down the stairs toward the front lobby when she thought better of it and turned toward the public works office. The director was one of her best inside sources at city hall. He'd worked in the department for nearly 30 years, under four different city managers and more than twice that many mayors. He was loyal only to his job and the island, where his family had lived since before the 1900 storm. And his son was a hot-shot TV reporter in Dallas, so he had a soft-spot for journalists.

When Kate walked into the office, the secretary waved at her to go on back. Eddie Vasquez was sitting at his desk, with the newspaper spread out in front of him.

"Looks like you'll get to add 'hurricane coverage' to your resume," he said, glancing up just long enough to see who it was.

"Ashleigh Tarver says you guys have everything under control, so I'm sure it will be an easy assignment," Kate smirked, leaning against the door frame.

Eddie snorted and rolled his eyes. "Only a few of us here have even been through a storm. Ain't no picnic, I'll tell you that."

"And we're due," Kate said, parroting the ominous warning she'd heard several times.

"That we are," Eddie said, eyeing her over the top of the newspaper. "People's gonna tell you this ain't nothing to worry about. But I've got a bad feeling about this one."

A tremor of unease fluttered in Kate's chest. "Why? Is it just because of the comparisons to the 1900 storm?"

He shrugged. "Not sure, exactly. Just a feeling I've got. I called my son last night and told him to expect a visit from his mother next week if this thing keeps coming the way they're expecting."

Kate's eyebrows shot up. "Your wife would leave?"

"Darn right! I can't do my job and look after her. Best thing would be for her to get the heck out of dodge."

"You really think it's going to be that bad?" Kate asked, trying not to sound worried.

He shrugged again and held her gaze for several moments before breaking into a smile.

"We'll come out okay. The island always does."

Kate smiled in return. The 1900 storm had given Islanders a sense of invincibility. If Galveston could recover from that, it could recover from anything. Of course, thousands of people didn't recover. Kate shuddered and pushed herself off the door frame to hide it.

"Alright, well, let me know if you hear anything the mayor doesn't want me to know," she said with a grin.

"You bet," he said, winking conspiratorially.

She was halfway down the hall when he called her back.

"Do me a favor. Go get yourself some supplies this weekend, before they all sell out."

Kate held his gaze, wide-eyed. Then she simply nodded and walked away.

After she filed her story for the day, a fluffy feature for the Sunday edition about a new neighborhood park, Kate snuck out of the office a little early. She had a date with Peter for dinner, and she still had to pick up a few things at the grocery store on her way home. Before going through the checkout line, she hefted a case of bottled water into her cart. From an end cap, she snagged a double pack of batteries. The cashier smiled knowingly as she rang up the items.

Kate felt foolish as she lugged the heavy water from the parking garage to her building under a cloudless sky and the sweltering evening sun. By the time she made it to the elevator, sweat drenched her back. She left the water just inside her front door, crammed the groceries into the refrigerator, and ran for the shower.

Thirty minutes later, she felt both cleaner and calmer as she stood at the kitchen counter tearing up lettuce for a salad. She'd been looking forward to this night all week.

A soft knock at the door sent her pulse pounding in her ears. She didn't need to bother looking through the peephole to know who was standing on the other side.

"Uber eats?" she called out teasingly as she slid back the deadbolt. Peter's chuckle made her breath catch in her throat.

"That would make a good disguise," he said, raising the dish in his hand. "I did bring food."

Kate laughed and stood aside to let him in. The savory tang of grilled chicken vied with the fresh scent of his cologne as he walked past. He set the dish on the table and turned to face her. They'd done this dance for a year. He extended an unspoken offer and waited to see if she would take the first step. Not a day had gone by that she didn't want to throw herself into his arms and give up her sham resistance. Too often, fear overpowered that desire.

But tonight would be their last time together for a while. She refused to go weeks without savoring a taste of what had grown between them. Just as he started to turn away, she took three quick steps forward and wrapped her arms around his waist. She could feel his heart hammering against her cheek as she pressed into his chest. His arms circled her back, and he took a deep, shuddering breath.

They stood that way for several moments. Kate willed him to understand everything she felt but was too afraid to say.

Reluctantly, she loosened her grip, glancing into his eyes as she pulled back. They glistened with unspoken promise and hope. He hadn't explicitly told her how he felt, not since his last faltering attempt in Cuba. But he didn't have to. It rang loud and clear from every glance, every smile. And it scared her to death.

She stepped back, widening the space between them to a safer distance.

"If you're thirsty, I've got plenty of water," she said lightly, pointing toward the door.

He turned slightly to follow her gaze. "Since when do you waste money on bottled water?" he asked, his teasing tone matching hers.

"Eddie Vasquez made me promise I would get some emergency supplies. He's convinced this is the big one."

"Well, supposedly we're due."

"So I've heard. Is everyone at the station talking about it?"

"Not really. I mean, it's a long way off. I'm surprised Vasquez is worried."

Kate shrugged. "He said he just had a bad feeling."

"Let's hope he's wrong," Peter said, picking up his dish and moving toward the kitchen counter. "Are you ready for me to cut this up?"

She nodded and pulled out a cutting board and knife. They chatted as they worked, falling into the comfortable rhythm they'd built up and relied on for months. After dinner, they settled onto the couch. Kate curled up in her usual corner, and Peter took the middle.

"How are you feeling about next week?" he asked, turning sideways so he could see her face.

Kate shrugged and looked toward the window. Outside, the setting sun had turned the sky to orange sherbet. She twisted her hands together in her lap and squeezed until her fingers felt ready to burst. Peter reached out and placed his hand over hers.

"It's going to be okay." He rubbed his thumb across the back of her hand until she released her grip.

She took a deep breath and turned back to meet his gaze. "Why does it feel like you and I are going to be the ones on trial?"

"Because coming after us is the only hope Gage has of getting any sympathy from the jury."

Kate shook her head. "Do you think it will work?" she asked after a pause. She hated the hint of desperation in her voice.

"I pray it won't. All we can do is tell the truth and let God take care of the rest."

She looked away again and chewed on her bottom lip. Peter squeezed her hand gently.

"He's done a pretty good job of looking after us so far," he whispered.

She'd spent a year trying to believe that. Peter needed her to believe it. He'd never said as much, but she knew accepting his faith would never be enough. She had to share it before they could move forward. Sometimes her desire to surrender thrashed so hard she could barely contain it. But her fear of letting go always came out a little stronger.

"I guess all the details of our trip to Cuba are going to come out now," she said with a grimace.

Peter laughed. "I don't think Mahoney will let it go that far. He'll object before we have to reveal anything too salacious."

Kate rolled her eyes and tried not to smile. "Good thing. Mattingly's getting all worked up about it again, just when I thought he'd finally let it go. If the whole story comes out, I'll never hear the end of it."

"You did exhibit a shocking lack of discretion."

"In more ways than one."

They both laughed. Kate looked down at his hand, still covering hers. She hesitated a moment and then laced her fingers through his. She tried to memorize the feel of his palm against hers and the warmth of his skin.

"It will be over before we know it," he murmured.

"Then what?"

"Then we don't have to worry about it anymore."

"I don't think the chief sees it that way," she said before she could stop herself.

"The chief—" Peter drowned whatever he was going to say in a sigh. "Let's just deal with one challenge at a time, okay?"

She nodded. But she knew that inevitable reckoning loomed on the horizon. They couldn't tip-toe around the edges of Sam Lugar's disapproval for much longer. Something would have to give.

"It's going to be a long few weeks," she said quietly.

"Tell me about it."

Chapter 3

Peter swiped at his alarm clock, sending several books tumbling off his nightstand. But the blaring noise that had dragged him from sleep didn't stop. He made another pass at the alarm clock before realizing the noise was coming from his phone. He slid his fingers across the screen to answer the call before he'd even pulled it to his ear.

"Johnson," he croaked.

"We need you down at the jail, detective," said a voice his brain slowly identified as belonging to his lieutenant. "We've had an escape."

Peter sat bolt upright, the fog of sleep immediately cleared.

"Who is it?"

"Tommy Gage."

Peter stared at the screen, disbelief paralyzing his vocal chords.

"Johnson?"

"I'm on my way," he stammered, tossing the phone onto the bed without bothering to hang up.

He glanced at the clock as he peeled back the covers and jumped to his feet. 6 a.m. The inmates would have finished breakfast already. He ran for the bathroom, grabbing a clean shirt and pants from the closet on his way. His surging adrenaline made his hands shake as he clipped his gun to his belt and grabbed his keys off the dresser. He debated calling Kate. If Gage was on the loose, she needed to know.

But surely they would have him back in custody before he could do any harm. No need to worry her, yet.

Twenty minutes later, he came to a screeching halt in the parking lot of the Galveston County Jail. His lights weren't the only ones strobing off the buildings in the early morning haze. Half a dozen squad cars parked at odd angles at the front of the jail. An ambulance held the closest spot, and Peter's chest tightened as he watched medics at work on someone lying on a gurney. Even from 50 feet away, he could see the drab khaki of a Sheriff's Department uniform.

He jogged up to a group of deputies and officers gathered near the jail's front door. In the middle stood Captain Mark Abbott, commander of the department's corrections division.

"What happened?" Peter asked as soon as he got close enough to talk without shouting.

"Gage jumped one of my men while he was taking him down to the infirmary," Abbott said. "He got into a fight during breakfast and acted like he broke his arm. Deputy

Travis Barker was taking him to have it checked out when Gage attacked him. He had a shank."

The man's voice broke, and Peter grasped his shoulder.

"I don't know if Barker's gonna make it. Gage stabbed him several times. He lost a lot of blood."

The paramedics who'd been working on the deputy hustled the gurney into the ambulance. Within seconds, it sped away, sirens wailing. Peter turned back to the group, fury bursting into flame. How had this happened?

"I'm going to go check things out inside. Is the sheriff on the way?"

Abbott nodded miserably. Not only was he facing the loss of one of his men, he had to know he might lose his job, too. Peter's stirrings of sympathy warred with his own anger. Gage should never have been allowed to interact with other prisoners, especially this close to his trial.

Inside, Galveston police officers and sheriff's deputies milled around the lobby like sheep without a shepherd. After a few moments of searching, Peter spotted Lieutenant Mark Jarrell. He stood in the corner talking to one of the Sheriff's Department investigators. Jarrell waved Peter over.

"We've already got people working on the manhunt," Jarrell said, as if he knew that would be Peter's first question. "They're setting up a checkpoint on the causeway to keep him from getting off the island. We're also working up a search grid for the city. I want you here, helping with the investigation into what happened."

Peter clenched his teeth to keep from protesting. Gage was already gone. Why bother wasting time now trying to figure out how he did it? All that mattered was getting him back in custody before he hurt anyone else.

Jarrell held up his hand. "I know you're probably worried about Bennett. We'll send an officer to her apartment."

Relief washed over him like a sudden summer rain. "Thank you, sir," he said, his voice tight with the strain of juggling the barrage of anger and worry.

"Now, I'm betting Gage had help," Jarrell said. "We need to know who knew about this and whether they have any idea what he might have planned next. This is the sheriff's investigation, but we're going to give them every bit of help we can."

Peter nodded at the ranking deputy in the group. He'd met Captain Alonzo Gutierrez several times, although he'd never worked with him. He knew the other deputies liked the barrel-chested captain, but at the moment, that didn't matter. All Peter cared about was that the man knew how to do his job.

"Good," said Jarrell, turning to the captain. "I'll leave you to it, then. I need to go brief the chief and check on the manhunt."

Gutierrez jerked his head toward the open door leading into the jail. "Let's go see what we can find out."

Peter followed him through the opening. Just inside, they had to step around a wide pool of blood.

"This is where it happened," Gutierrez growled. "Gage probably pulled out the shank on the way to the infirmary and forced Barker to keep walking until they got here. Then he made him open the door."

"He didn't need to stab him, but he did anyway," Peter said, his fury and fear rising like a storm tide.

Gutierrez looked just as angry, like he might tear Gage into tiny pieces if he could get his hands on him.

"What happened to the guy he got into a fight with?" Peter asked.

"Sent him back to his cell like everyone else. We'll have them bring him down."

Gutierrez waved a thick arm at a deputy standing nearby and told him to have the inmate brought into the chow hall.

"That way, he can show us exactly what happened," Gutierrez said.

Food, plates, and trays still littered the tables and floor of the large room. Peter narrowed his eyes as he looked at the mess. If Gage wanted a distraction, this was the best way to do it. Most of the deputies would have been busy restoring order while just one man took him to the infirmary. All he had to do was wait for the right moment to pounce.

About five minutes later, the deputy Gutierrez had dispatched came back, leading a subdued-looking prisoner. He still had a trail of blood down his cheek. Gutierrez motioned for the deputy to have the man sit.

"Name!" he barked, making the question sound like an order.

"Rudy Williams."

"What are you in for?"

"Drugs."

Gutierrez grunted. "So what happened this morning?"

"Gage tripped me when I was just mindin' my own business, trying to eat my breakfast real quiet like. Stupid little punk. Thought he was all that just because he killed his parents. He was always lookin' for trouble."

"So you jumped on him?"

"Straight up! I'm not playing around, man."

"What happened then?"

"We rolled around on the floor until guards broke it up," he said, shrugging. "Weren't no big deal. But when they pulled me off him, he starts hollering about his arm. Said it was broken. Too bad it weren't."

"You know what Gage did after that?"

"Course I know. Everybody know. But if he's out there, I don't know why you're in here hassling me. I didn't stab nobody."

"Rudy," Peter said, trying a softer tone than his temporary partner. "Did you know Gage had a shank?"

Williams shook his head. "If I'd a known that, I wouldn't have jumped on him, now would I?"

"Unless you knew he didn't plan to use it on you," Peter said.

Williams hesitated just long enough to bolster Peter's suspicions.

"That's crazy, man. How would I know that?" Williams said.

Gutierrez brought his meaty hand down on the table in front of Williams with a bang that made the man jump.

"Only way you would know that is if you knew he was planning to escape."

"Naw, not me." Williams shook his head, but the ghost of a smile tugged at the corners of his mouth.

"Gage needed a distraction and a reason to go to the infirmary," Peter said, the pieces falling into place in his mind. "What did he promise you in return for helping him?"

"You got it all wrong, man," Williams said with a laugh. "Why would I help that little punk? He don't mean nothing to me."

Peter watched him thoughtfully and then glanced up at Gutierrez. He shrugged.

"You got a family?" Gutierrez asked. "Maybe some kids? A mom? Did Gage promise to give them something if he made it out? Maybe some money?"

The laughter melted from the inmate's face. A wariness took its place.

"That's it, isn't it?" Peter asked softly.

Williams looked down but said nothing.

"We'll just have to pay his family a visit," Gutierrez said, his voice heavy with a veiled threat. "Maybe bring them in for questioning. Might need to get a social worker to check out the kids, make sure they're okay."

Williams glared at him.

"Rudy, if you're just here on drug charges, why risk helping Gage? You know this makes you an accessory to assaulting an officer, and whatever else Gage does before we catch him. Seems like a dumb choice to me."

"Y'all don't know what you're talking about," he muttered, staring at his shoes.

"Guess you'll be needing to get in touch with your lawyer, then," Gutierrez said. "You better believe the DA's going to be pressing charges."

"Can't prove nothin'" Williams scoffed, but his bravado sounded much less convincing than it had at the start of their conversation.

"And you'd better pray Barker doesn't die," Gutierrez hissed, leaning down until his face was just inches from the inmate's. "Man's got a wife and kids. If he dies, you're looking at a murder charge."

Williams kept his eyes glued to the floor.

"Get him out of here," Gutierrez barked.

The deputy who'd been standing behind Williams grabbed him by the arm and hauled him to his feet.

"Rudy," Peter called as the deputy led him away. "If you want to change your story, let us know."

Williams glared at them over his shoulder as the deputy led him through the door to the cell block.

"He's guilty as sin," Gutierrez said, kicking a bowl near his feet. It bounced across the floor with a clatter.

"We can go talk to his family, but I'm not sure how much good it will do. Might be better to have an undercover officer keep an eye on them, just in case Gage shows up. I can't imagine he'd be that stupid, though. He'd have to know that would be the first place we'd start looking."

Gutierrez grunted again. "We need to talk to his lawyer. See what he knew."

"And find out from the guards whether Gage had anybody that he'd developed a relationship with. Anyone else who might have known what he had planned and where he might be headed."

"I know you're worried," Gutierrez said. His voice didn't sound soft, but it lacked some of the edge it had carried up to this point. "We'll find him."

Peter nodded. But a growing dread lapped at the edges of his mind. Gage had proved there was nothing he wouldn't do to get what he wanted. Peter could only pray that didn't include hurting Kate.

Each ring of the phone doubled Peter's fear. Why didn't she answer? Between the first and second ring, he imagined Gage prowling up the stairs in Kate's building. Between the second and third ring, he was inside the apartment, swinging his deadly handmade weapon up to strike. Peter jumped to his feet, ready to bolt to his car, when Kate answered.

"Hey," she said. She sounded a little out of breath.

"Are you okay?" he blurted, abandoning all plans to stay calm to keep her calm.

"Yes, why wouldn't I be?"

"You didn't pick up right away, and it sounds like you were running."

"I just went downstairs to get the mail. I heard my phone ringing halfway up the stairs, so I jogged the rest of the way."

Any other time, her annoyance would have prompted him to tread gently. Today, it only added fuel to his own anxiety.

"Kate," he said, more sternly than he intended. "I need to tell you something."

"Okay." She only sounded slightly less annoyed.

"Tommy Gage escaped this morning."

Her sharp gasp tugged at his heart. He should have driven downtown to tell her in person. For several moments, silence hung between them.

"How?" she finally stammered.

"He orchestrated a fight in the mess hall and got himself a trip to the infirmary. On the way, he pulled out a shank, forced the deputy to open the door, and then stabbed him."

"Oh, no!" Kate gasped. "Is he dead?"

"I don't know. They rushed him to the hospital right after I got here. I haven't heard anything else."

"Peter..." Her voice sounded thin, filled with fear.

"Kate, listen, we're going to catch him. We've got everyone in the sheriff's and police departments on this. He won't get far."

She didn't say anything, but the ragged sound of her breathing echoed through the phone.

"Kate?"

"I'm here. And I'm fine. I mean, thanks for calling to tell me."

Peter frowned. She had retreated into her emotional safe room, where she pretended nothing could touch her and no one could see her vulnerability. But he had witnessed that trick too many times before.

"Kate," he murmured. "I know you're scared. I am, too. But we will get him. And we will keep you safe. There's already an officer at your building. He'll stay with you all day, at least until Gage is in custody."

"You think I need my own bodyguard?" The sarcastic edge to her voice didn't phase him a bit.

"For now, yes. If I know someone else is keeping an eye out for you, I can focus on trying to find Gage."

Kate sighed. "Okay. Just be careful."

"I will. I'm working with Alonzo Gutierrez to figure out if anyone knows what Gage has planned. The guys out searching are in much more danger than I am."

"Still," Kate said, the hint of a smile lightening her voice just slightly.

"Listen, I don't know what you have planned for today, but it would probably be best if you stayed at the newspaper and didn't go running around all over town."

"Mattingly's going to love that," she huffed.

"It's just for today."

"Fine."

"Thank you for your cooperation."

Kate laughed. "I'm a model of compliance."

"I'm pretty sure no one has ever said that about you. I certainly never have."

She snorted, making him grin. Her normal sass had returned, a sign that she'd at least recovered from the initial shock. Relief eased the tension in his shoulders.

"I'm sure Ben will be the one working on this, but call me this afternoon, just to let me know how it's going," she said.

"I will." He hesitated. He'd kept a tight rein on his feelings for the past year to avoid pressuring her. But that didn't seem to matter now.

"Kate," he whispered, struggling to come up with the right words.

"It's okay," she said. "I know."

Kate trudged up the steps to the *Gazette*'s front door, her temporary body guard right behind her.

"I'll just take a quick look around the building and then stay in the lobby," he said.

She nodded her thanks and pulled open the heavy glass door. She gave the wide-eyed receptionist a short explanation before fleeing to the newsroom. Her cheeks burned with embarrassment. It felt like everyone was staring at her. And she dreaded having to tell her boss that she now had a police escort.

"Bennett!" Mattingly's voice boomed before she was halfway to her desk.

Reluctantly, she dragged herself into his office. News Editor Hunter Lewis was already there, sitting in one of the chairs facing Mattingly's desk. A worried frown creased his forehead.

"I've just had a call from the police chief," Mattingly said as she eased herself into the other chair. "Helluva development."

His bushy eyebrows drew together, but not with the fury, indignation, or ever-present grumpiness she was used to seeing. This was genuine concern, and it made her squirm.

"Yeah, it's a huge pain," she said, hoping to cut off any outright expression of sympathy.

"Humph," Mattingly said. "Maybe. But necessary. I suppose you already know they're going to keep someone posted here all day. At least until he's caught."

Kate nodded.

"Right, well, I told the chief I'd make sure you stayed put, for today anyway."

A flutter of concern that had danced around the edges of her thoughts burst into full-fledged anxiety.

"What about tomorrow? What if they haven't caught him by then?"

Before Mattingly could respond, Lewis's phone blared with a nerve-rattling weather alert. Kate watched him as he looked down, his worry lines deepening into furrows.

"Looks like we've got a hurricane headed our way," he said.

BREAKING: Hurricane forms in Atlantic

Forecast models put Galveston in its sights | By Kate Bennett

The storm that spun to life two days ago off the coast of Africa is now Hurricane Julio.

As of Friday morning, it was about 200 miles east of Jamaica. Forecasters with the National Weather Service expect it to hit the Caribbean island tomorrow.

Models put Galveston squarely in the center of the cone of uncertainty.

"It's still way too early for anyone to panic," said Liam Arnold, a forecaster with the National Weather Service office in League City. "But certainly we want everyone to keep an eye on the weather and be prepared for a potential landfall toward the end of next week."

City of Galveston officials say they are in close contact with the weather service and will make a decision about public shelters once the storm's path becomes more clear. Spokeswoman Ashleigh Tarver said Mayor Matthew Hanes would not rule out ordering an evacuation but only if the storm looked like it would be a direct hit.

"Galveston is well-prepared for storms," she said. "We've certainly had plenty of them. Our crews will be out over the next few days checking all the city's vital systems, but residents should rest assured that we are ready."

Stephen Rush, the city's emergency management coordinator, encouraged all island residents to take time over the weekend to restock their storm supplies.

If Julio maintains its current speed, it could enter the Gulf of Mexico by the middle of next week.

Chapter 4

Peter's long strides carried him the length of the Sher-iff's Department conference room. When he reached the far wall, he spun around and paced back to where Alonzo Gutierrez sat at a sleek table. He was about to turn back to make another futile pass when the sheriff's deputy held up his hand.

"Stop." His firm voice wasn't harsh, but it held a note of command Peter couldn't ignore. "Save your energy for the investigation."

Peter gripped the back of a chair, squeezing all his frustration into its padded back. Every minute Gage remained on the loose compromised Kate's safety. He knew the officer assigned to watch her would do his job, but it was hard to know her life was in anyone's hands but his own.

Before he could do the chair any permanent damage, Sheriff Tyler Metcalf stalked through the door, followed closely by Police Chief Sam Lugar.

"Any word on Barker?" Gutierrez asked.

"Still in surgery," Metcalf said. "But it doesn't look good."

Gutierrez made no reply, but his jaw muscles bunched so tight it looked like he had a wad of gum in each cheek. Sympathy and fear warred in Peter's heart. If Gage didn't hesitate to kill a man he had no specific animosity toward, what would he do to the person he blamed for his arrest in the first place?

"We've got every deputy we can spare patrolling the neighborhoods around the jail," the sheriff continued, sitting down in the chair at the head of the table. "We're setting up a perimeter around a 20-block area. No one goes in or out without proof they live there. Anyone who looks suspicious will be searched."

Peter looked questioningly at Lugar.

"The Sheriff's Department is securing the perimeter," the chief said. "Our officers are going door to door."

"What did you two find out at the jail?" Metcalf asked.

"Pretty sure the man Gage picked a fight with was in on the plan," Gutierrez said. "We just don't know why. Yet. We need to find out what kind of family he's got and pay them a visit."

"What's he in for?"

"Drugs." Gutierrez held up several pages of the case file he and Peter had picked up when they got back from the jail. "Serial offender. Started when he was still a kid. This is his third stay with us."

"How long's his sentence?"

"Not long enough," Gutierrez sneered. "Three years."

"He's not a major dealer then."

"Case file said the narcotics team suspected he was dealing, but when they arrested him, he didn't have enough on him to make the charges stick. He pleaded guilty to possession for a lesser sentence."

"Any ties to Gage before they both ended up behind bars?" Lugar asked.

"We're not sure, but that's one of the things we need to find out," Peter said, trying to tamp down his growing frustration. The longer they stayed stuck in this building, the longer it would take them to find any useful information.

"Seems unlikely, but who knows?" Gutierrez added with a shrug.

"Right, well, go see what you can find out. We'll meet back here at three to debrief and plan the next phase of the manhunt, assuming we haven't caught him by then."

Gutierrez nodded and stood. Peter fell in behind him, but Lugar cleared his throat.

"One more thing," he said. "We can't ignore the possibility that Gage may have more on his mind than getting away. He may want to settle some scores first."

Peter's stomach twisted.

"We've already got someone watching Kate Bennett. It's probably worth putting someone on Gage's lawyer, too. He's another obvious point of contact. Be sure you talk to him, too. And soon."

The address in Williams' file led them to a rundown house north of Broadway and south of the port. It was a step up from the island's public housing projects, but only a small step. The house looked like it might collapse in a strong thunderstorm, but a shiny Dodge Charger sat in the driveway, its black paint glittering in the sunlight.

Gutierrez swatted open the tattered screen door that hung loosely on its hinges and pounded on the front door. A piece of weathered plywood covered one front window. Foil lined the glass of the other, making it impossible to see inside. Gutierrez took a step back, giving himself enough room to react to anything unexpected.

Peter breathed a sigh of relief when an older woman answered the door. Bright pink sponge curlers dotted her head, and she wore socks and fuzzy slippers, despite the heat. She didn't look threatening, but she frowned savagely at the two law enforcement officers on her stoop.

"May I help you?" she asked, loading each word with as much disdain as it could carry.

"Are you Lashonta Williams?" Gutierrez asked.

"I am."

"We'd like to ask you a few questions about your son, Rudy."

"You already got him locked up," she said, crossing her arms over her ample chest. "Why don't you ask him yourself?"

"Yes, ma'am, we did," Peter said quickly, before Gutierrez could say anything to alienate the woman even more. "But he was understandably cautious. We're just trying to explore all our options. And warn you about a potential danger."

The woman's eyes narrowed. "What kind of danger?"

"Rudy got into a fight with another inmate this morning. He wasn't seriously hurt, but the other inmate said he thought he'd broken his arm and needed to go to the infirmary. On the way, he stabbed the deputy escorting him and escaped."

A tiny hint of worry flashed in the woman's eyes. "What's that got to do with Rudy? He didn't try to escape, did he? Or do anything to a deputy?"

"No, ma'am, he didn't. But we think he might have known what this other inmate had planned. We think the fight might have been staged."

"Does the name Tommy Gage mean anything to you?" Gutierrez asked.

She frowned. "Isn't that the boy who killed his folks a few years ago?"

Gutierrez nodded.

"He's the one who escaped?"

"Yes, ma'am, and attempted to kill a deputy to do it," Peter said. "We're doing everything we can to find him, but right now, he's still on the loose. And he's very dangerous."

"Did your son know Gage before both of them ended up in jail? Maybe in school?" Gutierrez asked.

She shook her head. "I don't think so. Doesn't seem like the kind of boy Rudy would have associated himself with."

"What about drugs? Could Gage have been one of your son's customers?"

The woman's face puckered as though she's just bitten her tongue. "My son don't sell drugs, officer," she sniffed.

"Mrs. Williams, I know this is uncomfortable for you, and I'm sorry," Peter said. "We're only here because we don't know who Gage might contact and where he might try to hide. He's a dangerous man, and if there's any chance of him showing up here, you need to know your life is in danger."

She stared at him for a few moments, then turned over her shoulder and bellowed into the house.

"Keesha!"

A young woman sauntered out of the gloom and peered at them suspiciously over the older woman's shoulder. She held a baby on her hip.

"You ever heard Rudy talk about a Tommy Gage?"

"Who's asking? Ain't my business to be talking about Rudy to the police."

"Tommy Gage is an accused murderer who escaped from the Galveston County Jail this morning," Peter said, keeping his eyes fixed on the baby. He was holding his mother's bejeweled phone.

"What's that got to do with Rudy?"

"They think he might have helped this Gage escape," the older woman said.

"Now why would he do that?" Keesha asked, rolling her eyes. "Doesn't do him no good for someone else to escape."

"That's what we're trying to figure out," Peter said.

"Well, you came to the wrong place," she snapped. "Rudy's business is his business. Ask him. I ain't saying nothing."

"Rudy's looking after himself," Gutierrez barked. "He won't say anything that might add time to his sentence. But he's not the one who's in danger. If Gage comes around here, who's going to look after you and the baby?"

The young woman's insolent slouch snapped to attention, and she wagged her finger at them.

"Don't you be talking about him like that. Rudy looks after us just fine. We got nothing to be scared of. And we got nothing else to say to you."

She tugged the older woman back into the house and slammed the door.

Peter glanced at Gutierrez. His face had turned beet red, and the tendons in his neck stood out like ropes anchoring a boat in a gale. But he turned around without saying a word and marched back to his cruiser. Peter drifted after him, his thoughts churning. As they pulled away from the house, the shiny black Charger caught his eye again.

"What do you make of that?" he asked, nodding toward the car.

"Not what I would've pictured Mrs. Williams driving," Gutierrez said. "Or paying for."

"Right. That's what's bothering me. And the phone the baby was holding was the latest model iPhone. Not cheap."

"She said Rudy was looking after them. If so, where's the money coming from?"

"And does it have any connection to Tommy Gage?"

Gutierrez grunted. "Here's hoping we have more luck with his lawyer than we did with the Williams women."

Rhett Townsend had his office in a drab building near downtown, but several blocks on the wrong side of 25th Street. It was still waiting for the area's revitalization to reach it, just as the young lawyer was still waiting for his big legal break. So far, he'd mostly represented small-time thugs and mid-level criminals. Nothing that would get his name on the front page of the *Galveston Gazette*. But he'd earned a reputation as a bulldog in the courtroom, and his dubious client list was growing.

His secretary, a matronly woman who looked perfectly capable of keeping order in a room full of miscreants, greeted them as though she'd expected their visit.

"I'll let Mr. Townsend know you're here," she said, bustling down the hall and rapping loudly on a thick wooden door. She poked her head in for just a few moments. Peter couldn't catch her words, but when she turned to come back toward them, the lawyer was right on her heels. He held out his hand to Gutierrez, who introduced himself.

"How's the deputy Tommy stabbed?" Townsend asked.

"Still in surgery last we heard," Gutierrez said gruffly.

Townsend shook his head as if the news saddened him. "I've been thinking about his family all day. Sending many good vibes and happy thoughts their way."

Peter had to cough to cover a snort that escaped before he could stop it. Townsend nodded an acknowledgement in his direction.

"I did not think you would be the one asking me questions at our next meeting," he said. "Now our roles are reversed. Please, come back to my office where we can be more comfortable while we talk."

Townsend's office had a desk at one end and a conference table at the other. In the middle, two small couches faced each other across a narrow coffee table. The lawyer sat on one of the couches, leaving the other for the two officers. Peter hesitated as Gutierrez lowered himself onto one end. Neither of them were small men. They'd have to sit almost thigh-to-thigh, a ridiculously uncomfortable arrangement Townsend had no doubt calculated ahead of time. Peter quickly strode back to the conference table, snagged a rolling chair, and swung it around to the end of the coffee table. If the move surprised Townsend, he didn't show it.

"Have you heard from Tommy Gage since his escape?" Gutierrez asked.

"I have not," Townsend said. "And of course, if I do, I will contact the police immediately."

"How would you describe his state of mind as the trial approached?"

Townsend tapped his finger to his lips as though thinking it over. "I wouldn't call him agitated or anxious. Tense, perhaps. Tommy kept a very tight lid on his emotions, so it was sometimes hard to know what he was thinking."

"What had you told him about his chances in court? Did he expect to win?"

"What I told him is protected by attorney-client privilege. I'm sure you understand. But I can say that I believe we had prepared a good case. I certainly felt confident of it, and I thought Tommy did, too."

"But no matter what, he wasn't going to walk free," Gutierrez said.

"No, we didn't expect that. But time in a mental health facility would have been much more preferable to prison."

"Or death row," Peter said.

Townsend nodded curtly. "I do not mind telling you that I do not believe the jury would have given my client a death sentence," he said. "I believe the facts would have painted him in a much more sympathetic light than the coverage of the case in the *Gazette*."

"Sympathetic, huh?" Gutierrez growled. "Tell that to Travis Barker's wife and kids."

Townsend flinched just slightly before plastering on a look of sorrow.

"My client is mentally ill," he said. "And I don't think spending the last two years behind bars has improved his condition. He cannot be held responsible for his actions."

"We'll hold him responsible once we catch him," Gutierrez said.

Townsend offered no response, and an awkward silence filled the room for several heartbeats.

"Did you have any idea he might try to escape?" Peter asked.

Townsend cocked his head to the side and looked at Peter as though he were a child. "No, Detective Johnson, of course not. And if I had, I would have told someone. This doesn't exactly help his case, as Captain Gutierrez pointed out."

"What about other people in the jail? Did Gage ever talk about people he'd met, or maybe friends he'd made?"

"Not that I can think of. Why do you ask?"

Peter glanced at Gutierrez, who shook his head slightly.

"Just exploring all options," Peter said. "What about old friends and family?"

"Well, as you can imagine, not many of his family members wanted to have much to do with him. He did have a former girlfriend that he kept in touch with. She was one of our witnesses, as I'm sure the district attorney could tell you."

"Do you think she might help him, or even know he planned an escape attempt?"

Townsend pursed his lips. "I don't know, detective. Anything is possible."

"Based on what you know about Gage, and his mental state, what do you think he might try to do?"

"Well, I assume he intends to run. Isn't that the point of escaping from jail?"

"Unless he felt like he had something more important to do here, even if it meant risking getting caught again."

Townsend narrowed his eyes. "What would be worth that?"

"Revenge."

A slow smile spread across Townsend's face. It made the hair on the back of Peter's neck stand on end.

"I assume you're referring to Kate Bennett," Townsend said. "Tommy definitely didn't have any warm feelings toward her."

Peter's hands balled into fists in his lap.

"Do you think he would try to hurt her?" Gutierrez asked.

Townsend brought his finger to his lips again. "As I said before, Tommy Gage is mentally ill. I don't know whether he might try to harm Ms. Bennett. But I do know he seemed to fixate on her and the role she played on the night he was captured."

"He blamed her." Peter said flatly. His chest felt so tight he could hardly get the words out.

"Yes, he did, I'm afraid to say. It's not rational, of course, but people who are mentally ill rarely are."

Peter stood abruptly, propelling his chair backward. Townsend hadn't told him anything he didn't already know, but hearing him say it somehow made the danger more palpable.

Gutierrez heaved himself off the couch as Peter made for the door.

"I'm sure this goes without saying, but let us know if Gage tries to contact you," Gutierrez said. "Mentally ill or not, he's armed and clearly dangerous. I don't think anyone will be safe until he's caught."

Three o'clock came and went and the search teams had found no sign of Gage. The sheriff didn't make any changes to the search strategy after the debrief meeting. But Peter knew they'd have to expand their grid soon. Of course, if Gage wasn't in the area they'd already locked down, he could be anywhere.

The tightness in Peter's chest grew with every minute that ticked by.

Lugar caught up with him as he left the meeting.

"How's it going with Gutierrez?"

"Fine. He's a good investigator."

Lugar nodded. "One of the best the sheriff has. I want you to stick with him until we find this little punk. I wouldn't be surprised if he tried to come after you, and I'd rather you not be alone if that happens."

Peter couldn't hide his amazement. "You're worried about me?"

"I'm worried about anyone Gage may come after, including you."

Peter shook his head. "I'll be fine. I know how to defend myself."

But Kate didn't. Peter knew better than to say that out loud, though. Any reminder of his relationship with the reporter set Lugar off like fireworks on the Fourth of July. The older man sighed.

"Look, Johnson, I know you're not worried about yourself. Maybe that's why I am. If you aren't on your guard, you're vulnerable. Don't relax until we've caught him."

Peter pressed his lips together and nodded.

"I know who you're really worried about," the chief continued, his eyes boring into Peter's. "You know what I think about that, so I won't waste time repeating myself. But that will not affect any decisions I make about her safety. I will do everything I can to make sure she is not in any danger. If Gage intends to get to her, he'll have to get through us first."

Peter nodded again. The lump in his throat made any other reply impossible.

Chapter 5

Peter stood in the Sheriff's Department parking lot and let the sun bake the top of his head. The heat had the odd effect of calming his nerves, probably because it reminded him of all the carefree years he spent playing on the grassy African planes. Gutierrez had gone home to grab a bite to eat and see his wife and kids. Peter's stomach rumbled insistently, but more than anything else, he wanted to see Kate.

He pulled out his phone and pressed it to his ear.

"Have you found him?" she asked as soon as she answered, eager anticipation crackling through the speaker.

"No, not yet."

Her disappointment whooshed out in one breath, giving him the impression of a deflating balloon. She had sounded so hopeful.

"I'm sorry, Kate. We're doing everything we can."

"I know. I just hoped you were calling with good news."

"Well, it's not bad news, at least. I want to come see you. Do you have a few minutes to talk?"

"Here?" She sounded alarmed at the thought of him waltzing into the newsroom.

He smiled. "You can meet me in the parking lot. No one has to know."

She paused, and for a moment, he thought she was going to say no.

"Okay. Call me when you get here."

Ten minutes later, he watched as she drifted down the steps to the newspaper building. Despite the heat, she had her arms crossed tightly across her chest. As she walked toward him, she glanced around the parking lot. She would never admit it, but he could tell she was scared.

He smiled reassuringly as she opened the door and slid into the passenger seat. She offered a faint smile in return, then fixed her eyes on her hands twisted together in her lap. He reached over and put his hand over hers. She looked at it for a moment, almost bewildered, and then grasped it between her cold palms. His breath caught at the urgency in her grasp.

"We're going to catch him," he whispered.

"I know. It's just the waiting. It's driving me crazy."

"Me, too. That's why I wanted to see you."

She smiled up at him. "I'm sure Delilah is peering through the blinds at us now, and I'll never hear the end of it. But I'm glad you came."

He squeezed her hand. "I know you probably don't want to hear this, but you're going to have to put up with having an armed guard until Gage is in custody."

"I figured."

"Wow, you're being much more cooperative than usual! I'm going to enjoy this while it lasts."

She rolled her eyes. "Don't get used to it."

"I'll try not to," he laughed. "But it is kind of nice."

She pinched the back of his hand lightly in reply.

"I wish I could be the one staying with you, at least when I'm off duty, but I don't know when that's going to be at this point. The chief has me working with Alonzo Gutierrez to chase down any leads that might show where Gage would go."

"I know, and it's fine. Your job is to catch the bad guy, not babysit me."

"Protect, not babysit. And that is my job. Or at least I'd like it to be."

The silence that followed felt like a fog laced with lead. A sheen of sweat swept across his forehead. He should never have said something so direct, especially when she was already tense and worried.

He cleared his throat. "Sorry. I'm just—"

"Peter, it's fine." She smiled and squeezed his hand. "It's just hard to get used to, that's all."

"Well, hopefully this will all be over soon." He glanced at her out of the corner of his eye. Despite her assurance, she still looked uncomfortable.

"I'd better go back in before they start wondering where I am," she said, letting go of his hand and tucking her hair behind her ears.

"Of course. I'll let you know as soon as I hear anything."

She nodded and opened the door. But before she stepped out of the car, she looked back at him, her grey eyes clouded with worry.

"Be careful."

Those two words calmed the rising turmoil of anxiety his relational blunder had caused.

"Always."

Kate nearly ran back up the steps to the building. When she walked back through the newsroom door, Delilah looked up at her with a faint smirk but said nothing. No one else seemed to have noticed her absence. Kate breathed a sigh of relief. Peter's talk of protection left her feeling lightheaded. But it shouldn't have caught her off guard. She knew that's how he felt. And when she stopped to think about it logically, she knew she had no reason to get alarmed. So why did she continue to feel the overwhelming urge to flee any time things got too emotional? It was like all the years she'd spent running had made her incapable of any other response.

She was just lowering herself into her chair when Kenton Mattingly stomped out of his office.

"Is everyone here?" he barked, looking around the room at his reporting staff. "Good. Meeting in my office. Five minutes."

Kate looked over at Delilah with a raised eyebrow.

"You're about to get your first lesson in hurricane coverage," the older woman said. "Loads of fun. Just the thing to make a young reporter's career. Ask Dan Rather."

Kate shook her head. She'd heard Delilah tell the story at least three times in the last few years. Dan Rather was a lowly Houston television reporter in 1961 when Hurricane Carla roared ashore. His coverage of the storm earned him national acclaim and ultimately the attention of executives at CBS News.

"Yeah, but I don't have a TV camera following me around," Kate said. "Plus, I have a face for print."

"Nonsense! You have a face for television and a personality for print." Delilah cackled at her own joke.

Kate snatched a notebook and pen off her desk and made her way toward the managing editor's office. She could just see the dark blue uniform of her police guard through the glass in the newsroom door.

Mattingly stood at the head of his conference table, flipping through a three-inch binder filled to capacity.

"What's that," Kate asked as she flopped into one of the open chairs.

"Hurricane coverage plan," Mattingly grunted. "Didn't I make you read it when you got here?"

Kate raised an eyebrow and shook her head. "I'm sure I would have remembered that."

Mattingly grunted again and continued to flip through the documents while the rest of the editorial staff filtered in.

"Nothing like a little bad weather to liven things up around here," said Ben Denison, tossing his notebook down across from Kate.

"An escaped murderer isn't enough excitement for you?" Jessica Linton asked.

Ben shrugged. "I doubt that will last long. But a good hurricane can drag on for days."

Kate shook her head. Journalists just didn't look at things the way normal people did.

"Right," Mattingly said. "Ben and Delilah know the drill. But this will be new for the rest of you. This thing is a long way out and may come to nothing. But we need to sketch out the plans now, so they're ready if we need them."

"I call shotgun!" Ben said, flashing a grin around the table. "The rest of you can take the back seat."

"Well, I call mainland coverage," Jessica said. "I want to be as far away from this sandbar as possible if this thing turns into a major hurricane."

"We will divide into two teams," Mattingly continued as though no one else had spoken. "Hunter will head up the team on the mainland. I'll stay here on the island. My team should plan to be at the office during the storm and as long afterward as necessary. This building is like a bunker, so we'll be well protected. And if we need it, we have plans to bring in a generator so we'll have power."

"The city officials will stay at the convention center," Kate said. "I assume you'll want me there as well?"

Mattingly grunted. "That's the plan."

Kate narrowed her eyes. The way he said it made it sound like that wasn't really his plan.

"The mainland team will head as far north as possible while staying in the county. They'll report on damage there, and if necessary, take reports from the team on the island by phone."

"What do you mean, by phone?" Kate asked.

"We may not have internet service here, not to mention power," Delilah said. "We'll have to dictate our stories by phone, just like they did during Watergate."

"If our phones work, can't we just use them for internet access?"

"The cell networks sometimes go down, too. That's why we have a satellite phone."

Kate raised her eyebrows. She hadn't really thought about how hard it would be to get the news out if all the traditional communication networks were out of commission.

"Ben and Delilah will stay here. Cowel, you too," Mattingly said, nodding at the photographer.

Suspicion began to gnaw at Kate's stomach. "And me," she said. "Right?"

Mattingly sighed. "Maybe. Depends on whether they've caught Gage by then."

Kate's gasp sounded too loud in the suddenly silent room. "What does that have anything to do with it?"

"I'm not leaving you on the island while a murderer who has it out for you is still on the loose. I don't think the police chief will continue your dedicated security detail during a hurricane. If Gage is still on the run, I'm sending you to the mainland with Hunter."

"But I'm the city reporter! It's my job to stay."

"It's your job to do what I tell you," Mattingly barked.

Kate's simmering indignation burst into anger, sending a hot flush into her cheeks.

"Don't worry, kid," Ben said. "If it's a really bad storm, I'm sure you'll get plenty of excitement on the mainland, too."

Delilah shot him a warning glare he didn't seem to notice.

"You'd better hope she gets to stay," Mattingly said. "If not, you'll be a man down and might have to actually do some work."

"A woman down, which means he'll have to do twice as much work," Delilah said, punching Ben in the arm.

Ben snorted and waved her away.

"Right. That's it for now," Mattingly said, snapping the binder closed. "We'll meet again next week once we have a better idea where this thing is headed."

Kate lingered as her coworkers filed out of the office. She took deep breaths to calm her racing heart.

"What?" Mattingly growled when he noticed her still standing by the table.

"I'm not afraid of staying here," she said, concentrating hard to keep her voice from shaking. "It should be my decision. I want to do my job."

"Then you'd better hope they catch him." Mattingly pointed toward the door. "Now, go. I have work to do."

Peter picked up a burrito at a taqueria near the police station and wolfed down the last bite just before Gutierrez pulled into the parking lot.

"That your dinner?" the older man asked with a grimace as Peter slid into the passenger seat.

"Yeah. I had something to do after the meeting, so I didn't have time for anything healthier."

Gutierrez glanced sideways at him as he pulled onto Broadway. "You need a wife."

Peter chuckled. "Duly noted."

"What do we know about this girl we're going to interview?"

"She and Gage had a relationship in high school before he killed his parents. She's on the witness list for the trial, for the defense. Deputies at the jail confirmed she and Gage have traded letters. She's visited a few times."

Ten minutes later, they pulled into a long driveway that ran down the side of a beautifully restored Victorian on Avenue O. Gage's former girlfriend lived in a garage apartment behind the house. At one time, it had probably been the carriage house. But it now sat outside the fence of the bigger house, giving both properties privacy. A bright yellow Mitsubishi sports car sat in the driveway. Peter couldn't help but wonder what—or who—might be lurking in the large garage under the living quarters.

Gutierrez led the way up the wood staircase and knocked on the apartment door. A pale face with round, dark eyes peered out a crack in the curtains. But Gutierrez had to knock a second time before the door swung open a few inches.

"Yeah?" The young woman's voice sounded almost melodic, but it dripped with insolence. It struck Peter how much she sounded like Tommy Gage.

"Aleah Price?" Gutierrez asked.

"Who's asking?"

"I'm Captain Gutierrez, Galveston County Sheriff's Department. This is Detective Johnson, Galveston Police Department. We'd like to ask you a few questions about Tommy Gage."

"Why?"

"Were you aware he escaped this morning?"

The girl paused, as though trying to decide how much to say. "Yeah. I got an alert on my phone."

"Then I'm sure you can understand why we want to talk to you," Gutierrez said with just a hint of impatience. "Would you mind opening the door and coming out?"

Another pause. Peter's hand instinctively went to his gun.

But when the door finally swung open, the girl who emerged didn't look like a threat. She couldn't have weighed more than 100 pounds, and her tight skirt and short tank top left nowhere to hide a weapon. She probably could have been pretty, but her pale skin and hollow cheeks made her look almost ill. She'd pulled her unnaturally dark hair back from her face in a messy ponytail. Jet black eyeliner circled eyes that regarded them warily.

She stepped out onto the small landing and pulled the door closed behind her. Was she trying to keep out the insufferable heat, or keep them from seeing anything interesting inside? Peter glanced at Gutierrez, who was eyeing the door with the same suspicion.

"We know you and Gage were close before his arrest," Gutierrez began.

Aleah shrugged. "It's no big secret. Everyone who knows me knows that."

"And you planned to testify for the defense at his trial." Another shrug.

"Have you been in touch with him?"

"We write some."

Gutierrez drew in a long breath and let it out slowly, as though trying to keep his composure.

"Miss Price, as you can imagine, we are anxious to get Tommy Gage back into custody. Believe it or not, that's in his best interest. Now, this is a friendly visit. But if you decide you don't want to cooperate, we can make it an unfriendly visit."

"What's that supposed to mean?" she spat. "You gonna rough me up or something?"

Gutierrez rolled his eyes. "Hardly. But I'm happy to take you down to the station and hold you on suspicion of aiding an escapee. Have you ever spent a night in jail? It's not very comfortable."

The girl's eyes flashed with hatred. But after a few heartbeats, she seemed to make up her mind.

"What do you want to know?" She hurled the words like spit.

"Have you heard from Gage today?"

"No."

"Did he tell you he planned to escape?"

"No."

"Did he say anything that suggested he might try?"

The girl paused, then shrugged. "Of course he talked about wanting to escape. But I didn't take him seriously. It was like he used to talk about running away when we were in high school."

"You didn't think he would actually do it?"

"No. It's crazy. And even if he wanted to, it seemed impossible."

"Except it wasn't."

She smirked. "Guess not."

"Got any idea where he might go?"

"Nope."

She didn't even stop to think about her answer. She's lying, Peter thought. Conviction tingled across the back of his neck. If she didn't know, she had a good idea.

"Tommy doesn't have any family on the island," he said. "You may be the closest thing he has. Are you worried he might try to come here?"

She narrowed her eyes. "Why would I be worried?"

"He murdered his parents."

"He doesn't have any reason to hurt me."

Peter focused on her face and tried to keep his blank. She seemed to think Gage's parents deserved to be murdered.

"If he does come here, what are you going to do?"

She shrugged again, but this time slowly, as though mocking him.

"I guess I'll call the police."

"You don't think that would make him want to hurt you?"

She looked at him wide-eyed, then rasped out a laugh that sounded like tearing paper.

"I guess I'll have to do whatever he says, you know, to protect my life."

Peter inhaled so sharply the sides of his nose pinched together and cut off his breath. He hadn't felt so frustrated with anyone since the first year he'd known Kate. Aleah laughed again.

"You know, I'm not the one you should be worried about."

"What do you mean?"

"I know who you are. You're the cop who shot him and..." she threw up her hands and bobbed her fingers in air quotes "...rescued that stupid reporter. Guess she's your girlfriend now or something. I don't know what Tommy has planned, but I know he thinks he has unfinished business with you. And her."

Rage, fueled by fear, rocketed through Peter's body. Black spots danced at the corners of his vision and he forced himself to take a deep breath.

Gutierrez shot him a warning look. "Did Gage tell you he wanted to hurt Miss Bennett?" he asked.

"He didn't have to. She's the reason he was in jail in the first place."

Peter barely heard her over the blood rushing past his ear drums.

Gutierrez pulled a business card out of his pocket. "If Gage contacts you, or you think of anything else you want to share, give me a call."

He turned to go, but Peter kept his eyes on the girl's face. She smirked back, her glittering dark eyes filled with the most animation he'd seen since she walked out the door.

Chapter 6

Peter closed his eyes and leaned back in his seat, letting the motion of the car rock the tension out of his back and shoulders. His heart still thudded against his ribs. He sensed Gutierrez shift in the driver's seat.

"That girl is trouble," the older man said.

Peter sighed. "She's hiding something. I'm just not sure whether it's Gage in her garage or just knowing ahead of time that he planned to escape."

"We should get an officer to keep an eye on her. If Gage shows up, we'll spot him."

"Unless he was already there. We should have gone to her first and not wasted time on Williams' family." Peter balled his hands into fists in frustration.

"The Williams link was solid," Gutierrez said. "And we still aren't done chasing it down. Gage could just as easily be there as with his old girlfriend. After all, he had to know we'd look at her before too long. In fact, that's a big reason for him to stay away from her."

Peter nodded absently. His mind galloped through the last 12 hours, re-evaluating everything they'd learned, looking for red flags.

"We still don't know why Williams was willing to help Gage. He had no incentive to, as far as I can tell."

"Did he plan to escape with Gage? Is that why he helped him?"

"I don't think so," Peter said. "It wasn't worth the risk. He doesn't have that much time left to serve. He had to know he'd get caught eventually, and then he'd be in for a very long time."

"So, if Williams didn't want to escape, Gage must have had something to buy his help. Maybe not money, but something he wanted."

"Or something he didn't want anyone else to find out."

Gutierrez glanced at him with one raised eyebrow. "Like blackmail?"

"Maybe."

"What could a prisoner have that he didn't want discovered?"

Peter thought about the car that seemed so out of place in front of the Williams house.

"He's in on a drug charge, right? But investigators suspected he was dealing. They just didn't catch him with enough to make the charges stick. What if he's still dealing?"

"You mean running his operation from the inside?"

"Or on the inside."

Gutierrez let out a low whistle. "Smuggling drugs into the jail is risky business."

"And hard to do without help," Peter said.

"You mean one of the deputies?" Gutierrez growled.

"I hope not. But it's possible."

Gutierrez swore under his breath. "This just gets better and better."

"I have an idea. I know an inmate I could talk to who might be able to tell us what's going on. Or at least confirm whether Williams is smuggling drugs inside."

"Sounds like you have some friends in low places."

Peter chuckled. "Not exactly. I busted this guy for burglary. But he wasn't your typical small-time criminal. College educated. He'd just had a long run of bad luck. I helped persuade the DA to go easy on him. It's not a big deal. He didn't deserve to have the rest of his life ruined for one stupid decision. But he seems to think he owes me. I'm sure he'll be happy to talk, as long as I can keep my visit quiet so Williams doesn't think he snitched."

"Have them bring him down to the infirmary. That's where I used to meet with one of my informants. He would fake an asthma attack."

Peter nodded appreciatively. "That's a good idea. Two of us will draw more attention than one. Why don't I do this interview alone? I'll meet you back at the station."

"Fine," Gutierrez said as he pulled into the justice center complex. "I'll go type up the notes from the Price interview and see you in a few."

Peter strode across the parking lot toward the jail entrance. Plotting out his next move had helped calm the hurricane of anxiety Aleah Price had whipped up. He breathed a prayer for Kate's protection and then stuffed his worry into a back corner of his mind. He could still feel it, trembling in the background as though ready to erupt at any moment. But for now, he had it under control.

After he explained his errand to the ranking deputy, Peter ducked into the infirmary. The surprised nurse showed him to an exam room where he would have some privacy. While he waited, he replayed the interview with Gage's former—or possibly current—girlfriend. Her comments about Kate threatened to unleash his worry, but he reminded himself she had an officer watching over her. If Gage planned to attack, he'd likely wait for an opportunity when she was alone. Peter just had to make sure that never happened.

About ten minutes later, the exam room door opened and a tall man with tightly cropped black hair and a fearful expression shuffled into the room. When he saw Peter, his frown melted into a smile.

"Detective Johnson! You had me worried, man! I didn't know what was going on."

Peter held out his hand, and the prisoner shook it. Manny Chavez looked like he'd lost some weight in the six months since Peter had last seen him at his sentencing hearing.

"Sorry for all the secrecy. I wanted to talk to you, but I figured you wouldn't want the other inmates to know about it."

"Dang," Chavez said, drawing the word out in proportion to his relief. "You got that right. Thanks for looking out for me."

"You doing okay? You look a little thin."

"I gotta be honest, detective. The food's not so good in here, you know what I mean?" He laughed ruefully and rubbed his head. "I miss my mama's cooking."

Peter kicked himself for not thinking to bring something with him.

"Sorry, man," he said, feeling the inadequacy of his sympathy. "I'll mention that to the sheriff."

"Naw, don't worry about it. I'm sure it's better than prison food, which is what I would be eating if it weren't for you. I owe you one."

Peter smiled. "You don't owe me anything. You didn't deserve to go to prison."

"Well, maybe I did and maybe I didn't. But I'm sure glad I ain't there," Chavez said. "But I'm sure you're not here just to check on me. What can I do for you, detective?"

"I'm working on this morning's escape, trying to figure out who knew what and how it all happened. What do you know about Rudy Williams?"

"He's not someone to mess around with," Chavez said, his smile vanishing. "He's not a real tough guy, but he's got power, you know what I mean?"

"Why's that?"

Chavez crossed his arms and regarded Peter in silence for a few moments. "Now I know why you wanted to see me down here. You know more about Williams than you're letting on."

"I have some suspicions, but I need confirmation. Is he smuggling drugs into the prison?"

"Drugs and just about anything else you could want, as long as you've got the money."

A mixture of satisfaction and dismay swirled in Peter's chest. It definitely wasn't the first time he was sorry to be right, but it was probably the hunch that would have the most lasting effect on the department.

"That's no easy task. He must have help from one of the corrections officers."

"Right you are, detective. But I don't know who it is. I swear. I would tell you if I did. Might get me out of here sooner."

Peter's satisfaction devolved into anger. Smuggling contraband was one thing, but if the deputy helping Williams knew about the escape, he was responsible for setting a monster free. He took a deep breath to keep his voice even.

"I assume Williams isn't taking cash and stuffing it in a hole in his mattress. How does it work?"

"Sometimes he does. But mostly guys have people on the outside send money to Williams' baby mama. She runs the show on the outside."

"How does he communicate with her? Does he have a cell phone?"

Chavez shrugged. "I don't know, honest. It wouldn't surprise me. But he might have whoever's helping him carry messages back and forth."

That made more sense and would be much less risky.

"How was Tommy Gage involved?"

"He wasn't, as far as I know. I didn't think he and Williams were friends. He mostly kept to himself."

"How did the other prisoners treat Gage?"

"They mostly left him alone. The one time I saw someone try to pick a fight, he got all up in the guy's face, bragging about what he done to his parents. He made it seem like you wouldn't want to mess with him, even though he was just a little guy. He acted like a maniac."

Peter nodded. Bluffing worked just as well with a bunch of bullies in the jail yard as it did in the school yard. Except, in Gage's case, it might not have been bluffing.

"Did you ever hear him say anything about escaping?"

"Just that one time the other guy got up in his face. He was raving about getting back at the cop who put him in here, and some girl."

Chavez's words hit Peter like acid. His face burned, and he had to force himself to take a breath.

"What's wrong?" Chavez sounded genuinely concerned, a testimony to the goodness Peter had seen in him after his arrest. "Oh, snap! Are you the one who arrested him?"

Peter nodded grimly.

"I'm sorry, man. I didn't know. I would have said something right away if I had."

"That's okay," Peter forced the words through lips that felt numb. "It's not important now. I just need to know whether anyone had an idea about where he might go."

"If I hear anything, I can try to let you know. Everyone's talking about it. But I haven't heard nothing about his plans."

"Alright. You've been really helpful. You didn't owe me anything, but if you did, we're square."

Chavez smiled and held out his hand again for Peter to shake. "Watch your back, okay?"

"I'll try. Let's get you back upstairs. The nurse is going to give you a cover story, so hopefully no one will be suspicious. If you run into any problems or need anything, let me know."

When the nurse gave him the all-clear, Peter slipped out of the infirmary and through the front entrance. By this time in the evening, the inmates should all be in their cells, but he didn't want to run into anyone out on an unexpected work duty assignment. And since he didn't know which deputy was working with Williams, he had to be extra careful not to raise suspicions.

The anxiety he'd kept at bay while talking to Chavez came roaring out of its lock box as he walked across the parking lot to the station. Two people in a row had confirmed Gage's desire for revenge. How could he keep Kate safe from someone determined to hurt her? His pulse screamed in his ears. He knew the officers assigned to protect her would do the best they could. That was their job. But it was just a job. For him, it was the whole world.

He knew Kate didn't want to leave the island, but somehow, he had to convince her to go.

Kate swirled the wine in her glass and looked resentfully at her windowsill. It was her favorite seat in the apartment. From it she could see all the way to the port and a slice of downtown. Perching there, she felt like an eagle in its nest. But when she sat down on its wide ledge tonight, she felt like a duck in a shooting gallery. Unable to shake the feeling that someone was watching her, she retreated to the couch.

Mattingly's threat to send her off the island still smarted like a slap in the face. Despite the tingle of fear she could not deny when she thought about Tommy Gage prowling around in the dark, she refused to retreat like a coward. Surely that's exactly what he wanted. She would not give him that satisfaction.

A phrase had been running through her mind ever since she got home, something Peter had read to her not long ago. It was one of his favorite Bible passages. Something from Psalms, but she couldn't remember the reference. All she could remember was the words, "I will fear no evil." She was just about to pull out her phone to google it when someone knocked on her door.

No, not someone. Peter. She set down her glass and ran to the door, opening it without even bothering to check.

"Did you look to see who it was?" he asked, stepping quickly inside and shutting the door behind him. He sounded annoyed.

"No. I didn't need to. I would recognize your knock anywhere."

She frowned at him, her own annoyance rising. But her anger melted as her eyes searched his face. Deep lines of worry creased his forehead, his lips set in a grim line. She stepped toward him and put her hand on his chest, looking up at him.

"I didn't expect to see you, but I'm glad you're here."

He closed his eyes and wrapped his arms around her, resting his chin on the top of her head. His heart thudded against her fingertips. She took a deep breath and pressed into his embrace, drawing strength and comfort from his nearness. Keeping up her charade of emotional distance seemed silly now.

He released her slowly and guided her to the couch.

"I'm guessing by the look on your face you haven't caught him yet?"

"No. And several people we interviewed this afternoon confirmed he's bent on revenge."

Her tingle of fear exploded like a lightning bolt through her heart. Goosebumps rippled along her arms.

"Who told you that?" she whispered.

"Gage's former girlfriend and another inmate at the jail."

Kate swallowed and nodded, not trusting herself to say anything.

"Look, Kate, I've added a second officer to keep an eye on your building, but I'm worried. If Gage is really intent on hurting you, I'm not sure we can keep you safe here, especially with me distracted by trying to track him down."

She rubbed her arms and then crossed them, squeezing her biceps to keep from trembling. "I'll be careful. Promise."

He sighed. "I don't think that's going to be enough. I want you to go see your dad for a while, just until we catch him."

"What?" Kate shifted from where she'd been sitting, pressed close to Peter's side, and turned to face him. "You can't be serious. Leave the island when a hurricane is brewing? I can't do that. Mattingly would fire me."

"I'm sure he would understand. He doesn't want to see you hurt any more than I do."

Kate shook her head with increasing force. "No, Peter. This is my job. I can't just bail on it, and I don't want to. I understand it's risky, but I do not want to let Tommy Gage chase me away."

Peter jumped off the couch and stomped to the window. When he spun back to face her, a red flush covered his face.

"It's only for a little while." His voice sounded strangled, as though he were squeezing it as hard as he could to keep it under control. "That storm's at least a week away, if it even comes here at all. It's more likely to turn than not."

"What if it doesn't? Then the whole week will be filled with covering the storm prep! I can't just run away, skip all that work, and then sail back in to cover the exciting stuff. Mattingly will just have someone else do it all, and I'll be stuck on the mainland doing nothing!"

"Kate, this is one story!" Peter lost the grip on his voice and it rose with every word. "You cannot seriously be trying to convince me that one story is worth more than your life."

"I'm not," Kate roared, springing off the couch to stand opposite him. "It's not just one story. It's all the stories. It's my job! You say I would only have to leave for a few days, but what if it's longer than that? What if you never catch him?"

"We can deal with that when it happens, if it happens." Peter's nostrils flared. She'd never seen him so angry.

"I can't run forever, Peter. There's always going to be something dangerous to face. If I run every time, I'll never do anything."

"This is different! Just this once, Kate. I'm asking you to be reasonable just this once."

"Reasonable!" she exploded, her anger and frustration boiling over. "What does that even mean? Doing what you want me to do, no questions asked? Well, I'm sorry, that's not how it works. You can't just order me around."

"I'm trying to keep you safe!" he shouted.

"I don't want to be safe. I want to be free!"

For a moment, a heavy silence filled the room. He stared at her with his mouth half open. Then he swallowed hard.

"You're never free when you care about someone," he said so quietly she had to strain to understand. "You're always tethered to them."

Heat flushed her cheeks. "Maybe that's why I've always been better off alone."

Peter flinched like she'd kicked him. He took a deep breath. "You weren't made to be alone."

"Well, I wasn't made to be ordered around either," she snapped. "And if that's your idea of caring for someone, I don't want any part of it."

His face contorted, and he looked away. The silence dragged out, stretching Kate's heart like a rubber band forced past its breaking point. She wished she could rewind the past few minutes and rethink her words. Let the anger and surprise dissipate before they drove her headlong over a cliff.

Peter turned back to face her. "If that's how you really feel, then I'll leave you alone. But I..." He trailed off and looked away again. Then he shrugged. "What's the point? You already know."

Before she could respond, he charged toward the door. It slammed shut with the finality of a guillotine. Kate ran to the window, searching the street below until she saw him jog across to his waiting car. The engine roared to life, and he peeled away from the curb, leaving a trail of tire marks in his wake.

The weight of what had just happened pressed down on Kate's chest. She struggled to catch her breath. The tether between them had frayed, and she'd realized too late the tie she thought was binding her had actually been her lifeline.

Chapter 7

K ate spent the night tossing from one nightmare to the other. They all featured Tommy Gage, either in bodily form or a threat that loomed from the shadows. In some of them, he came after her. In others, she watched helplessly as he turned his wrath on Peter. She woke up again and again, trembling and gasping for breath. She tried to break the cycle by staying awake, but the darkness of her worst fears kept sucking her back under the surface of consciousness.

Her last dream had nothing to do with Gage. It was just Peter staring at her wordlessly, sorrow filling his eyes, before turning and walking away. She called to him to come back, but he just kept walking. She woke up yelling his name.

Outside her window, the steely light of dawn tinged the horizon. Kate groaned as she sat up. Her eyes felt like she'd fallen face-first into a sand dune, and her head throbbed. But she refused to get dragged back into any more dreams.

She stumbled to the coffeepot with the dregs of sleep still clinging stubbornly to her brain. It took her five minutes of fumbling with the filter before she finally turned it on. As the dark black liquid began to drip into the pot, she decided it was a miracle she only managed to spill a few tablespoons of grounds in the process.

Five minutes later, steaming mug in hand, she trudged over to the window. Now that the sun bathed everything in an optimistic glow, she no longer feared her favorite perch. She spotted several downtown residents she recognized walking their dogs. Otherwise, the streets were empty. The two police cars sitting at the curb stuck out like pelicans on a fishing pier. No doubt her neighbors wondered what was going on.

She settled into the windowsill, knees pulled to her chest, and leaned her head back against the cool brick. A replay of the previous evening's fight rolled across her mental screen. Her throat tightened at the memory of the look Peter gave her before rushing out of the apartment. Hot pinpricks peppered the back of her eyes. She squeezed them shut to block the impending flood.

How could everything good in her life implode in less than 24 hours? And, more importantly, how would she salvage anything from the ruins?

Two tears slipped past her defenses and slid down the side of her face. She sat very still, afraid if she moved, the rest of her emotional fortress would come crashing down.

A relentless buzzing finally drew her off the ledge.

It took her a few moments to locate her phone, halfway under the couch. It must have tumbled out of her lap during the argument. A surge of hope made her almost dizzy as she flipped it over to see the caller's name scrolling across the screen. Dad.

With a groan, she tossed it onto the couch. It stopped buzzing for a moment and then started again. Slowly, she picked it up, took a deep breath, and answered.

"Katie!" he said before she even managed to croak out a hello. "Are you okay? I saw Ben's story about the escape. I've been trying to call you. When you didn't answer, I called the police station and persuaded them to patch me through to Detective Johnson."

Kate put her hand to her forehead and cursed silently. Her father had a suspicion she was seeing someone, and she guessed he had an inkling it was Peter. But she'd said nothing about it, and the two men had never talked. Until now.

"Dad, that was totally unnecessary! I'm fine."

"Well, I didn't know that. Why didn't you answer your phone?"

"I was probably still asleep when you called the first time. And I might not have heard the second time."

"Or the third?" Her father let out an exasperated humph. "Peter said he thought you were probably still asleep."

So now they were on a first-name basis? Kate wrestled with the urge to kick her coffee table.

"I assume he also told you I've got two armed guards?"

"He told me he'd assigned two officers to keep an eye out for any trouble, yes. That seems reasonable to me. I'm not sure why you sound so bent out of shape about it."

"I feel ridiculous! And conspicuous."

"Well, you ought to feel safe. Peter said he had credible evidence Tommy Gage might try to get revenge. It makes perfect sense that the police department would assign officers to protect you. I'm sure they would do it for anyone, regardless of any other factors."

Kate glared out the window. "What other factors?"

Her father sighed. "Katie, I did not fall off the turnip truck yesterday. I assume you have your own reasons for keeping your business to yourself. But I can read between the lines."

His words settled over her like a lead blanket. If her father, who lived four hours away, knew about her personal life, everyone who saw her on a daily basis surely knew as well. She'd gone through the last year believing people bought her "just friends" dismissals to their winks and hints.

"Look, I did not call to pick a fight," her father said. "I wanted to make sure you were okay. But I also wanted to suggest you come home for a while. Just until they catch him."

"Did Peter put you up to this?"

"What? No. I managed to come up with the idea of protecting my daughter all on my own."

Kate blew out a long breath. "I had this exact conversation with him last night. I'm not going anywhere."

"So he thinks you should leave, too?"

"Yes, but I'm not leaving. I already told you."

"Well, no wonder you feel ridiculous. That's exactly how you're acting."

She gasped as all the anger she'd felt the night before returned to swirl around her like high tide.

"I'm not going to run away like a coward," she yelled. "I have work to do here. This is where I belong. Tommy Gage is not going to chase me away."

"Do not raise your voice at me, young lady," her father barked.

Suddenly feeling like a sullen teenager again, Kate dropped onto the couch and glowered at the image of her father's face in her mind.

"For what it's worth, I did not expect you to take my advice," he huffed. "But I had to try. If you weren't being so unreasonable, you'd understand that. You're my daughter. I don't want to think about you being in any danger."

Kate bit her bottom lip. She knew how much her father loved her, and she usually tried not to think about what it cost him to have her so far away, physically and emotionally. The fortress she'd built around her heart since her mother died kept him out, along with everyone else.

She took a deep breath and let it out slowly. "Fine, I'm sorry. Just don't ask me to leave, okay? We have a hurricane coming, in case you missed that story, and the paper's going to need all hands on deck. Plus, thanks to my two guards, I'm probably safer than I'll ever be."

"Peter told me he'd do everything he could to keep you safe, otherwise I'd come down there myself."

Kate groaned. That was all she needed.

"What else did he say?"

"Just that you rejected his suggestion to leave pretty forcefully."

Kate picked at the fraying hem of her shorts but said nothing.

"I'm sure you don't want my advice. In fact, I know you don't," her father said. "But you can't fault a man who cares about you for doing his best to protect you. He can't help it."

She swallowed against the lump forming in her throat. "I'm not going to be ordered around. I don't expect you to understand."

Her father snorted. "When has anyone ever ordered you around? Seems to me you've always done exactly what you wanted. Getting your back bowed up because you're afraid someone's going to give you a helpful suggestion doesn't count."

Kate rubbed her forehead with her free hand. The pounding in her head felt like a jackhammer that had broken loose from its operator.

"Look, can we just call a truce?" she said. "I'm sure you have something better to do than continue to browbeat me."

"Well, as a matter of fact, I do, now that I know you're safe. It's a beautiful day with a nice southerly wind."

Her father spent all his spare time working on his sailboat, or cruising her across Canyon Lake. The thought of him zipping along with the bright blue jib stretched tight in the sun made Kate smile.

"That sounds wonderful. Much better than being stuck inside, where I'll be."

"It won't last forever. Just promise me you'll be careful. And give Peter a break, okay? He seems like a good guy."

That was easier said than done, after everything that had passed between them the night before.

"Okay, Dad. Have a good day on the lake."

"I love you, Katie. Don't ever forget that."

She shook her head in disbelief as she disconnected the call. She never expected to have that kind of conversation with her father, especially not now. How ironic that he'd finally gotten a window into her personal life just as she'd managed to blow it all up.

Kate spent the next half hour perched on the windowsill, watching the world below her come to life. After she finished her second cup of coffee, she went to the front door to retrieve her morning paper. The young officer standing outside gave her a friendly wave. She offered a small smile in return and retreated to the couch. She spread the paper out on the coffee table and read it from front to back, even though she already knew the gist of all the stories.

After she finished reading, she wandered back to the window. Restlessness crashed over her like a breaker. Through the thin panes of glass she could hear the murmur of laughter and the strumming of a guitar. A few blocks away, the monthly farmer's market sounded like it was in full swing. The thought of food made Kate's stomach growl. She walked to the refrigerator and swung open the door. The mostly empty interior didn't surprise her, but it offered little hope for breakfast, let alone lunch.

She stood debating for a few moments before making up her mind. No one told her she couldn't go out. And she had to eat.

Thirty minutes later, she'd showered, tucked her hair under a cap, and grabbed several shopping bags out of her pantry. Her young guard looked mildly surprised when she stepped out the front door.

"Running some errands?" he asked, a cautious frown crinkling his forehead.

"I have no food," she said, trying not to sound like a petulant child chafing against a grounding. "There's a farmer's market on Postoffice. I thought I could run over and pick up a few things. It's just a few blocks."

The officer smiled. "Sure, okay. I'm sure that's fine. Detective Johnson said he thought you might need some fresh air today. I know he doesn't want you to feel like a prisoner."

The thought of Peter talking about her to his coworkers made her feel very much like a prisoner.

"How kind of him," she snapped.

The officer's eyes widened. "Oh, I didn't mean... It's just..." He trailed off, seemingly at a loss about how he'd made her mad.

"Don't worry about it," she said. "I'm just feeling a bit stifled. And hungry. What's your name?"

"Dylan Conner," he said, holding out his hand. "Detective Johnson asked me specifically to take this shift, and I was happy to do it."

The young man practically oozed admiration for Peter. The appreciation must have been mutual. Peter would never have asked Officer Conner to guard her if he didn't trust him.

"Well, thanks," she said. "I'm sure it's not exactly a riveting assignment."

He grinned. "It could be a lot worse. Being on patrol during the summer isn't much fun. Everyone's hot and cranky. That only leads to trouble."

"I know what you mean," Kate said with a laugh. "I've had to babysit the police scanner for the newspaper during plenty of Saturday shifts. It's entertaining, but then I'm not the one having to bring order to the chaos."

She headed down the building's wide staircase, Conner at her side.

"How long have you been with the department?"

"About two years."

"Do you like it?"

"For sure! It's all I ever wanted to do my whole life."

His enthusiasm made Kate smile. That's exactly how she felt about the newspaper. "You want to stay on patrol or move into investigations?"

"Investigations. Probably cyber crimes. I've gotten a chance to work with Detective Johnson a few times." Conner gave her a sideways glance. "He's awesome."

Kate squashed a smirk as they stepped out into the mid-morning steam bath.

Five minutes later, they turned onto Postoffice. A line of pop-up tents stretched along the sidewalks on each side of the street, the tables under them brimming with fresh produce and baked goods. Kate moved slowly past each one, Conner by her side. A few vendors cast curious glances their way. Kate tried to focus on her shopping and not wonder what they were thinking. But the man at the booth selling local honey just wouldn't stop gawking. Kate leaned toward him over a table covered in pale yellow felt.

"I'm in the witness protection program," she said in a stage whisper. Several other shoppers turned to look at her.

Surprise lit the man's eyes, then skepticism. She could feel his gaze boring into her back as she walked to the other side of the street.

"Nice," Connor said with a chuckle. "I know I'm drawing a lot of attention. I thought about waiting at the end and giving you some space. But I don't think I could get to you fast enough if Gage suddenly showed up and tried to grab you. Detective Johnson would never forgive me if something happened to you."

Kate's cheeks burned. Even the lowest ranking officers in the police department knew about her private life. She was about to tell him it wasn't Peter's business to worry about what happened to her when a familiar tinkling laugh caught her attention. A few booths away, Kenton Mattingly's wife was inspecting a basket of tomatoes, chatting with the vendor. The *Gazette*'s managing editor hovered a few steps behind, looking like he'd rather be anywhere but there.

Kate watched him for a few moments, debating what to do. Then, before she could change her mind, she strode toward him.

"Hey, boss," she said when she got close enough. She tried to infuse as much cheerfulness into her voice as she could.

He scowled at her, his bushy eyebrows arching over the top of his round-rimmed sunglasses.

"I thought you were supposed to be lying low," he growled.

"I just came out to get a few things to eat. And besides, I have a police escort. I've never been more safe in my life."

Mattingly glanced at the young officer and grunted.

"Listen, I know you said you might want me to head off the island for any hurricane coverage that comes up, but I really don't think that will be necessary. As you can see, I'm well protected. And if I stayed on the island, I'd be right in the middle of a bunch of police officers. The whole force, actually, since they shelter with the city officials at the conference center. In fact, this is the best place for me to be. If you send me to the mainland, I wouldn't have any kind of protection."

Mattingly said nothing for a moment, and with his eyes hidden behind his sunglasses, she couldn't tell what he might be thinking. But out of the corner of her eye she spotted his wife headed toward them, the cloth bag on her shoulder bulging with her purchases.

"Hello, Kate," she said as she raised her sunglasses to push back her ash blonde hair. "I hope Kenton's not giving you an assignment. He was grumbling about something this morning as he read the newspaper over our tea and grapefruit."

Kate laughed. Mattingly was probably grumbling about his breakfast. His wife, an environmentalist devoted to all things organic, had dedicated herself to reversing the effects of his previous hard living with healthy food, green tea, and as much exercise as she could entice him to endure. For all of his snarling and snapping in the newsroom, Mattingly submitted to her efforts with remarkable docility. But that didn't mean he liked it.

"No, I was actually trying to get him to give me an assignment. Covering this hurricane, if it makes it to the island."

"Well, of course! Why wouldn't you?"

"He wants to send me to the mainland because of this escaped prisoner. Everyone seems to think I'd be safer there. But I'm just trying to do my job. I'm sure if I was a man, he wouldn't think twice about having me stay. That hardly seems fair, does it?"

"Now, look here, Bennett," Mattingly growled.

Angela Mattingly looked sideways at her husband, one perfectly plucked eyebrow raised.

"I agree, Kate, that doesn't quite seem fair," she said. "Especially since I know how much my husband supports women's rights."

Mattingly pressed his lips together.

"And really, she's one of the best reporters you've got," his wife continued. "It seems silly to put her on the side-lines when she obviously wants to be in the game."

"I'm only trying to look out for her," Mattingly huffed. "She doesn't seem to have enough sense to look out for herself."

Angela patted her husband's arm. "So chivalrous. That's one of many things I love about you. But really, she should be allowed to make her own mistakes."

Kate couldn't tell whether that was a subtle dig or a vote of confidence, but she didn't care. Just as she thought Mattingly was about to give in, he shook his head.

"I'll think about it. That's the best I can do right now. I have to think about the newspaper's interests as well. If you can't focus 100 percent on your job, I need someone who can."

The expectant bubble that had filled Kate from the moment she spotted her boss at the market popped. Her disappointment landed with a resounding thud in its place. She nodded wordlessly as the couple walked on to the next booth. She turned to find Conner watching her. Sympathy filled his eyes.

"I guess I'm done here," she muttered. She spun around before he could say anything that would make her feel worse.

He trailed her back to her building but caught up to her in time to open the door. The young officer maintained his silence all the way up the stairs. When they got to the top, he paused.

"I know this is hard, but it won't last forever," he said with an encouraging smile.

Kate looked at him for a moment, then nodded. She knew he was right, but right now it was hard to tell the difference between forever and a few days. She'd lived under Tommy Gage's shadow for less than 48 hours and it already felt like a year.

Chapter 8

Peter brought the palm of his hand down on the table with a slap that left his ears ringing. Rudy Williams, sitting in the chair across from him, flinched.

"You lied to us," Peter yelled, his voice reverberating off the walls of the interrogation room. "You knew exactly what Tommy Gage had planned yesterday morning, didn't you?"

"I already told you I didn't," he said. "Why y'all hassling me again? I can't help you."

"Really? I think you can, and I'm going to give you one more chance to do it."

"Or what?" the inmate scoffed, leaning back in his chair with studied nonchalance.

Peter put both hands on the table and leaned over it. "Or I'm going to tell everyone that you've been working for us this whole time. That your little drug smuggling operation is really a sting targeting all your best customers."

The man's eyes flew open, unvarnished shock blanching his face before he wrestled his mask of caution back into place.

"I don't know what you're talking about," he mumbled.

"Let me refresh your memory," Peter growled. He rarely took such an aggressive stance during interrogations. But the tension that had built over the last 36 hours had stretched his nerves so tight he thought they might snap. The anger and helplessness he felt over Kate struck his soul like a match to tinder. He hadn't felt this close to an explosion since the day he'd learned Fulani herdsmen had attacked the village he'd called home for 13 years. Violence, righteous anger, felt like the answer then—an eye for an eye—but that had triggered a slide into a darkness that almost consumed him.

He couldn't fall into that tomb again.

Peter sat back in his chair, chest heaving. Rudy watched him, wariness and the slightest hint of fear shading his face.

"I know you've been smuggling drugs into the jail," Peter said after his breathing slowed. "Drugs and just about anything else inmates want. And I know you're working with one of the deputies. I'm sure Gage knew about your little operation, too. Maybe he threatened to rat you out. Maybe you offered to help him escape to keep him quiet."

Williams crossed his arms and glowered.

"Sound familiar now?" Peter asked.

The inmate didn't respond, but under the table, Peter could hear his foot tapping the floor with nervous energy. He was considering his options.

"Look, either way, your inside job is over. We can file charges against you for dealing, and keep you locked up for a lot longer. Or, you can cooperate and we'll give you another chance. That might be especially valuable after we catch Gage, in case he turns on you. Then we'd have to charge you as an accessory."

Williams kept his silence for several more heartbeats, then leaned over the table, locking eyes with Peter.

"I didn't know Gage was going to kill nobody," he said. "He told me his plan was to get to the infirmary, where it would be easier to escape. He said he might even try to get himself taken to the hospital, which would give him another chance to get away. All he wanted from me was a distraction."

"In exchange for what?"

"Not ratting me out."

Peter nodded. He'd guessed right.

"What did he plan to do if he got out?"

"Man, I don't know. That's the truth. He raved about a lot of stuff. That kid is crazy. Even planning to escape. Crazy. You wouldn't catch me trying a stunt like that."

"What kind of things did he rave about?"

"How he wasn't gonna spend the rest of his life behind bars. How he was gonna convince the jury he was crazy. He had my vote, for sure."

"He never said anything about where he might go?"

Williams shrugged. "As far away from here as possible."

"We think he might have a reason to stick around. He didn't ask you to find him somewhere to hide out?"

"Naw, man. He didn't trust no one. He woulda been way too easy to catch if someone like me knew where he was. I'd tell you in a heartbeat if I thought I could shave some time off my sentence."

"You think he knew that?"

"I said he was crazy. Didn't say he was stupid."

Peter sighed. This conversation was proving to be much less fruitful than he'd hoped.

"He did have a girl he kept up with," Williams said. "She visited him every so often. I think he even had her bring him money a couple of times."

"I guess you would know about that."

Williams grinned, apparently no longer concerned about consequences. "I'm a businessman. And it's my business to know when people have money to spend, and when they don't."

Peter shook his head. "So he never said anything about getting revenge on anyone?"

Williams frowned with what appeared to be genuine confusion. "Like who? He'd already killed his parents."

"The people he blamed for catching him."

"Oh, you mean the police? Well, sure, he talked about that. But everyone does. Not me, you understand. But a lot of the other guys. It's just talk."

"Right," Peter said. "I'm sure."

"Look, man, I told you I didn't know nothing. If I was Gage, I'd get off this island as fast as I could and never look back. You may think he's still here, but I'm betting he's long gone. He could be halfway to Mexico by now."

Peter looked at the inmate for a long time, trying to figure out whether he'd held anything back. He had no reason to, as far as Peter could tell.

"Alright," he finally said. "I'm sure you'll be hearing from another investigator soon. The DA's going to want to know all about who's been helping you."

"You tell him I'm a reasonable man. I'm more than happy to make a deal if the price is right. I don't got much time left. Maybe we could just call it even, know what I mean?"

Peter grimaced. Gage was on the loose, and an unrepentant drug dealer would soon be back on the streets. Today was one of those days when it felt like the bad guys were winning.

He opened the door of the small room and waved for the deputy to take Williams back to the jail. He rubbed the back of his neck as he headed toward his office. Maybe Tommy Gage really was long gone. That would explain why he'd seemingly vanished into thin air after leaving the jail. But how had he made it off the island? He didn't walk across the causeway. Peter wanted to believe Gage was halfway to Mexico, but he couldn't shake the feeling that he was much closer than that.

Sheriff Tyler Metcalf and Police Chief Sam Lugar sat at the end of a long conference room table deep in conversation as Peter filed into the room with the other officers and deputies leading the search for Gage.

Once they were all seated, they went around the table, giving reports on their progress. Gutierrez offered their update. Peter kept what he'd learned from Williams to himself until he could talk to the sheriff privately. He didn't want word getting back to the inmate's connection before Metcalf could make a plan to bust him.

None of the search teams had spotted even a hint of Gage.

"I'm inclined to think maybe he did make it off the island before we locked everything down," the sheriff mused, a deep frown creasing his forehead.

"Well, we can't keep the neighborhood blocked off much longer," Lugar said. "And if he did somehow make it over the causeway, we need to increase the search on the mainland."

The sheriff nodded. "If we still haven't made any progress here by tomorrow morning, we'll hold a news conference to remind the public to stay vigilant. Then we'll announce we're shifting our focus."

Peter listened with a sense of defeat. The bulk of two law enforcement agencies were hunting for one man, who still managed to evade detection. Now that this much time had passed, they weren't likely to find him until he did something to attract attention. Thinking about what he might do made Peter feel like he'd swallowed a shot glass full of vinegar.

Gutierrez raised his hand.

"Sir, I recommend we keep an eye on Aleah Price. Around the clock surveillance. We had a feeling she was hiding something. Maybe in a few days she'll show her hand."

"Yes, good plan," Metcalf said. "We'll leave that to the police department and focus our attention elsewhere."

"We'll set up a team," Lugar said. "We'll also keep watching Kate Bennett, in case he shows up near her. I'm betting if anything could entice him out of hiding, she could."

Peter didn't realize he'd made a sound until everyone in the room turned to look his way. The chief narrowed his eyes.

"Something you'd like to add, detective?"

"No, sir," Peter mumbled, even though he had plenty he wanted to say. The chief had promised to ensure Kate's protection, but now it sounded like he wanted to use her as bait.

After the sheriff dismissed the meeting, Peter and Gutierrez lingered while everyone else filed out. Lugar fixed Peter with a scowl, probably anticipating another conversation about Kate. Peter tried not to think about where that would lead.

"Sheriff, I have another update I wanted to save for you alone," he said.

"Go ahead."

"Rudy Williams, the inmate who started the fight with Gage before his escape, is running a smuggling operation inside the jail."

The sheriff blanched as though he'd bitten his own tongue. "Drugs?"

"And other things. But that's not the worst of it. He's got help on the inside. From one of the deputies."

Metcalf's face turned from pink to crimson in seconds.

"What does that have to do with Gage?"

"Gage found out about it and threatened to rat Williams out. That's why Williams agreed to help him with the escape."

The sheriff swore. "Did he give you a name?"

"No. He intends to bargain for an early release. He's going to save his information for the DA."

"Almost makes me wonder whether that was his plan all along," Gutierrez grumbled. "He mighta been using Gage as much as Gage was using him."

Metcalf grunted. "I'll talk to the DA. We'll have to set up a sting operation to get solid evidence. Otherwise, the case will never stick."

"Let me know if I can help," Peter said.

The sheriff nodded and motioned for Gutierrez to follow him as he headed out of the room.

"Good work, Johnson," Lugar said, his earlier scowl replaced by a slightly less angry looking frown.

"Thank you, sir."

"We're putting surveillance teams on both Aleah Price and the Williams family. If Gage shows up at either place, we'll know about it."

"What about Townsend?"

Lugar's scowl returned. "I may regret this, but I'm going to trust his legal integrity to turn Gage in if he gets the chance. He has nothing to gain by helping him."

Peter nodded. "What do you want me to do?"

"For now, nothing related to this case. If something turns up, I'll let you know."

Peter stared at his boss for a moment, trying to figure out whether he was getting sidelined as punishment.

"Sir, I can keep working this case. It may be the most important case of my career."

Lugar put his meaty hands on his hips and blew out an exasperated sigh.

"I understand that, although I don't like the implication," he said, his eyes boring into Peter's. "I hope you think long and hard before you do anything you might regret in a few months. This department needs men like you."

Peter dropped his gaze. He'd sensed an ultimatum was coming, but it still felt like a punch in the gut to hear the chief make such a direct reference to his possible departure.

"I'm not taking you off this case for any reason other than that there's nothing you can do at this point," Lugar continued. "We just have to wait until Gage comes out of hiding."

Peter sighed, relief mingling with frustration. He hated doing nothing.

"Can I at least check in with the surveillance teams?"

"I'll let you sit in on the daily updates, in an advisory capacity only," Lugar said. "Is that clear?"

Peter nodded. "Thank you, sir."

Lugar turned to go, but then paused. "One more thing. I'm going to keep a security rotation on Bennett for a few more days. But if we still have no sign of Gage, I'm calling it off. The longer this drags on, the more convinced I am that he's not on the island any more."

Peter nodded again, trying to keep his concern off his face.

"If he's not here, he's not an immediate threat," Lugar said, clapping Peter on the back. "Which means you can stop worrying."

Peter chuckled. It sounded hollow even to him. Lugar shook his head as he marched out of the room.

"Go home and try to get some sleep," he said, casting one last look of exasperation over his shoulder.

"Yes, sir," Peter said, suddenly so tired he wasn't sure he could drag himself to the parking lot.

Five minutes later, Peter unlocked the door of his cruiser and slid into the driver's seat. The stifling heat sapped the last of his energy, and he sat there for a moment, letting the waves radiate over him. Just as he was about to start the engine, his phone buzzed. Dylan Conner's name flashed across the screen.

"Hey boss, the next shift arrived about 10 minutes ago. I'm headed home."

"Everything okay?" Peter couldn't bring himself to ask directly about Kate.

"She's fine," Conner said, clearly reading between the lines. "I thought she might give me some trouble this morning. She's pretty feisty."

Peter smiled. "Sorry about that. I'm sure she feels like a caged animal."

"She went to the farmer's market, which seemed safe enough. I think it was a good distraction, until she ran into her boss. Evidently he's told her she'll be covering this storm from the mainland, if it keeps heading our way. She's trying to talk him into letting her stay."

Peter closed his eyes and leaned his head back against the seat. No wonder she'd blown up at him the night before. Mattingly had already taken away her coveted hurricane assignment. When he asked her to consider leaving, it must have stung like alcohol on an open wound.

"Did she talk to him?"

"Yeah, and she's pretty persuasive. Even Mattingly's wife sided with her. But just when it seemed like she'd talked him into letting her stay, he held his ground. She looked completely crushed. I felt bad for her, even though I know she'll probably be safer off the island."

"What'd she do after that?"

"Went back to her apartment and stayed there the rest of the day. She didn't even come out when I knocked to tell her I was leaving. Just told me goodbye through the door."

Peter groaned. Kate had retreated to her inner safe room, a habit he'd methodically worked to undo over the past year. One fight at the wrong time had erased all that progress, leaving her to seek sanctuary behind her old emotional barriers. How hard would it be to get her to come out again?

"Thanks, Conner," he said, clearing his throat to ease the sudden tightness. "I appreciate you keeping watch."

"Sure thing, boss. I don't mind a bit. Hopefully, we can catch this guy soon and everything can get back to normal."

It had been less than two days since Gage's escape had upended their lives. But normal seemed like a dream of a dream, impossible to return to no matter how hard he tried. Kate's anger from the night before, and his own, had left a searing tear in the cord they'd been weaving between them. He wasn't sure the remaining threads would hold long enough to make a repair before the whole thing snapped.

Julio batters Jamaica

More than half the island without power as cleanup efforts begin | By Kate Bennett

Hurricane Julio raked across the length of Jamaica on Saturday. The storm passed directly over the capital, Kingston, in the morning and spun off the western coast by nightfall. Much of the island remains without power, but local officials say the storm damage could have been much worse.

Julio made landfall as a strong Category 2 storm, with maximum sustained winds of 98 mph. But the heavy rain and storm surge caused most of the damage.

Officials say villages near the coast fared the worst. Residents in those smaller communities sent word to the capital of flooded streets and landslides. The storm surge swept away homes and businesses. At least six people are confirmed dead, but officials expect the death toll to rise when search and recovery teams gain access to coastal communities.

After losing energy over Jamaica, Julio was briefly downgraded to a tropical storm.

But Liam Arnold with the National Weather Service office in League City warns the storm won't stay that weak for long.

"All the forecast models show Julio strengthening over the next few days, potentially into a catastrophic storm," he said. "The waters of the Gulf of Mexico are extremely warm, and storms like this feed off those conditions."

Models still show Galveston in the center of the cone of uncertainty, but Arnold said it's too early to say for sure where Julio will make landfall.

"The one thing we can say is that it will almost certainly be on the Texas coast," he said. "There's still a small chance it could make a dramatic turn toward Louisiana or even northern Mexico, but at this point I would say that's not likely."

Forecasters expect Julio to cross the Gulf of Mexico by this time next week.

Chapter 9

Kate stood at the edge of a crowd of reporters filling the lobby of the Sheriff's Department. Normally she would have elbowed her way to the front of the pack, more than happy to irritate the television reporters who had staked out their claim in front of the podium. But her security detail, as she'd come to think of the officer assigned to protect her, created an added complication. She had no interest in drawing attention to him. Standing at the side of the room, he almost seemed like he was just here for the news conference.

After another night of fitful sleep, Kate felt like her arms and legs were made of lead and her head was full of cotton. She'd lain in bed, staring at the ceiling, for a long time after she awoke for the last time. It was the first Sunday morning in quite a while that she hadn't gone with Peter to church. She told herself she only went for him, so skipping it this week should have felt like getting off the hook. Instead, a bereft emptiness surrounded her like a cloud.

When her phone buzzed on her bedside table, she'd snatched it up, hoping to see Peter's name on the screen. Delilah's name appeared instead, and it took all Kate's willpower not to vent her disappointment on her coworker. The sheriff's communications director had texted Ben about the news conference, but after a late night at his favorite dive, he wasn't in any shape to cover it. Kate thought about letting Delilah pick up the assignment. She didn't want to go out in public with her police escort. But she had even less interest in staying in her apartment for another day. She told herself the possibility of seeing Peter had nothing to do with it.

At eleven o'clock on the dot, the door to the office wing swung open and Sheriff Tyler Metcalf marched through with Police Chief Sam Lugar on his heels. Kate held her breath as several other deputies followed them. She spotted the top of Peter's head before she saw his face. That should have given her time to prepare, but the blood still rushed to her cheeks when he walked through the door. Even from across the room, she could see the dark smudges under his eyes. Evidently, he had slept no better than her.

He kept his eyes down until he took his place behind the sheriff. But when he looked up, he spotted her immediately. His raised eyebrows registered surprise, and the set of his mouth suggested concern. But his eyes shone with something she'd gradually grown used to seeing, even if she wasn't willing to put a name to it yet.

"Good morning, everyone," Metcalf said, adjusting the microphone before gripping the podium with both hands. "I wish I could tell you that we have our escaped prisoner back in custody, but we do not. Tommy Gage remains on the loose."

He paused to let that news sink in. Camera shutters clicked in the silence as the few photographers in the room captured the sheriff's grim expression.

"Both the Galveston County Sheriff's Office and the Galveston Police Department have worked around the clock for the last two days searching for him. We have found no signs, no clues as to where he might be. Initially, we thought he remained here on the island, and that's where we focused our efforts. But at this point, we believe he must have slipped over the causeway shortly after his escape. How he did that, we still don't know."

Kate froze, her pen digging into her notebook. If Gage was gone, he must not intend to come after her. The fear that had pressed in on her since Friday morning suddenly lifted. She felt unbalanced, just like she did every time she returned to shore after spending an afternoon on the lake with her dad. She glanced up at Peter, telegraphing a silent question. When he nodded almost imperceptibly, goose bumps tingled up her arms.

"We are shifting our focus to the mainland and have alerted law enforcement agencies across the state," Metcalf continued. "Although we don't know where he might go, we are urging all members of the public to be vigilant. We consider Mr. Gage to be armed and dangerous. Anyone with information should call us or their local law enforcement agency."

Metcalf stood aside and let Lugar take his place at the microphone.

"As of this morning, we are lifting the perimeter set up in the neighborhoods around the jail. As the sheriff said, we believe Gage has left the island. But we won't know for sure until he's caught. Everyone should stay on their guard. Lock your doors. Check your sheds and garages for any sign that someone might have broken in. If you see anything, call 9-1-1. Do not—I repeat, do not—investigate anything unusual yourself. We will have increased patrols on this end of the island. We can have an officer to you, if needed, within just a few minutes."

The sheriff leaned over and whispered in Lugar's ear. The chief nodded.

"All that said, we do not believe there is any immediate danger," Lugar continued. "We encourage everyone to go about their daily lives as usual. And certainly, we want to assure all our visitors that they have no reason to postpone any trips they might have planned. Galveston is open for business."

Lugar stepped back, and a dozen hands went up around the room. When Metcalf didn't immediately respond, several television reporters started calling out their questions.

"Do you have any idea how Gage escaped?" asked a perky blonde whose bright red lipstick probably looked fine on camera but seemed garish in the morning light.

"We are still investigating," Metcalf said. "We have a good idea, but we're not ready to release any details yet."

Metcalf ignored half a dozen other shouted questions about the escape and called on the reporter from the *Houston Chronicle*, who held up his hand and waited patiently.

"What about the deputy that Gage stabbed? Can you give us an update on his condition?"

Metcalf nodded. "I can, and I'm happy to say it's cautiously good news. Deputy Travis Barker remains in intensive care, but he came through surgery well, and doctors are optimistic about his recovery. As you know, he has a wife and two young children. I would ask that you keep them in your thoughts and prayers. He still has a long recovery ahead of him."

Kate closed her eyes and breathed a sigh of relief. It was as close as she could manage to a prayer of thanks.

After answering a few more questions, Metcalf thanked everyone for coming and led his entourage out of the room. Peter cast one more glance her way before he disappeared through the door. She could tell by the look he'd given her when he walked in that he wasn't angry, but he hadn't tried to call her either. Maybe he'd actually believed her when she said she was better off alone.

Or maybe he thought she was right.

Kate chewed on that possibility as she drove to the newspaper office to write her story. The cavernous newsroom, empty on a Sunday morning, echoed with her footsteps as the accusations that bombarded her echoed in her head. She'd strung Peter along for a year. She gave him just enough hope that their relationship would develop into something more serious, but never fully committed. It reminded her of the time she'd gone with friends to the cliffs at Lake Travis. She'd stood on the edge looking over for a long time, gazing into the water below. She'd tried to imagine the feel of her body careening into the water. Her friends all cheered her on, but in the end, she'd backed away. She just couldn't force herself to face the free fall.

She thought Peter understood. But he couldn't wait around forever.

Kate closed her eyes and squeezed the bridge of her nose to keep back a storm of regret that threatened to overwhelm her. It shouldn't surprise her that he would keep his distance after everything she'd said. And if he thought it was better for them to go their separate ways, how could she blame him?

It took her several minutes to wrestle her emotions under control enough to concentrate on her story. It took three times as long as it should have to write. But finally, an hour later, she sent it to the copy desk. She was packing up her laptop when she heard the door scrape open. She glanced up to see Mattingly walking in.

"What are you doing here?" he barked, although with less ferocity than normal.

"I covered the sheriff's presser this morning. Just filed my story."

Mattingly scowled. "Ben hung over again?"

Kate shrugged noncommittally. It wasn't her job to rat Ben out, even though she knew Mattingly wouldn't do anything about it.

The managing editor grunted and shook his head. "So, what'd the sheriff have to say?"

"They're shifting the search to the mainland. They don't think Gage is still on the island."

Mattingly raised one bushy eyebrow. "If he got across the causeway, there's no telling where he could be."

Kate nodded. "That about sums it up."

"I see you still have a uniformed escort." Mattingly jerked his thumb over his shoulder toward the officer who stood just outside the newsroom door.

"For now, at least. I haven't heard how long it will continue, but I'm sure the chief has a better use for his officers' time, especially if he doesn't think Gage is still here."

Mattingly cleared his throat. "Well, I guess that's good news for you. If it's true, there's no need to send you off the island."

Kate sucked in a breath. "Does that mean I'll be staying here to cover the hurricane?"

"I suppose so," Mattingly said, looking almost as though he might smile. "But don't get your hopes up. I have a feeling this storm is going to turn."

Kate didn't bother trying to suppress the triumphant grin that spread across her face. Her boss turned abruptly and stomped into his office, as though he feared her jubilation might spill over and contaminate his perpetually dour mood.

"Thanks," she said to his retreating back.

He didn't turn around, but waved his hand in acknowledgement.

Kate felt like rolling her windows down, cranking up the radio, and singing at the top of her lungs as she drove back toward downtown. She didn't, mostly because she didn't want the officer following her to see. Without an outlet, her joy bubbled just under the surface, occasionally erupting in a grin or shout of laughter. She couldn't remember the last time she'd felt so elated.

She trotted up the stairs to her apartment well ahead of her escort, whose heavy footfalls suggested he had already grown weary of his assignment. Kate unlocked her door and shut it behind her with a sigh of satisfaction. But as she looked around the room, an emptiness began to seep into her soul. She had no one to share her triumph. Her effervescent joy evaporated like a sea fog under a relentless sun.

With a sigh, she trudged to the couch and threw herself into one corner, kicking off her shoes and tucking her legs up under her. She slipped her phone from her back pocket and stared at the screen. A view of the streets of Havana glowed back at her. She'd taken the photo last year, during the trip that had cemented her tie to Peter. They'd left Cuba with a sense of anticipation. But over the last year, that anticipation had stretched thin from lack of fulfillment. It no longer drew her toward something yet to come. She'd refused to face the future, afraid of its demands. Now that it seemed too late, she finally thought she might be ready to embrace it.

Kate rested her head on the cushion at her side and closed her eyes. The tension and lack of sleep during the last few days had taken a toll. Before she realized it, reality had morphed into dreams. Back in Havana, she wandered with Peter under the soaring ceiling of the Catedral de San Cristobal. The golden rays of the Caribbean sun filtered through the windows and pooled around them. Enchanted by the dancing light, she wandered away from Peter into the bowels of the church until darkness surrounded her. Confused, she turned back, only to come face-to-face with a closed door. The walls of the church melted away, and she was back in the jail cell where she thought she might have to spend the rest of her life, alone and forgotten.

A knocking on the cell's damp wall stilled her mounting alarm. She knew that knock. Peter's knock.

Before she could search for the sound's source, Kate woke with a start, disoriented as the mist of her dream faded into reality. Long shadows filled the room. She had slept through the rest of the afternoon.

The knock from her dream sounded again, this time with a hint of urgency, and she realized with surprise it was coming from her own front door.

She sprang off the couch and ran, hesitating only when her hand reached out to grasp the handle. Her ears told her it was Peter, but her brain screamed with doubt. She glanced through the peephole and caught her breath. Peter stood on the other side, a worried frown creasing his forehead. He raised his hand to knock again, but she wrenched open the door before his knuckles made contact.

They stood staring at each other for several moments. Uncertainty filled Peter's eyes, but it lifted as Kate took his hand and drew him into the apartment. The door swung shut behind him. She said nothing as she led him to the couch. They sat facing each other, just as they had two nights before. Silence settled over them, and Peter leaned toward her.

"Kate, I'm sorry," he said, squeezing her hand. "I know how much your job means to you. I just couldn't get past worrying about what might happen."

She smiled. "I know. And I shouldn't have punished you for it."

"I'll never get over wanting to protect you, you know."

She took a deep breath and nodded. She wanted to tell him that she would learn to live with it, but the words stuck in her throat.

"I knew this would not be easy, but I'm not ready to give up," he said.

The cord that bound them together coiled around her again. Kate relished its familiar tug.

"Me neither," she whispered.

He pulled her toward him until she was nestled against his side, her head resting on his shoulder. Her heart thudded with gratitude for a second chance. She closed her eyes and breathed deeply, savoring the faint scent of his cologne.

The blaring of a weather alert from her phone snapped her out of her reverie. Reluctantly, she scooped the device from the floor and stared at the screen.

"Looks like I won't have to worry about hurricane coverage after all," she said.

Julio heads south

Forecast models show hurricane trending away from Galveston | By Kate Bennett

Storm track models from the National Weather Service (NWS) now show Hurricane Julio turning away from Galveston and heading toward South Texas.

Liam Arnold, a forecaster in the NWS League City office, said the island likely won't feel more than minimal effects from the storm.

"Right now it looks like we may get some of the far outer bands, which could mean some heavy rain and intermittent wind gusts," he said. "And depending on when the storm comes ashore, we might have some higher than normal tides. But Galveston can heave a big sigh of relief."

Julio formed off the coast of Africa on Wednesday and grew to hurricane strength on Friday. Officials in Jamaica are still assessing the damage from Saturday's landfall there but say as many as two dozen people remain unaccounted for. The storm struck the Caribbean island as a Category 2 hurricane.

Arnold said he expects the storm to strengthen quickly once it hits the warm waters of the Gulf of Mexico toward the end of Monday. Before then, Julio will pass over the eastern tip of Cuba and brush by Mexico's Yucatan Peninsula.

Officials in Rockport and Corpus Christi have urged their residents to start making preparations over the next few days.

Julio is expected to make landfall somewhere along the Texas coast by the end of the week.

Chapter 10

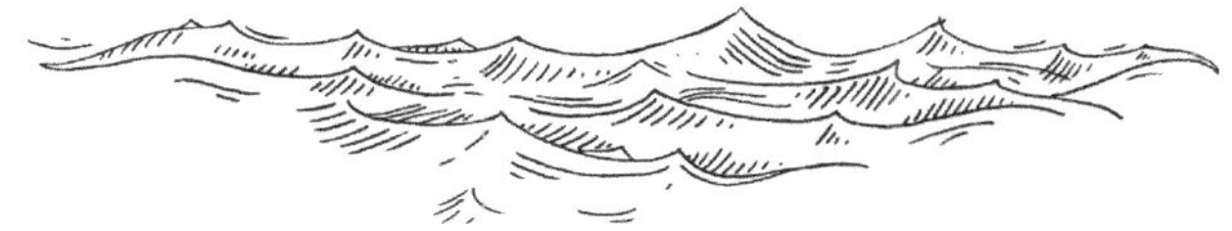

Peter went to bed early Sunday night and woke up Monday morning feeling more rested than he had since the news of Gage's escape jerked him out of bed Friday morning. He didn't have the sense of peace he would if Gage was back in custody. But the pressing dread of imminent danger had lifted enough that he could breathe more freely.

His talk with Kate the night before gave him a renewed sense of purpose. It had also restored his hope that she would eventually surrender to feelings he believed she desperately wanted to embrace. The call from her father had come as a complete surprise. But he sensed he had an ally in his quest to break through her barriers. The man clearly adored his daughter and wanted what was best for her. And he'd asked Peter to keep him updated on the search for Gage. Maybe that would be an opening for future conversations about other things.

But first things first. Gage was still on the loose, and even if he was headed for Mexico, he remained a threat. Peter knew they wouldn't be truly free until Gage was back in custody.

The police chief had taken him off the immediate search team, but that didn't mean he couldn't do a little reconnaissance on his own. He rolled out of bed, threw on a tank top and running shorts, and grabbed his shoes. His two dogs raced him to the front door, eager for the early morning exercise they'd missed the last few days. They were used to their routine trip to the beach just a few blocks away, so they stumbled in confusion when Peter turned north and headed toward the center of the island. But they soon warmed to the idea of exploring new territory and lifted their heads to take in the sights and smells.

They jogged for several blocks until they reached Avenue O and turned west. Peter concentrated on his breathing, syncing it with the thump of his feet on the sidewalk. He whispered prayers for wisdom and insight, but mostly protection, first for Kate and then for anyone else in Gage's path. By the time he reached the block where Aleah Price lived, he felt calm and focused.

He slowed to a walk, a break even the dogs seemed to appreciate. He squeezed a stream of water into his mouth from the bottle he'd carried with him, then turned it toward the dogs. They'd gotten adept at gulping the flow even though they preferred to lap. While they stood panting, Peter turned his attention to the fence surrounding the property. Tall oleander bushes blocked most of the view, but by peering through the leafy stalks, he could get a look at most of the yard.

The carriage house apartment stood on the opposite side of the grassy expanse. He scanned the side and back of the building, lingering on the downstairs garage. Nothing looked different than it had on Friday, when he and Gutierrez had interviewed Gage's former girlfriend. He sauntered toward the corner, pausing occasionally to pat one of the dogs or pull his foot up in a quad stretch. Another peek through the oleanders revealed the front of the carriage house. The drawn blinds still covered the front windows. The yellow sports car parked a few feet from the front steps offered the only evidence of life inside.

Just as he was about to turn around and jog home, the apartment's front door opened a crack and Price slipped out. After pulling the door closed behind her, she turned and inserted a key into the lock, sliding the deadbolt into place. She trotted down the steps without a backward glance and slid into the car's driver's seat. Moments later, the car crawled down the long driveway and turned onto the street.

Across the intersection, another car engine fired up. The surveillance team Peter had spotted as soon as he jogged onto the block pulled away from the curb and headed in the same direction as Price.

Peter turned back toward the apartment. The temptation to steal up the driveway and try to get a look inside the garage pulled at him. But he had no probable cause. Sighing in frustration, he tugged on the dog's leashes and headed home at a brisk jog.

An hour later, Peter strode through the front door of the police station. The cloud of tension that had filled the building a few days earlier had dissipated. In its place, the usual bustle and drudgery of daily law enforcement had returned. In the break room, officers ending their shift traded a volley of friendly insults. No one mentioned Gage. The missing prisoner had already become someone else's problem. Peter poured himself a cup of coffee and checked his watch. The chief said he could sit in on the daily briefings, and he had no intention of missing the first one.

At a few minutes to nine, he stepped through the conference room door, nodding to several of the officers already there. A few shot curious glances his way, but no one questioned his presence.

Lugar lumbered in with a curt greeting and dropped into the chair at the head of the table. The others took seats close to him, but Peter hung back, hoping the chief would interpret the distance as respectfully following his order.

"Well, any sign of our fugitive?" Lugar asked.

"No sir," Lieutenant Jarrell said. "We continue to get tips and calls to the hotline, but nothing obviously points to Gage."

"What about the surveillance on Aleah Price?"

"They report nothing unusual at her apartment, or at her job."

"Where does she work?"

"She's a waitress at Pelican's Landing."

The chief grunted. "No sign that she's done any unusual shopping or brought home more groceries than normal?"

"No."

The chief nodded. "How about the detail on Kate Bennett?"

Peter tensed. Jarrell surely knew he'd been to Kate's apartment last night. If he reported it, Peter would be in for a haranguing, or worse.

"Nothing unusual there, either," Jarrell said, glancing at Peter. "No sign of Gage or any other threat."

Lugar nodded. "Keep an officer there until the end of tonight's shift. If nothing happens between now and then, I think we can assume Gage has other plans."

Peter tightened his grip on his coffee mug and pressed his lips together to hold back the protest that almost slipped out. He knew the department couldn't provide private security, but the threat against Kate wasn't over, even if it had diminished.

Lugar raised an eyebrow in his direction, as if daring him to mount an argument. He held the chief's gaze but kept his own neutral.

"Has the sheriff's department heard anything on the mainland or from other agencies?" Lugar asked, turning his attention back to the other officers.

"No. It's all quiet there as well."

Lugar grunted. "It's like the man vanished into thin air. But sooner or later, he'll show himself. He can't stay hidden forever."

Jarrell nodded and closed the manila folder sitting in front of him. Lugar stood, and the others followed suit. But while they filed out of the room, he hung back and fixed Peter with a look that told him to stay put. Once they were alone, Lugar's already pointed gaze narrowed.

"I'm guessing you might be tempted to take on some extra security work tomorrow," he said.

Peter hesitated. He refused to lie and say he wouldn't keep watch over Kate. But he wasn't ready to have a confrontation either.

"I highly recommend you don't do that," Lugar continued, as though he hadn't expected a reply. "I was willing to cut you some slack these last few days. But that time has just about run out. So has my patience."

The elephant lurking at the edge of every interaction with his boss for the last year blew its trumpet in warning and stomped into full view. Peter knew he couldn't ignore it much longer. He took a deep breath.

"Yes, sir," he said.

"You're one of my best detectives," Lugar said, pinning him in place with a hard stare. He paused, as though debating what to say next. Peter braced himself for an ultimatum. But Lugar just shook his head and walked out of the room.

Peter let out a breath he didn't realize he'd been holding. His boss obviously didn't want to draw a line in the sand, probably because he felt sure Peter would step over it.

The thick breeze that rolled over the seawall and down the tree-lined street did nothing to dim the oven-like heat blazing down on Kate as she stepped through a wrought-iron gate and up a path pocked with weeds. She did her best to ignore it and the officer who lingered on the sidewalk next to his patrol car. Having someone to keep watch gave her comfort, but she hated explaining the situation to everyone she bumped into.

Half way up the path, she paused and looked up at the austere building that loomed ahead. Its once-butter colored brick had faded thanks to a century's worth of salty air, and its tall windows looked out on an overgrown lawn with sad resignation. Children had once pounded up and down its long stone staircase all day. But for the last almost 20 years, it had sat vacant, another relic of the island's storied past.

"Ms. Bennett! I'm so glad you could make it."

The tall man who hailed her from the top of the steps had a smudge of dirt across his white button-down shirt. He had loosened his tie and rolled up his sleeves as though preparing to begin work as soon as their interview was over. Bill Presley's enthusiasm for his renovation project had a contagious quality that had saved it from certain ruin at the city's planning commission. The Gothic-style building, finished just a few years after the 1900 storm, had been home to the Galveston Orphan's Home until the mid-1980s. Its next owner tried to turn it into a private residence, but found the maintenance costs far outweighed its prestige. Presley bought it with plans to turn it into a premiere wedding and event venue. But to do that, he needed a special use permit.

Kate trudged up the steps and forced herself to smile when she got to the top, pretending she didn't feel the trickle of sweat working its way down her back.

"Sorry about the heat," Presley said, extending his hand and shaking hers vigorously. "But it's cooler inside, believe it or not. It's all the high ceilings."

He led her through the front door and into the foyer. The ceiling soared 20 feet overhead, and a musty heaviness hung in the air.

"Wow," Kate said, glancing from the white-tiled floor to the honey-colored woodwork adorning every other surface. "It's in a lot better shape than I expected."

"Beautiful, isn't it?" He smiled and rubbed his hands together.

"I bet you can't wait to get started," Kate said with a laugh.

"I can't. We have contractors scheduled to arrive on Friday."

The city council planned to vote on the permit Thursday, as Kate's story in tomorrow's paper would explain.

"Sounds like you're pretty sure you've got the votes," she said.

"Well, anything can happen, of course. But I think now that most of the neighbors have dropped their objections, there's no reason for the city to hold us back. It's a wonderful project that will bring in plenty of extra tourism dollars."

Kate smiled. The mighty tourism dollar wasn't a panacea for every city council objection, but it covered a multitude of sins. And Presley had worked tirelessly during the last few months to convince neighbors the venue wouldn't create the traffic jams and noise problems many feared.

"Let me show you around," he said, bouncing on the balls of his feet and grinning from ear to ear.

Several large rooms took up almost the entire ground floor. One had once been a dining room, another the girls' dormitory.

"They do seem perfect for parties and events," Kate admitted as they came to the foot of the wide staircase leading to the second floor.

"Can't you just picture this place decked out for a wedding? Hor d'ourves in the front room, a sit-down meal in the dining room. Ceremonies could be outside, in the garden. It's not much to look at now, but in six months it will be a tropical paradise."

Presley led her up the staircase and through several more wide-open rooms.

"It's surprisingly beautiful for an old orphanage," Kate said, as they walked back down. "I wouldn't have expected the building to have so much character."

"Well, you know, the original building suffered quite a bit of damage during the 1900 storm. Newspaper magnate William Randolph Hurst held a ball in New York to raise money to rebuild. Mark Twain was the guest of honor. They really spared no expense. They even tripled the thickness of the outer walls as a defense against future storms."

"That should help cut your insurance rates," Kate said with a laugh.

"I don't know about that, but at least I'm relatively certain the building will withstand the next major storm."

"You weren't nervous about Julio?"

"Not exactly nervous. I was mostly worried it would interfere with our restoration schedule."

"How long do you think it will take, assuming you get the council's approval?"

"I'm expecting about a year. If we're on track by the first of January, we'll start taking wedding bookings for next summer."

Kate nodded and flipped her notebook closed. "I don't have any more questions, but I appreciate the tour."

"Let me just show you out back, so you can see how much of a buffer we have between us and the closest houses."

Swallowing her protest, Kate followed him through the back door onto a landing set into the back of the building. A stone staircase almost identical to the one in front led down to a grassy expanse that took up half the block. A rickety looking shed sat in one back corner.

"We'll put the parking lot there. And the rest will be professionally landscaped. That will go, of course," he said, pointing to the shed.

Kate tried to show interest, but all she could think about was getting back to the air conditioning.

"Oh, dear," Presley said with a frown. "It looks like the door's come open again. I'll have to go shut it before I leave. But I don't want to keep you any longer."

"I do have a story to write," she said with a smile. "But all of your plans sound really well-thought out. I'll look forward to seeing the end result."

"It really will be such an improvement over what's here now. How could the neighbors object? Plus, it's not making the city any money in its current state."

Kate squelched a smirk and just nodded. "I'll be sure to quote you on that."

At five o'clock, Peter stood up and stretched. After the commotion of the past few days, the routine of reviewing case files and incoming reports felt like running in molasses. He was so tired he could barely keep his eyes open. He plucked his keys from his desk drawer and headed for the parking lot. All day he'd tried to avoid thinking about Kate. He would not leave her unprotected, but he hadn't figured out how to do that without risking a confrontation with the chief. He debated stopping at her apartment, or inviting her to meet him for his nightly walk on the beach with the dogs. But since she still had a police escort, at least for one more night, neither seemed like a good idea.

Forty-five minutes later, the thundering of the dogs paws on the sand as they chased ball after ball helped to clear the fog of his monotonous day and ease the tension of his worry over Kate. When the animals finally flopped down at his feet to rest, he pulled out his phone and dialed her number.

"Sounds like you're at the beach," she said as the wind rumbled across the phone's mouthpiece. Peter cupped his hand over it to block the noise.

"I am. I wish you could have joined me, but that would have caused unnecessary hassle for your escort."

Kate snorted. "I dragged this one around town all day, so I'm sure he appreciates the break. I think he's counting down the minutes until his shift ends."

"Did you have an assignment today?"

"I went to the old orphanage for a tour. Remember that developer who plans to open an event venue?"

"Oh, right," Peter said, reaching out to pat one of the dogs.

"What's up?" she asked, the sharp edge in her voice cutting through his distraction. "You're thinking about something else."

He smiled and shook his head. She knew him better than he realized.

"The chief is calling off your extra security detail, starting tomorrow morning."

Silence filled the line for several moments.

"Oh," she finally said. "Well, I guess that's a good thing. Lugar must really think Gage is long gone."

Peter sighed. "There's been no sign of him, here or on the mainland. But that doesn't mean he's not lurking somewhere. I don't like leaving you unprotected."

"I know, but I can't hide forever. And I can't have an officer tagging along with me every day."

"I'm mostly concerned about the night," Peter murmured. "I don't like you being in your apartment all alone."

"Well, I would ask you to stay over, but I know how you feel about that." He could see her wicked grin just as clearly as if she were sitting next to him on the sand.

"This is serious, Kate. I would absolutely stay with you to keep you safe. But if word got back to the chief, I'm pretty sure I'd be forced to have a conversation with long-term consequences."

She didn't respond for several moments, and he put his hand to his forehead. Why did this have to be so difficult?

"I see," she murmured so softly he almost didn't hear her.

"Kate, I won't hesitate to do whatever it takes. You know that. All you have to do is say the word."

This time the silence lasted so long he wondered if she'd hung up.

"Kate?"

"I'm here," she whispered, followed by another long pause. Then she cleared her throat. "I'm sure I'll be fine. I'll be extra careful and lock my door. We're probably worrying about all this for nothing. What are the chances he's kicking back on a beach in Mexico by now?"

Peter took a deep breath to push against the familiar tightening in his chest. She wasn't ready to move forward, but he wasn't sure how much longer he could keep up this balancing act. He squeezed a handful of sand into a hard ball. He couldn't force her to make a decision. Until then, or until Gage was back in custody, he'd have to figure out another way to keep her safe.

"We'll see what happens tomorrow," he said, trying to force a lightness into his voice that he didn't feel. "If there's still no sign of him, maybe you're right."

She let out a shaky sigh. "I hope so."

WEATHER BULLETIN

Hurricane Julio advisory number 28

NWS/TPC National Hurricane Center, Miami FL

200 a.m. CDT - Tuesday, August 29

... Julio just east of Mexico's Yucatan Peninsula ...

At 2 AM CDT ... A hurricane warning is in effect for Cozumel, Cancun, and surrounding areas. Heavy swells are expected offshore. Preparations to protect life and property should be rushed to completion.

All interests in the Yucatan Peninsula should closely monitor the progress of this hurricane.

Julio is expected to pass just north of the Yucatan Peninsula and enter the Gulf of Mexico by mid-afternoon.

Julio is moving toward the west at 15 mph and a west to west-northwest motion, but a turn toward the north is expected over the next day or two. On this track, the center of Julio will move across the Gulf of Mexico over the next four days and will make landfall along the southeastern Texas coast on Saturday. All interests between Corpus Christi and Galveston be advised.

Maximum sustained winds are near 100 mph ... with higher gusts. Julio is a Category 2 hurricane on the Saffir-Simpson scale. Additional strengthening is expected over the next few days.

Hurricane-force winds extend outward up to 60 miles from the center ... and tropical storm force winds extend outward up to 200 miles.

Storm surge flooding of 2-4 feet is possible in the Yucatan Peninsula, subsiding toward the end of the day.

Julio is expected to produce rainfall accumulations of 6 to 12 inches throughout the Yucatan Peninsula ... with isolated amounts up to 20 inches. These rains are likely to cause life-threatening flash floods and mudslides over mountainous terrain.

Chapter 11

Television news crews already filled the lobby of city hall when Kate pushed through the doors a little after nine o'clock. The early morning bulletin from the National Weather Service had launched the city into full hurricane prep mode. The crackle of anticipation and low-level anxiety that filled the lobby mirrored the conflict churning through Kate's mind. At least it took her thoughts off Tommy Gage and her canceled security detail.

She headed for the edge of the crowd, avoiding the preening reporters and grouchy cameramen. Toward the front of the room, near the podium where the mayor would deliver his remarks, Ashleigh Tarver stood talking to Eddie Vasquez and Stephen Rush. Kate headed straight for them.

The press-friendly public works director waved as soon as he spotted her.

"I told you I had a bad feeling about this, didn't I?" Vasquez said with a somber nod.

"Looks like you were right," Kate said. "I'm not sure whether to be excited or worried."

"Doesn't matter how you feel," he said, wagging his finger at her. "Just be sure you're prepared. No doubt you'll be staying on the island to cover the carnage. Just be sure you don't do anything stupid. My bad feeling's only getting worse."

The city spokeswoman's forehead puckered in disapproval at Vasquez's words, but her "official" smile didn't waver.

"And be sure you don't downplay the seriousness of this storm in your stories," Rush added. "People always debate whether they should leave. If news reports make it sound heroic to stay, we'll have a bunch of people gathering on the seawall to drink beer and watch the waves crash ashore."

Kate glanced at Ashleigh. Her smile now stretched so thin it looked like it might crack her face. She forced out a hollow laugh.

"Remember, the storm is still forecast to make landfall south of here," she said. "There's no need to panic."

The emergency management director huffed, but said nothing more.

Kate frowned. She knew Ashleigh would stick to the Mayor's talking points. But it sounded like the city's more experienced staffers didn't agree with the public messaging. Before she could ask anything else, Mayor Matthew Hanes stepped out of his office.

"Looks like we're ready to start," Ashley trilled, looking pointedly at Kate. "I hope you can still find somewhere to stand in this crowd."

Kate wondered what the young woman would do if she refused to move. Deciding it would do her no good to cause an uproar or make an enemy just before a major news event, Kate smiled, waved, and picked her way toward an empty spot in front of the cameras. Before the cameramen could start protesting about her blocking their view, she dropped into a squat, balancing her notebook on her knee.

"Good morning, everyone!" Hanes crowed. He sounded as though he were welcoming them to a ribbon cutting instead of a weather emergency. "As you all know, Hurricane Julio took a slight turn to the north overnight. While Galveston is now on the edge of the cone of uncertainty, it does not look like we will feel the worst of the storm's effect."

Hanes flashed his camera-ready smile around the room. Kate ground her teeth. She wished she'd stayed at the back of the room. Close proximity to Hanes always made her want to hit something.

"The storm could still turn south again, so if you have plans to come to the island this weekend, please keep them," Hanes continued. "But maybe have a Plan B, just in case."

Kate rolled her eyes when several of the TV reporters who were chummy with Hanes chuckled at his lame attempt at a joke.

"We are obviously keeping a close eye on the storm tracking models and are getting regular updates from the

National Hurricane Center. At this time, we do not anticipate ordering any evacuations. Believe me, the last thing I want to do is ask Galvestonians to leave their homes. But on the advice of our emergency management staff, I have ordered buses to evacuate anyone who wants to leave but doesn't have reliable transportation. We could be in for a few days of rain and wind, and that could mean power outages. So if you have medical equipment that might be affected, I would urge you to take that into consideration."

"When will the buses arrive?" an older reporter asked, without bothering to raise his hand.

The slightest hint of a frown darkened the mayor's face momentarily before his smile returned.

"This afternoon at 2 p.m. We've made arrangements for anyone who wants to leave to stay at a temporary shelter the Red Cross is opening in Houston. So nobody will have to travel too far from home. Really, this is just a precaution, to make sure all our citizens are comfortable and cared for over the next few days."

Hanes waved to Rush, who strode to the podium.

"I'd like to introduce Stephen Rush, our emergency management director," Hanes said. "He's going to say a few words about getting prepared."

"Thank you, Mayor Hanes," Rush said as he stepped up to the microphone. "Even though it does not look like Julio will come too close to Galveston, we all need to be prepared. As the mayor said, we might have heavy rain and strong winds. We could experience power outages. Make sure you have plenty of non-perishable food items and water on hand. Over the next few days, take a look around your yard and secure any loose items that could become projectiles. And obviously, check for updates frequently. I know our friends in the media will stay on top of this story."

Kate smiled. At least some people at city hall valued the press.

"This storm has already changed track once, and it could do it again. In fact, it probably will do it again. The real question is when and how much will it move? That will make a big difference in the kind of weekend we have ahead of us."

Hanes stepped forward and put a hand on Rush's shoulder.

"Thank you, Stephen," he said, a slight hint of annoyance in his voice. "The takeaway here is be prepared but don't panic. Galveston has withstood many storms before. This is no different. I'll take a few questions now."

Hanes called on several reporters behind Kate, ignoring her raised hand.

"I have time for just one more," Hanes said, scanning the back of the room.

Kate shot to her feet and didn't bother waiting for him to acknowledge her.

"Mayor Hanes, the storm that struck Florida last year caused a significant amount of damage and loss of life in low-lying areas. We're already prone to flooding here. Are you worried that if the storm turns north again later in the week, people won't have enough time to leave?"

Hanes' smile twisted into a ferocious snarl before he wrestled his animosity under control.

"Miss Bennett, you are new here. You've never gone through a storm on the island, am I correct?"

Kate nodded slightly. Her disgust for the man standing just a few feet from her kindled a fire of anger in her chest so hot it made her cheeks burn.

"Islanders know how to handle a hurricane," he sneered. "And we are not afraid of a little wind and water."

Hanes turned away with a sniff and flashed his smile at the TV cameras.

"I would encourage all island residents and visitors to keep an eye on our local television stations for the latest updates. Thank you."

After delivering his final dig at Kate and the *Gazette*, Hanes turned on his heel and marched back to his office.

"Wow, he really doesn't like you," a pretty brunette reporter in a tight red dress said when Kate turned away from the podium. "What did you do to get on his bad side?"

"Told the truth," Kate snapped, her frustration with Hanes spilling over before she could rein it in.

While the other reporters packed up and headed for the door, Kate slipped up the back staircase and headed for Eddie Vasquez's office. His secretary waved her back, as usual. The public works director was standing behind his desk, a map rolled out in front of him.

"Looking for an escape route?" Kate quipped.

Vasquez looked up and offered a brief smile. "Not exactly. I was just looking over the flood map survey we had done last year."

"And?"

He shook his head. "It's not good."

He motioned her around the desk and pointed to the shaded areas on the map. They covered more than half the city.

"This is a model showing what could happen if a Category 4 storm came ashore over Galveston at high tide."

Kate ran her finger over the downtown area. "How high is this water?"

"Depends," Vasquez said. "Could be three feet. Could be ten feet."

Kate traced the edge of the grey zone that covered all the city's poorest neighborhoods and many of the others.

"Has the mayor seen this?" She knew the answer before she even asked.

Vasquez nodded. "He called it an exaggerated, worst-case scenario."

"What do you think?"

"It is worst case, but it's not an exaggeration. We've got storm drains that are long overdue for cleaning out. That's only going to make this worse."

"If this storm turns north again..." Kate trailed off as she looked over the map.

"It could be really, really bad," Vasquez said. "I'm sending my wife to the mainland tonight."

"But the storm's not expected to make landfall until Saturday," Kate said.

"Right, but if it looks like it's going to be anywhere close to a direct hit, lots of people will be leaving at the same time. Talk about a mess."

"You think the mayor should have issued a stronger warning? Even called for a mandatory evacuation?"

Vasquez looked at her through narrowed eyes. "Off the record?"

Kate sighed. "Come on! You're the one who brought this up! Why tell me if you didn't want me to report on it?"

Vasquez pressed his lips together for several moments. "Because I want you to know what could be coming. Keep it in the back of your mind when you're writing your stories. You were right to ask the mayor about Florida. All it takes is a few bad decisions to cost a lot of people their lives."

"Can I quote you on that?"

Vasquez shook his head. "Not right now. I'm still going to need a job when this is all over."

Kate took a deep breath. "Fine. When you're ready to talk, you know where to find me."

He smiled. "You're a good reporter, Bennett. Keep asking those tough questions."

"Asking questions is easy. Getting answers is the hard part."

Peter pulled up outside the old orphanage and tried to wall off the nagging worry clamoring for attention at the back of his mind. The call had come over the scanner thirty minutes earlier. An officer doing a welfare check had discovered a body. Four squad cars sat parked along the curb, two with lights flashing. Peter climbed out of his own car and stared up at the building. Its vacant windows stared back. A tingle of apprehension evaded his defenses and danced across the back of his neck. Kate had been there just twenty-four hours earlier.

He put his hands on his hips and breathed a prayer for her continued protection. He was about to head up the stone staircase when a uniformed officer came around the corner of the building.

"The body's around back, sir," he said. "In the shed."

Peter's unease grew as he followed the officer to the back. They walked through a wrought-iron gate that must have been beautiful at one time, but now looked like something from a horror movie. Across the overgrown lot behind the building, Peter spotted three other officers standing outside a large ramshackle structure. Unless you walked through the gate, you would never know it was there.

The officers nodded a greeting as Peter walked up. The ranking officer, Greg Walker, motioned Peter over to the door.

"We only went inside to verify he was dead. We didn't touch anything else."

The man lay on his side. Peter couldn't see any visible wounds until he got closer. A dark purple bruise across the man's throat suggested he'd been strangled. Broken pots and rusted shovels and rakes littered shelves on either side of the shed. A heavy coating of dust covered everything. But one corner of the floor had been swept clean. Peter stepped around the body and bent down to inspect the space. Whatever had been there was gone.

Peter straightened and turned back toward the officers. Walker was making notes on a small pad.

"Who did the welfare check?" Peter asked.

"I did," Walker said, looking up from his notes. "Dispatch said someone from the man's office in Houston called when he didn't return from a trip to the island yesterday. He wasn't answering his phone."

"I assume this is him?"

"Yes, sir," Walker said. "I pulled up his driver's license information. Bill Presley. Looks like the same guy."

Walker held up his phone for Peter to inspect the photo.

"Didn't I see a story about him in the newspaper today?" one of the other officers asked.

Peter nodded and tried not to think about having to tell Kate the man she'd just interviewed was dead.

"Let's get the coroner out here," Peter said. "And set up a grid to go over every inch of this property. The high grass isn't going to help. But we need to see if our killer left anything behind."

Walker nodded and reached up for the radio mouthpiece clipped to his shoulder. The other two officers headed for their cars to collect crime scene tape. Peter turned back to the shed.

Any number of things could have led to Presley's murder. But something about the secluded outbuilding on the vacant property made Peter's skin crawl. It would be the perfect place for someone to hide.

"What makes you think Gage was there?" The police chief leaned back in his chair and regarded Peter through narrowed eyes.

"Just a hunch right now," Peter said. It took all his self-control to keep his voice even. "We're going over every square inch of that shed. We haven't found anything obvious yet. If he stayed there for any length of time, he covered his tracks well. I just have a bad feeling about this."

Ever since he'd seen the swept-out corner, Peter was sure someone was sleeping there. It was the perfect size for a makeshift bed. Of course, it could be a homeless person. But whoever it was had the presence of mind to remove all traces of his or her presence. In his experience, not many homeless people thought that far ahead.

"Don't jump to any conclusions yet," Lugar said. "You've still got more questions than answers."

"I'd like to send officers through the neighborhood to warn residents and ask them to keep an eye out."

Lugar grunted. "If it was Gage, he won't stick around to get caught."

"No, but at least we can tighten the net." Peter's pulse quickened at the thought of bringing Gage in and ending this nightmare of uncertainty.

"Fine, but Jarrell can handle that," Lugar said. "I don't want you anywhere near the search for Gage."

"But, sir!" Peter sputtered.

Lugar held up his meaty hand in warning. "You are too close to this to see it objectively. You may be making an assumption about Gage's involvement here because you want some kind of evidence that could lead to his capture."

Indignation made Peter's chest burn. But the logical part of his brain, sidelined temporarily by his emotions, whispered that Lugar was right. Peter took a deep breath.

"I guess that's fair," he said. "But we shouldn't dismiss the possibility just because I want to see Gage caught."

Lugar raised an eyebrow. "We all want to see him back in custody, detective. I just don't want to see another potential murderer escape because we jumped to the wrong conclusion."

Peter nodded. "I will work this case as though Gage were not a consideration."

"Good. Jarrell can handle the rest."

Peter stood to go, but paused before he took a step.

"Just one more thing. If Gage was hiding in that shed, he must be sticking around for a reason. Maybe he was lying low until things died down and we pulled back the search."

"And?" Lugar's face looked like the horizon darkening before a storm.

"Anyone in danger before could be in even more danger now."

"By anyone, you mean Kate Bennett."

"Yes."

"I'll have Jarrell increase patrols around her apartment."

"Thank you, sir. But that may not be enough."

The storm brewing on his boss's face broke.

"That is not your concern," he thundered. "Lieutenant Jarrell can handle that."

Amid the explosion of Lugar's anger, certainty coalesced in Peter's heart. He'd struggled for months to walk the tightrope between Lugar's disapproval and Kate's mixed messages. It was finally time to jump off.

Chapter 12

Two boxy white tour buses sat idling outside the community center when Kate pulled into the parking lot that afternoon. She expected to see a crowd milling about, but she counted less than two dozen people gathered along the edge of the building in the shade of its overhang.

One woman sat in a wheelchair, a tank of oxygen in a stand at her side. Nearby, another woman with a long white braid snaking over her shoulder sat on a bench. She clutched an enormous canvas bag in her lap, and as Kate walked past, a tiny, trembling dog poked its head out the top. Kate smiled but got nothing but sorrowful stares of resignation in response.

Assuming the rest of the crowd must be waiting inside to beat the heat, Kate headed for the community center's front door. It took her eyes a few moments to adjust to the relative gloom of the low-ceilinged interior. But the mass of people she expected to find didn't materialize.

"Huh," she said, stopping in confusion and putting her hands on her hips.

"Can I help you?" a woman called from a nearby office.

Kate poked her head inside. The woman, whose mass of dark curls bobbed around her face like a writhing mobile, peered at her through thick glasses.

"Where is everyone?" Kate asked, glancing back toward the front door.

"Everyone?" The woman looked a little alarmed, as though she'd just been told she'd lost a group of people left in her charge.

"For the evacuation buses. I was expecting a big crowd."

"Oh!" The woman laughed. "This is it so far. We might have a few more people show up in the next hour. That's when the buses are going to leave. But I don't know that we'll get many more."

Kate frowned. "Really? Why not?"

"Evacuating is a hassle. Nobody wants to do it unless they really have to. This far out, nobody feels much sense of urgency."

"But it's only three days away," Kate protested. "And the storm is probably going to keep moving north."

"Or it could turn south. I'm sure that's what most people are thinking."

Kate pictured the map spread across Eddie Vasquez's desk. No one liked making decisions based on the worst-case scenario, but surely they should at least consider it.

"You with the newspaper?" the woman asked, eyeing the notebook Kate clutched in her hand.

Kate nodded. "This will be my first hurricane, so I don't really know what to expect. But I definitely thought more people would want to leave."

"Well, I grew up here. Seems like we go through this every few years. Nobody ever used to leave. The evacuations are new."

"Really? What did they do when you were a kid?"

"Just hunkered down at home. I remember one storm my dad put us kids in the bathtub and set a mattress over us. I think he was worried the roof would blow off."

Kate shook her head to clear the image of terrified children huddled in a bathtub.

"So, are you going to leave this time?"

The woman shrugged. "Depends on how things look on Thursday, and whether the city says we can leave work. I can't just take off whenever I want. I'd get fired."

Embarrassment flushed Kate's cheeks. Of course, people couldn't just leave whenever they wanted to. And if city officials didn't think a mandatory evacuation was necessary, employers probably wouldn't give workers extra time off to evacuate. That made the mayor's nonchalance even more dangerous. He was making it nearly impossible for most of the city to leave, even if they wanted to.

"Well, I guess I'd better go talk to the people who are leaving," Kate said. "Thanks for your help."

"No problem. Sorry it's not much of a story yet. Give it a few days. Maybe you'll get some excitement then."

Kate grimaced. "I think Galveston is the only place that considers natural disasters exciting."

The woman grinned. "They definitely break up the monotony."

Kate walked back into the sweltering afternoon and surveyed her interview possibilities. The woman with the dog in her bag was the closest. She eyed Kate with suspicion as she approached.

"Hi," Kate said, preparing to sit down on the bench beside her. But before she could, the little dog popped its head out of the bag and started barking. The woman jumped and tried to push the animal back into hiding. But it fixed its beady eyes on Kate and continued its high-pitched yapping. The woman scowled at Kate.

"Go away," she hissed. "If they see him, they might not let us get on the bus."

"Sorry," Kate said, backing away. She turned around to look for someone else to talk to and stumbled over the oxygen tank standing next to the woman in the wheelchair. She looked up at Kate, mild surprise filling her watery eyes.

"Be careful," she said. "That's the only one of those I've got until I get to Houston."

Kate glanced at the tank in alarm. "You don't have a backup?"

The woman shook her head. "That's why I decided to get out now. If the power goes out, I'll be in trouble fast."

"I guess this isn't your first storm." Kate squatted down next to her and balanced her notebook on her knee.

The woman chuckled, but it sounded more like a rasping cough. "I lost count of all the storms I've been through on this sandbar. It ain't as easy as it once was, and there's no one left for me to call for help."

"You don't have family here?"

"Not any more." She said it with such sad finality that Kate couldn't bring herself to ask why.

"I'm surprised more people aren't joining you on these buses."

The woman shook her head. "All they're worried about is the inconvenience. And they don't want to leave their houses. If something does happen, they want to be here to start making repairs right away. I remember the time a storm blew part of our roof off when I was a kid. My daddy was out there on a ladder with a sheet of plywood before the wind had even died down." She smiled at the memory.

"Sounds dangerous."

"He was crazy. An old shrimp boat captain. He refused to let any storm get the best of him."

"Were you scared?"

"Probably was. I don't remember that, though. I just remember the family being together. Seemed like we could weather anything."

"And now?"

"Now I'm old and alone and I don't want to sit in the dark for days and days."

Kate nodded. "I'm glad you're going somewhere safe."

"Hopefully, this is a whole lot of trouble for nothing. I been in my house sixty years. I just hope it's still standing when I get back."

"Me, too," Kate said. "Where do you live?"

"Right next to English Bayou. Grew up in that house. It's survived quite a few storms. But our streets flood even in a heavy rain these days. After what happened to those poor people in Florida a few years back, I ain't gonna risk it. I'd rather not drown in my own living room."

"What about your neighbors?"

"No one seems worried, even though our front doors are 75 yards from the water as it is." She paused to cough, shaking her head. "My next door neighbor dropped me off here this afternoon. He told me I should stay, that he and his wife would look after me, but I don't want to be a burden. And anyway, there's only so much he can do with no power."

"They're not worried?"

The woman shook her head. "Just like all the rest of 'em. Carl Neal told me he's sure this storm will turn at the last minute. Maybe it will, but it seems like people just want to stick their heads in a sand dune and pretend there's nothing out there."

Kate glanced up at the cloudless sky. Maybe it wasn't that hard to understand, especially since it had been several decades since the last really bad storm.

"I hope he's right, but I'm glad you're not waiting around to find out."

The woman smiled, deep wrinkles fissuring her cheeks. "Don't you go sticking your head in any sand dunes, you hear? It may look safe right now, but there's a monster lurking out there."

A chill shot down Kate's back and she shivered. She knew the woman was talking about the storm, but her warning immediately made Kate think of Tommy Gage.

Peter eyed the man sitting at the top of the steps leading to the door of the old orphanage. His disheveled hair, slumped shoulders, and pale face all suggested genuine shock and sorrow. Peter had called Bill Presley's office from the police station to confirm they'd found his body. His business partner, Fitzgerald Isaacson, had agreed to come to Galveston right away to answer some questions.

His eyes followed Peter as he walked up the steps, but Isaacson didn't offer any visible acknowledgement until Peter sat down next to him.

"Mr. Isaacson?"

The man nodded and passed his hand over his face as though trying to wipe away a bad memory.

"The coroner was just leaving when I drove up," he croaked. "I still can't believe it was Bill on that gurney."

"When was the last time you saw him?"

"Yesterday morning, early. He came into the office just briefly before heading down here to talk to a reporter with the local newspaper."

The back of Peter's neck tingled at the mention of Kate.

"Did anything seem unusual?"

Isaacson shook his head. "Bill was excited. He poured his heart into this project. He was so excited about it. The neighbors objected at first, but Bill had worked hard to win them over. It seemed like all those problems were behind him. The Planning Commission gave its approval.

And he felt pretty confident the city council would as well."

"What can you tell me about Mr. Presley's personal life?"

"There's not much to tell, to be honest. Bill spent a lot of time working. He didn't date much. No serious relationships since college. We were roommates at A&M."

"Did he have any problems with anyone? Any serious conflicts?"

Isaacson shook his head.

"What about pastimes not related to work? Was he involved in anything that might have gotten him in trouble?"

Isaacson shook his head again. "He was a really tame guy. He played tennis at the country club and liked to travel. And garden. That was where he spent most of his time when he wasn't working. He used to tell me his life wasn't interesting enough, and that's why no one wanted to date him. But he always said it with a laugh, like he didn't really care."

"Tell me about your business," Peter said, searching Isaacson's face for any sign of a lie.

"It's a 50-50 partnership."

"And what happens to Mr. Presley's half of the business now?"

Isaacson showed no sign of concern. "It reverts to me, until I can find someone else to partner with. I can't do this on my own, which is why Bill and I teamed up in the first place. We worked really well together, and neither one of us wanted to run a business by ourselves."

He rubbed the back of his neck. His face looked pinched, as though he were trying not to cry.

"Did you expect Mr. Presley back in the office yesterday?"

"I didn't really think about it. I had a meeting in Clear Lake yesterday afternoon with another client to talk about a project we're trying to finalize there. That kept me busy all afternoon and then we went to dinner in the evening. I didn't get home until late, and I didn't expect to see Bill until this morning. When he didn't come to the office and didn't answer his cell phone, I called you guys and asked if someone could swing by and check on him."

"What made you think he was still here?"

Isaacson smiled sadly and held up his phone. "Location tracking. We've had it set up since college. I could see his phone was here. Honestly, I was worried maybe he'd had an accident. There are a couple of spots in the building that are a bit dicey."

Peter glanced at the list he'd jotted in his notebook. If Isaacson was telling the truth, nothing obvious in Bill Presley's life pointed to murder.

"Did you have any problems here at the property with anyone trying to break in, maybe to sleep or take shelter?"

"You mean like a homeless person?" Isaacson sounded surprised.

"Or someone looking for a place to do drugs."

Isaacson shook his head. "The previous owner had someone who kept an eye on the place to prevent that kind of thing. Even though it needs a lot of restoration work, it never suffered any vandalism. That was one of the things that appealed to Bill. All things considered, it's in great condition."

"What about the shed out back?"

Isaacson's eyes widened. "Where they found Bill's body? I didn't think of that. I don't know. He planned to tear it down, so I don't think he was concerned about what shape it was in. I'm honestly not sure he ever went in there."

Peter frowned. Something made him go into the shed yesterday morning. Did he spot someone, or signs that someone had been there?

"If you think of anything else, please give me a call." Peter pulled a business card from his pocket and held it out. "I'll be in touch soon. I'd like to come up to Houston in the next few days and talk to some of Mr. Presley's other friends."

Peter stood to go, then turned and held out his hand. "I'm sorry this happened to your friend."

Isaacson nodded, and his forehead crinkled as though his face wanted to fold in on itself. His voice caught in his throat when he tried to speak. Peter squeezed his hand and hurried down the steps. He walked around to the back of the building, where yellow caution tape stretched all the way to the edge of the property. Several crime scene investigators stood outside the shed, comparing notes. Another one was inspecting the grid the responding officers had marked off in the high grass. Even though his officers had done an initial sweep, the specialists would do a more thorough analysis.

Peter waved at the men and one of the two standing by the shed carefully picked his way toward the tape. Peter tapped his foot with impatience while he watched the man's slow progress.

"Find anything?" he finally asked when the technician, Vic Romero, got close enough to hear him.

Romero shook his head. "Nothing newer than 20 years old, from the looks of it. Some of the broken pots and general disarray probably happened during the struggle. But even that's minimal. It doesn't look like the victim put up much of a fight."

"The element of surprise is a big advantage," Peter said. "Do you think someone was sleeping in there?"

"It's hard to say. Except for the spot in the corner that you noticed, there's no other evidence. If the killer was hiding here for any length of time, he did a good job removing any trace."

Peter sighed and squinted through the afternoon glare at the shed.

"We're not done yet," Romero said. "The next step is to comb through all these weeds. If the killer dropped something on his way out, it would be easy for him to miss."

Peter swallowed his disappointment and nodded. "Let me know if you find anything."

The possibilities churned through Peter's mind as he strode back to his car. Despite Isaacson's claim that his friend led an uninteresting life, Bill Presley still could have been killed by someone he knew. That was much more likely, statistically speaking, than an attack by a stranger.

And even if he surprised someone staying in the shed, the odds were against it being an escaped prisoner. But Peter couldn't shake the feeling that the odds in this case were wrong.

He slid his phone out of his pocket and scrolled to Alonzo Gutierrez's name in his contact list.

"I was just about to call you," the sheriff's deputy said as soon as he answered. "News must travel faster than I realized."

A volcano of hope erupted in Peter's heart, stopping him in his tracks.

"Did you catch him?" His voice sounded unnaturally high, and he held his breath to slow his racing heart.

"Aw, sorry, man. No. Gage is still on the loose."

Peter's excitement vanished as quickly as it had come, like a rug pulled out from under him. He closed his eyes and forced himself to take a deep breath.

"But we did arrest the deputy helping to run the smuggling ring in the jail. The sheriff's about to hold a press conference in thirty minutes."

"That's good news," Peter said. "Not the good news I was hoping for. But still good news."

"Yeah, sorry about that. We're still looking for Gage."

"That's actually what I was calling you about. I'm working a murder case that seems like it could have a connection to Gage. We haven't turned up any evidence yet, and the chief is skeptical. But I can't shake the feeling Gage didn't make it off the island after all."

"Hmmm..." Gutierrez said. He didn't sound any more convinced than Lugar had been.

"Look, I just wanted to give you a heads up. I know you're putting all your resources on the mainland, and he could be hiding right under our noses."

"I hear ya. But the truth is, he could be hiding anywhere."

Peter closed his eyes and willed his rising frustration into retreat.

"Sure," he said. "I know you've got your hands full. I'll let you get back to it. I'll call you if I have anything more concrete to share."

"Thanks, detective. I know you want to get this guy. Just keep at it. He'll show himself eventually."

Peter ended the call and glanced back at the crime scene. Goosebumps pricked his arms. He felt like the mouse to Gage's cat. No amount of doubt from Lugar or Gutierrez could shake his conviction that the escaped murderer had been here. And if he was hanging around the island, he must have a reason.

BREAKING: Deputy arrested in jail smuggling case

Ringleader had ties to escaped inmate | By Ben Denison

Galveston sheriff's deputies arrested one of their own on Tuesday. Corporal Zack Dalton is accused of working with inmates at the Galveston County Jail to smuggle and distribute contraband, including drugs.

"This is a very serious offense that strikes at the heart of everything law enforcement stands for," Sheriff Tyler Metcalf said in an exclusive interview with the *Galveston Gazette* shortly after Dalton's arrest.

The smuggling ring came to light following the escape on Friday of an inmate about to stand trial for murder. Tommy Gage is accused of killing his parents two years ago. Investigators believe Gage found out about Dalton's involvement in the smuggling ring and used the information to bribe another inmate into helping him escape. Metcalf said investigators did not believe Dalton had any direct involvement in Gage's breakout.

"Nevertheless, his activities helped make Gage's escape possible, which only makes it worse," Metcalf said.

During his escape, Gage stabbed Deputy Travis Barker with a knife he made out of razor blades and a toothbrush. Barker is still in the hospital, but doctors expect him to make a full recovery.

Gage remains on the loose, and investigators haven't found any evidence showing where he might have gone. After at first focusing their efforts on the island, the sheriff's department expanded its search to the mainland. Although tips come in to the hotline every day, Metcalf said none of them have turned into solid leads.

"But we know he's out there, and it's just a matter of time before we find him," the sheriff added.

Chapter 13

Kate turned her car's air conditioning to full blast as she pulled out of the community center parking lot and headed back toward the newspaper. The woman's warning still rang in her ears and she glanced in her rearview mirror. No threats loomed, and she forced herself to laugh. The hollow sound disappeared as quickly as it came, like a stone tossed into deep water. She didn't want to stick her head in the sand, but she would only drive herself crazy if she kept looking over her shoulder every few minutes.

As she neared the intersection of 59th Street, she slowed. Her story about evacuees looked pretty thin, and Mattingly was counting on it to hold a spot on the front page. She could hear his outraged roar if she had to tell him the story didn't pan out. That did not sound like a great way to end the day.

She swerved into the turn lane, waving an apology to the truck she cut off in the process. The driver blared his horn in reply as he sped past. She ignored him and cut across Broadway into the English Bayou neighborhood. She turned right and cruised down the street at its outer edge. On one side, big houses backed up to the water. On the other side sat modest bungalows built in the '50s and '60s.

Kate slowed as she drove, peering into driveways and backyards as much as she could. No one seemed to be in a hurry to secure those loose items Stephen Rush had warned about. Halfway down the street, she slowed and started looking for the house numbers. When she found the one she was looking for, she pulled over and stopped the car.

A man holding a garden hose over his front flower bed waved as she walked toward him.

"Are you Carl Neal?" she asked, holding her notebook to her forehead to shield her eyes from the sun's glare.

"I am. I hope you're not here to sell me something or collect any money. My bank account's empty."

Kate laughed. "Your wallet's safe. I just want to talk. My name's Kate Bennett. I'm with the *Gazette*. I met your neighbor over at the community center a few minutes ago. She's getting ready to evacuate. She told me you and your wife were staying put, so I thought I would come meet you and see if you would talk to me for my story."

Carl turned off the water and set down the hose. "Evie's a gem. I told her she would be perfectly safe to stay, but she insisted on going. We would have looked after her. Come on inside. It's too hot to stand around out here."

Kate followed him through the front door into a brightly lit living room. A television in the corner blared an afternoon talk show. A woman sitting on the couch looked up in surprise, although the clicking cadence of the knitting needles in her hands didn't slow.

"Who's this?" she asked, sending a puff of air toward several errant strands of hair that had escaped her ponytail to gather around her face. A few silver streaks in her black hair offered the only hint at her age.

"Kate Bennett. She's a reporter from the newspaper who met Evie over at the community center," Carl said, picking up the remote and turning off the television. "She wants to talk to us about why we're not evacuating."

"Evie worry too much," the woman said. "We no worry."

"This is my wife, Gigi," Carl said, motioning for Kate to sit down on a chair opposite the couch. "We've been married for 45 years. I don't think she's ever worried a day since I met her."

Gigi tsked at her husband. "Silly man," she said, as though that explained everything Kate needed to know.

"Have you lived in Galveston that whole time?"

"No. I was in the merchant marines and met Gigi in the Philippines. We married there and have lived all over the world. We came back to Galveston after I retired."

"You grew up here?"

"Sure did. And I've seen plenty of storms here and everywhere else. Julio isn't keeping me up at night."

"I know it seems like a long way off right now, but if it keeps turning north, it could be a problem. You're not worried about the possibility of a direct hit?"

Carl waved his hand dismissively. "Even if it comes right over us, we're a long way from the seawall. Just had the roof replaced last year, so it's nailed down tight. Only other thing we'd have to worry about is flying debris breaking a window. I'll close the shutters if it looks like it's going to be bad."

Kate glanced out the front window toward the houses across the street. "What about the bayou? It's right there. You're not worried about flooding?"

"Nah. The streets fill up in a heavy rain, but the water always drains."

"We no worry," Gigi said again. Her clicking needles seemed to magnify her assurance.

"What would be the downside of leaving?"

Carl chuckled. "It's a pain, and it's not free! I'm not staying in any shelter, which means we'd have to get a hotel room. Why go to all that trouble and cost when I can stay in my own home for free? I'm not worried about power outages."

"Do you have a generator?"

"Don't need one. Just costs more money in gas. I'll get ice for a cooler, and we'll fill up the bathtub. It'll be like camping."

Kate glanced out the window again. She could see the bayou's dark water glistening between two houses. The neighborhoods devastated by that storm in Florida had looked a lot like this. She turned back to Carl and smiled.

"Hopefully you're right. Seems like most people share your opinion of the situation. Only a few dozen people showed up to take those evacuation buses."

Carl shook his head. "They'd be much better off staying put. You know, it's not just the inconvenience. The other issue is the potential for looting. If everyone leaves, and the police are busy dealing with other things, all those empty houses would be easy prey for criminals. And if you leave only to have the storm turn, you might come back to a disaster, anyway. Given the opportunity, some people turn into animals."

From the couch, Gigi tsked and nodded vigorously.

Kate looked around the room at the things the couple wanted to protect. Nothing looked particularly valuable. Then she noticed the wall covered in photos.

"Is that your family?"

Carl nodded, and the incessant clicking of knitting needles stilled. Gigi hopped off the couch and glided over to the wall. She beamed as she pointed to a photo of a young woman holding a baby.

"This our granddaughter," she said, raising her knitting for Kate to inspect. "I knit sweater, blanket, bootie."

In the photo, the baby girl sported a pink hat that Kate felt sure was also Gigi's handiwork.

"Couldn't you visit them while you evacuated?"

Carl laughed. "That would be a long drive. They live in Alaska. Our son works on the fishing boats up there."

Kate decided to admit defeat. If a beloved grandchild couldn't convince them to leave, nothing could. For the next 10 minutes, she listened to Carl narrate an abbreviated version of their life story. The frames adorning the wall chronicled each significant event.

"We've been through a lot, haven't we, old girl?" He draped his arm around Gigi's shoulders and kissed the top of her head. "Whatever happens, we'll face it together. And we'll add another photo to the wall."

Kate smiled as she headed out to her car. She stopped to turn back and wave before sliding behind the wheel. Carl stood in the doorway, hands in his pockets. Through the window, she could see the back of Gigi's head as she resettled herself on the couch. The couple's security might not be based on reality, but Kate couldn't help longing for a taste of it.

Most of the tables on the deck at Pelican's Landing sat empty when Peter walked up the gangplank leading from the sidewalk along Seawall Boulevard. The late afternoon sun still beat down like an inferno, but the restaurant shaded all but the outer edge of the deck from its rays. A waitress in tight black shorts and a bright blue tank top sashayed over to him.

"You can sit anywhere you like," she drawled.

"Actually, I'm here to see Aleah Price. Is she working this afternoon?"

The girl's eyes flicked to the gun on his hip. She looked like she wanted to ask a question, but then thought better of it.

"I'll get her," she said.

Peter walked to the deck's railing and gazed out over the Gulf of Mexico. It still showed no sign of the storm brewing beyond the horizon. People dotted the sand, unperturbed by the weather reports. He turned around just in time to see Tommy Gage's former girlfriend slipping out the door at the back of the restaurant. She frowned when she saw him watching her. He wondered if she'd intended to sneak off while his back was turned.

She made her way toward him slowly, her face filled with suspicion.

"What do you want?" she spat when she got close enough for him to hear her without raising her voice. "You can't just harass me at work. I haven't done anything wrong."

"I'm not trying to harass you. I just wanted to check with you to see if you'd thought of anything that might help us find Tommy."

"I already told you I don't have any idea where he is." She crossed her arms and jutted out her chin.

Peter hadn't expected her to tell him anything useful, but he wanted to gauge her reaction. Her belligerence seemed a little exaggerated, even for someone who chaffed at authority.

"We found someone murdered today," Peter said, studying her face. "Looks like he might have surprised someone hiding in the shed in his backyard."

Aleah's eyes widened just enough for Peter to notice. A hint of emotion flitted across her face before her mask of grievance slid back into place.

"What does that have to do with me?"

"I guess that depends on whether it has anything to do with Tommy."

The girl shifted her weight and put her hand on her hip. "I still don't see what it has to do with me."

"If Tommy Gage is still on the island and he hasn't contacted you, I'm betting he will. If he just lost his hideout, he's going to be looking for a new one. I just thought you would want to know."

Aleah snorted and shook her head, but not before Peter caught a glimmer of fear in her eyes.

"Like I told you before, I haven't heard from him."

"You know he's dangerous, don't you?" Peter murmured, willing her to let her guard down.

"He wouldn't hurt me," she snapped. "I'm not a threat to him."

"I don't think he sees threats the way normal people do."

She glared in reply, but said nothing.

"Look, I know you don't trust the police, but I don't think you should trust Tommy Gage, either. If you hear from him, please call us. Even if you don't think you're in danger. If you help him in any way, you'll be considered an accessory to anything he does until he's caught."

Aleah hesitated, but only for a split second. "I'll keep that in mind," she said. Then she turned abruptly and marched back into the kitchen.

Peter's chest tightened as he watched her go. He couldn't tell whether she was telling the truth about not knowing where Gage was, but she couldn't hide that hint of fear. Was she scared of what he had done, or of what he might still do? If Gage was already at her apartment, Peter's warning might have come too late. As he walked back to his car, he prayed Aleah would have the courage to reach out for help. Then he pulled out his phone and dialed Lieutenant Jarrell's number.

Kate had just typed the last word in her evacuation story when her cell phone buzzed and Peter's name flashed across the screen. She scooped her phone off the desk and trotted into the break room where her colleagues were less likely to listen in on her conversation.

"Are you on deadline?" he asked as soon as she answered.

"I just turned in my story. It's been a busy day, but uneventful as far as you're concerned. The most dangerous thing I faced was a ferocious but very tiny dog."

Peter chuckled, and the warmth in his voice caressed her cheek.

"Do I need to start sending Coral and Simba on assignment with you?"

"Since they only seem to notice my presence when I have a ball or a bone, I'm not sure they would be much help."

He chuckled again, and she leaned into the phone. She still marveled that no matter the circumstances, or even what they were talking about, Peter managed to convey a sense of peace and strength. Then he sighed, and the peace crumbled like a sandcastle kicked by a petulant toddler.

"Listen, Kate, I called to tell you about a murder that happened this morning. Bill Presley."

"What?" The question whooshed out of Kate's mouth as though someone had punched her in the stomach. She swayed and put out her hand to catch the edge of a nearby table. "I was just with him yesterday."

"I know. That's why I wanted you to hear it from me. I just got off the phone with Ben. He's working on the story."

"What happened?"

"I'm not sure. It looks like someone attacked him in a shed behind the old orphanage. We don't know who or why."

Kate's mind reeled. She closed her eyes and pictured the overgrown yard with the shed in the corner.

"I saw it when I was interviewing him. He was showing me what he planned to do with that space. I wasn't paying close attention because I just wanted to get back to the newspaper, but I remember him saying something about the door being open."

When Peter didn't respond right away, Kate's skin started to crawl.

"Do you think whoever attacked him was there? While we were talking?" Her voice came out in a strangled whisper.

"I don't know. Did you walk across the grass?"

"No. We never left the back porch."

Peter sighed with what sounded like relief. "We're still combing through evidence. Nothing is off the table at the moment. For all I know, it could have been a disgruntled contractor or someone else who had a beef with Presley."

Something in his voice made her tremble. "But that's not what you think, is it?"

"No. I don't have any reason to believe this, but my gut tells me Tommy Gage was hiding in that shed and Presley found him."

Kate squeezed her arms to her sides in a vain attempt to stop shaking. All she could think about was going home to her empty apartment with no police officer to guard the door.

"What am I supposed to do?"

"Finish up with work and come straight home. I'll be waiting for you."

"Then what? Do you think the police chief will agree to reinstate the guard?"

"No. He thinks I'm overreacting. I'm going to stay with you tonight. And I'll bring the dogs."

A mixture of relief and alarm swirled in her chest.

"Are you sure?"

"Absolutely. There's no way I'm leaving you alone."

Kate took a deep breath and let it out slowly. She knew he wasn't asking anything of her, but it still felt like she was about to take a step she wasn't ready for.

"What if the chief finds out?"

"I'm not worried about the chief." His voice held an edge Kate hadn't heard before in their discussions about the challenges their relationship posed to their careers.

"Maybe you should be," she whispered, afraid of what his new determination meant.

"All I'm worried about right now is you. Listen, I need to tie up a few loose ends here before I head home to get the dogs. Don't leave the office until I text to let you know I'm headed downtown."

"Okay." She wanted to protest, but couldn't find the words.

"I'll see you soon."

Kate sat in the break room, clutching her phone, for a long time after Peter hung up. She didn't make a move to get up until she heard the managing editor bellowing her name.

"Bennett!" Mattingly careened around the corner and scowled when he saw her. "What are you doing in there? Get back to your desk. You've got another story to write."

BREAKING: Julio's track shifts closer to Galveston

Communities along the middle Texas coast encouraged to evacuate | By Kate Bennett

Hurricane Julio brushed past the Yucatan Peninsula and entered the Gulf of Mexico on Tuesday afternoon. As forecasters feared, the storm has maintained its northerly track, putting it much closer to Galveston than originally expected.

"I would say it's increasingly likely that the Houston-Galveston area will see significant effects from this storm," said Liam Arnold, a forecaster with the National Weather Service office in League City. "And if it continues to strengthen like we think it will, we could be in for a very uncomfortable few days."

Julio is still a Category 2 storm, but just barely. With wind speeds already topping 108 miles per hour, forecasters expect it to strengthen to a Category 3 overnight.

The storm track still shows Julio making landfall south of the island. Officials in Port Lavaca and Palacios have ordered mandatory evacuations for people living on the edge of Matagorda Bay.

But the City of Galveston spokeswoman, Ashleigh Tarver, said Mayor Matthew Hanes has not changed his directive to island residents.

"We are still taking a wait and see approach," she said. "A lot could change in the next 24 hours, but for now, the mayor feels Galvestonians are better off preparing to hunker down and weather this storm at home."

Julio's brush with Mexico left a trail of debris along its coast, with travelers forced to take refuge in their hotel rooms. But because the storm stayed offshore, it did minimal damage.

Julio is the tenth named storm of this season, but none have struck the U.S. mainland. The last major storm rolled ashore last year in south Florida. Most of the 36 people who died lived in houses near the water.

Arnold urged people to take Julio seriously.

"People tend to get lulled into a false sense of security when we haven't had a storm in a while," he said. "But that's the kind of thinking that gets people killed."

Chapter 14

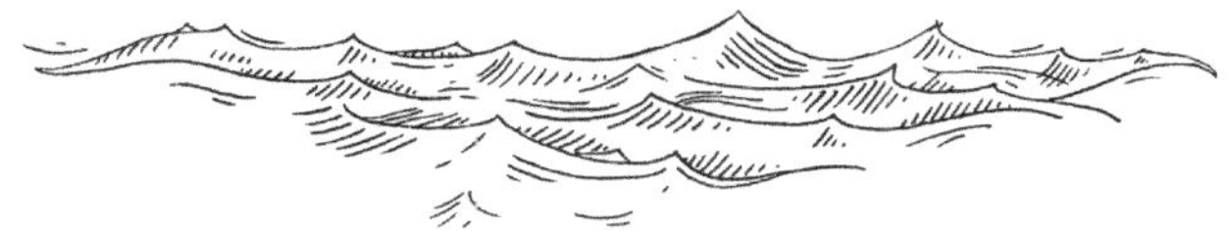

Peter planned to go straight home, but as he neared the cross street that ran by the old orphanage, he swung into the right turn lane. The crime scene techs should be done with their sweep of the area around the shed. He didn't want to wait until tomorrow to learn if they'd found something.

The two men were standing by the back of their SUV when Peter pulled up at the curb. Romero waved at him, a clear plastic bag pinned between his fingers. Peter's heart pounded against his ribs.

"What did you find?" he asked as soon as he jumped out of the car.

"Orange fibers," Romero said, squinting at the bag. "We won't know until we can get them tested, but they look to me like the same color as prison uniforms."

Peter's breath caught in his throat. It could take the lab weeks to confirm a match. But he didn't need scientific confirmation to fan the worst of his fears into flame. Tommy Gage was still on the island, and there was only one reason he wouldn't try to flee.

"Good work," he said. "Where did you find them?"

"Snagged on a branch near the fence. It was well hidden by the grass. If he was moving quickly, he might not have noticed."

"I'll let Lieutenant Jarrell know, but could you also write up a brief memo? With this storm coming in, it will take even longer for the lab to process those fibers. I want the chief, and the sheriff's department, to be aware of this as soon as possible."

Romero nodded. "I'll do that when I get back to the office. We can get this expedited to the lab tomorrow."

Peter waved his thanks and jogged back to the car. With the sun sinking lower in the sky, twilight would come on fast. He refused to leave Kate unprotected after dark.

He was standing outside her building when Kate's car pulled up to the curb. The anxiety twisting knots across his shoulder blades eased, and he took a deep breath. He'd talked to her less than 15 minutes earlier when she left the newspaper, but he couldn't rest until she made it safely home. He opened her door and took her hand, drawing her out so swiftly her eyes widened.

"Is everything okay?" she asked, glancing around them.

"It's fine. I just want to get upstairs before it's dark."

He swung the car door shut and led her toward the building.

"I don't know what we're going to do about dinner," Kate said. "I'm pretty sure there's not much to work with in the kitchen."

He smiled. "We'll have plenty. I cleaned out my freezer. If the power's out for very long when this storm comes through, it would all go to waste, anyway."

Two throaty and menacing growls greeted them when they got to the top of the stairs. Peter made a clicking noise, and they immediately stilled. When he opened the apartment door, the dogs stood expectantly, tails wagging.

"Good boys," Peter said, caressing them both behind the ears.

"I don't think I've ever heard them growl before," Kate said, setting her computer bag next to the kitchen table.

"They can sense the tension, so they're on alert. Plus, they're in a new place." He snapped his fingers and pointed toward a blanket next to the door. The dogs flopped down obediently and put their heads on their paws.

Peter pulled several packages out of the refrigerator and rummaged in the cabinets for the right pans. Kate watched him with narrowed eyes.

"What aren't you telling me?" she finally asked.

He turned around and looked at her. Worry creased her forehead and pinched the corners of her mouth. Light smudges under her eyes testified to the toll the past few days had taken on her sleep. He didn't want to add to her burden, but he couldn't lie.

"The crime scene techs found orange fibers in the yard behind the orphanage. It's not much, but it's enough to convince me Tommy Gage was there in his prison uniform. I have no doubt he killed Bill Presley."

Kate swallowed and pressed her lips together. Peter took a step toward her, but she held back. Fear and determination waged war across her face before she turned away.

"I'm going to get cleaned up," she said over her shoulder as she headed toward the bathroom.

He watched her go with a sense of resignation. He would lift every burden he could. But some battles had to be fought alone.

While he worked on dinner, his mind wandered back to the day they'd first met, amid the ruins of someone else's tragedy. He could tell right away that the story she'd been sent to cover as her first assignment held a personal significance. In the two and a half years since then, he'd never asked her about it. He'd gathered hints, but never the whole story. All he knew for sure was that she went to a lot of trouble to keep something hidden. And it made her keep everyone she knew at arm's length, even him. Several times he'd sensed the dam of revelation about to break, but each time, she'd pulled back from the edge.

Anyone else probably would have given up waiting, but he had secrets of his own. How could he ask her to unlock the door to her darkest memories when he couldn't bring himself to do the same? No matter how much it cost, he knew he had to be the one to take the first step.

Thirty minutes later, Kate emerged from the bathroom with wet hair and pink cheeks. She smiled weakly as she walked over to where he stood at the counter.

"Thanks for cooking dinner," she said, glancing up at him briefly before looking away again. "And for being here."

Peter reached out and lifted her chin. Her eyes held a hint of hesitation, but behind it he sensed a sea of longing. It drew him toward her like a magnet.

"There is nowhere I would rather be," he whispered.

She reached up and took his hand. Her quick smile almost hid the tremble in her lower lip. The beeping of the kitchen timer broke the tension. He gave her hand a quick squeeze and turned to take the food out of the oven. While he tossed a salad, Kate set the table. They lingered over their meal, and Kate filled him in on everything she'd learned about the storm and the reasons people gave for their decision to stay.

"I just keep thinking about the storm that hit Florida last year," she said. "So many people died unnecessarily."

"Does Vasquez really think that could happen here?" Peter had been so focused on Gage, he hadn't paid much attention to the danger posed by the storm. If it was as bad as the public works director feared, he would have his hands full keeping Kate safe, along with everyone else.

"Both he and Stephen Rush are convinced the mayor made a mistake by not calling for a voluntary evacuation at least. If people wait too long to leave, they may get stuck."

They washed dishes in silence. Peter's thoughts flitted from one danger to the next. Threats loomed on all sides.

And yet, the biggest challenge hung in the silence between them.

When they finished drying the last two pots, he took her hand and drew her toward the couch. She followed without a word, but questions filled her face. He sat down in one corner and motioned for her to take the other. The expanse of cushions between them felt like a raging sea.

"I want to tell you a story," he said. He'd meant to start strong, in hopes the momentum would carry him through to the end. But his voice cracked under the weight of what he knew was coming. "I should have told you a long time ago."

He held her gaze for several heartbeats. She sat motionless, but her wide eyes swam with concern. He passed his hand across his forehead and took a deep breath.

"I've never told anyone the whole thing. People from my past know what happened, but not because they heard it from me. I've wanted to tell you for the past year, but I kept putting it off. It's partly because I didn't want to relive it. But mostly I just—" he paused as he searched for the right word. "I feared what you would think."

Kate drew her knees to her chest and wrapped her arms around her legs. A protective pose. Her obvious alarm made him want to shovel every word he'd just spoken back into his mouth and forget the whole thing. But he couldn't turn back now.

"I was five when my parents moved to Nigeria to be missionaries. We settled in the north in a really rural area. My dad came from a farming family and studied agriculture in college, so he worked with the village elders to improve their planting and harvesting techniques. My mom set up a medical clinic and provided care not just to our village but the surrounding ones as well. Eventually, several other missionary families came to join us and the whole area just flourished."

He closed his eyes and pictured the rolling hills undulating with grass under the hot sun.

"The area had been peaceful for a long time, but during years when the rains dried up, herdsmen would drive their cattle long distances in search of food. They sometimes destroyed crops or made trouble in the villages. The elders appointed guards to keep watch when they knew the herdsmen were around, but the trouble never got too serious."

He opened his eyes and found Kate's glued to his face. He wanted to take her hand, but he didn't want to feel her pull away when he got to the hard part.

"I loved every minute of my life there. Everyone treated me like just another child in the village. The chief's son, Danjuma, was my best friend. Our birthdays were just a few weeks apart. Every year they included me in the big celebration. We were inseparable. But when I turned thirteen, my parents sent me to a boarding school in Kenya so I could get a more Western education. Danjuma spent more time with his father, and mine, learning about farming. He had big plans for expanding their fields and improving the village. So while I was being bored to tears by algebra and world history, he was learning how to lead with an eye to the future."

He smiled at the memory of his friend explaining his ideas to the village elders, full of enthusiasm and hope.

"Since we were kids, he had known his parents planned for him to marry the daughter of one of the village elders. Her name was Asabe. We used to laugh about it back then. It was hard to imagine getting married and having a family. But when I came home from school during the holidays, I could sense a change. Danjuma was growing up fast, faster than me, anyway. He had fallen in love with Asabe. I knew it wouldn't be long before they were married."

He paused and looked out the window at the inky dark of evening. He felt like the night sky was drawing the last of the light from his own heart.

"But that wasn't the only thing that changed while I was away at school. The herdsmen had gotten more aggressive. What began as a feud over land morphed into an ethnic and religious conflict. The herdsmen were Muslim, and they had no interest in coexisting with the Christian villages that stood in their way. The attacks started as small raids. They would ride through the village at night on motorbikes, shooting in the air and starting small fires. Danjuma organized defense teams to respond. At first they just chased them out of the village, but soon they went on the offense. If the herdsmen raided the village, the defenders would attack their camps."

Kate's eyes held a hint of dread, as though she feared what was coming. His breath caught in his throat and he had to swallow hard before he could continue.

"My parents begged the elders not to retaliate but to seek help from the local authorities. They did try, but it's not like the rural areas have an active police force. And besides, most of the local officials sympathized more with the herdsmen than with the villagers. So the cycle of raids and attacks continued. The other two missionary families left because of the violence. When I was seventeen, I came home for the summer and barely recognized the village. They had built walls and fortifications. Most of the men carried rifles slung over their shoulders everywhere they went, even in the fields. I had only been back for a few days when another raid came. This time, they caught an old man outside his house and killed him. Danjuma insisted we had to strike back or the death toll would only be worse next time. He organized a party, and I went with them."

He stopped and took a deep breath. It suddenly seemed as though all the oxygen had seeped out of the room.

"The herdsmen were ready for us, and we ended up in a firefight. I don't know how many of them we killed, but we didn't lose anyone on our side. That victory emboldened Danjuma, who persuaded the elders that the best defense was a strong offense. Our attacks on their camp continued, almost every night. We didn't target any people, just dispersed their herds and destroyed their equipment. Our goal was to drive them away, make them think twice about continuing to harass the village. But it just made them even more angry."

He covered his face with his hands as the memories he'd buried for so long came roaring back to life.

"I continued to go out with the defense force, but I'd started to have second thoughts about Danjuma's strategy. It wasn't decreasing the violence, only escalating it. I argued with him, but he refused to listen. Then one night, the herdsmen came again with a much larger force. They had joined with another group, and they were bent on total destruction. They set fire to every building in the village. The men fought, and the women frantically tried to put out the flames. But there were just too many of them. We were so busy fighting that we didn't realize the extent of the damage until the herdsmen finally left. So many people were dead or wounded, including Asabe. My dad suffered serious burns trying to save the medical clinic and the storage buildings that contained seeds and much of the farming equipment."

He took a shaky breath and plunged on before he lost the will to finish.

"I'll never forget the sight of my mom running from one victim to the next. I didn't think my father would live, his burns were so bad. I was in shock. Couldn't even think straight. Danjuma was wild with anger and grief. He insisted we give chase and make them pay. We piled into the trucks and tore out of the village. He refused to even wait to put out the fires. We'd always taken a measured approach when we attacked their camp. But this time, Danjuma ordered us to drive straight through and shoot at anything and anyone we saw. Women. Children."

His voice broke, and a sob forced its way through his lips. He doubled over, racked by the pain of reliving that moment.

"I stood in the bed of that truck and watched it all, too horrified to do anything to stop it. I never fired a single bullet. But I had blood on my hands just the same. Innocent blood."

For a few moments, all he could hear was the explosion of bullets and the screams of people dying all around him. Then he sensed Kate's presence beside him, her hand on his back.

"Peter," she whispered. He could feel her trembling. "It wasn't your fault. You didn't kill anyone."

He shook his head. He'd heard it all before. But it didn't make him any less guilty. "I went along with all of it, right up to the moment we drove into their camp. God help me! I don't know what I thought would happen. There was a time Danjuma would have listened to me. I could have prevented the whole thing. But I encouraged him! I helped make a monster. And he ended up devouring everything in his path."

Kate said nothing. But her arm still circled his back, and she showed no sign of pulling away. He drew strength from her nearness and willed himself to go on.

"By the time we got back to the village, a medical team had arrived from a nearby town. A garrison of soldiers arrived shortly after that. They flew the injured, including my dad, to the nearest city. Asabe was already dead. So were Danjuma's father and mother. He was inconsolable. Wailing filled the village all night. In the morning, we buried the dead. The soldiers recommended we move, but Danjuma refused to leave the village land. He vowed to die defending it. Some of the men wanted to take their families and go, but he threatened to kill them if they did. He needed them to stay and fight."

Peter leaned back and closed his eyes. He could picture his friend's face, twisted into a snarl of hate and vengeance.

"One of the missionary families who once lived with us in the village had relocated to the city where they took my dad. They were sending me updates on his condition. He was still alive, but they didn't think he would make it unless they flew him to Europe for treatment. They encouraged me to come before he was scheduled to fly out. But Danjuma refused to let me go. He said I had a duty to fight like everyone else."

"How could he keep you from leaving?"

"He threatened to kill me. And I had no doubt he would do it. He didn't care about anything but getting revenge. Of course, he called it justice."

Kate looked away. Justice had always been her plumb line. Now she knew why he refused to rely on man's interpretation of right and wrong.

"How did you escape?" she whispered.

"Our friends hatched a plan with help from a missionary pilot's group. They used to fly supplies into the village fairly often. So one of the pilots who knew my parents offered to fly a rescue mission using a supply run as cover. With the clinic destroyed, the village badly needed medical supplies. That's probably the only reason Danjuma agreed to let the plane land. After they unloaded the delivery, I climbed into the back and hid under a pile of blankets. Like a coward."

Kate sucked in a breath. Tears filled Peter's eyes as he searched her face.

"I'm not the hero you thought I was."

Her eyes widened, and she grabbed his hand. A flash of defiance lit her eyes.

"Is that what you think? Well, you're wrong. Heroes aren't made in a moment—or destroyed by one."

Her words poured oil on his wounded soul. The firm grip of her hand anchored his mind to the present, and the past receded into the background. She hadn't flinched away, even after hearing the worst of his sin. Rays of light began to seep into the dark crevices he'd worked so hard to avoid. He felt like he was floating.

Kate tucked her legs under her and laid her head on his shoulder. He closed his eyes and prayed for forgiveness, a plea he'd made a thousand times before. But with Kate pressed to his side, he finally allowed himself to believe God had heard him—and answered.

WEATHER BULLETIN

Hurricane Julio advisory number 36

NWS/TPC National Hurricane Center, Miami FL
    400 AM CDT - Wednesday, August 30
    ... Watches and warnings issued for the Gulf Coast ...
    At 4 AM CDT ... A hurricane watch has been is-
sued from Cameron, Louisiana, westward to Galveston, Texas, and south to Port Mansfield. Hurricane
conditions are likely within the watch area by Friday.

Julio has gained strength over the last 12 hours and
is expected to become a major hurricane in the next 24
hours. Maximum sustained winds are near 110 mph,
with higher gusts.

The storm is moving to the west-northwest at about
10 mph. If it continues to slow, damage could increase
exponentially. Heavy rain is expected to lead to wide-
spread flooding.

A mostly west-northwest motion is expected as Julio
crosses the central and western Gulf of Mexico. But the
storm could take a northward turn as it nears land.

Hurricane-force winds extend outward up to 90
miles from the center and tropical storm force winds
extend outward up to 215 miles.

Coastal storm surge flooding of 3 to 5 feet above normal tides, along with large and dangerous waves, can be expected within the hurricane watch area. Above normal tides are expected along much of the Gulf Coast during the next few days and will increase as Julio approaches.

Chapter 15

For a few moments after she woke, Kate lay still, gazing at her ceiling through the grey of early morning light. It seemed almost peaceful. Then she glanced at her couch and the previous night's torrent of emotions flooded back over her. Peter sat looking at his phone, the glow of its screen lighting up his face. His sagging eyelids and the grim set of his mouth screamed exhaustion. She realized with a stab of regret that if he'd slept at all, it hadn't been much.

She had stayed curled up by his side for a long time after he finished telling her his story, willing him through proximity to absorb her empathy and respect. She knew how much it had cost him to tell her everything. He'd exposed his deepest regret and shame for her to inspect, opening himself to the possibility of rejection and judgement. She'd known for a year that he loved her, but last night's confession proved just how much.

She sat up, and he looked up from his phone with a smile that stirred pin pricks of hot tears behind her eyes. She slipped out from under the covers and padded across the floor. Tucking herself at his side again, she rested her head on his shoulder and wrapped one arm around his chest. She could feel it rise and fall in a deep, shaky breath. He put his hand over hers and she closed her eyes.

"Good morning," he finally murmured, giving her hand a gentle squeeze.

"You didn't sleep, did you?"

"I did, a little." He paused as though unsure how much more to say. "I used to have nightmares every night. It only happens occasionally now, but after talking about it..."

The tingling behind her eyes returned, and she lifted her head to look at him. "I'm sorry."

He reached up to brush her hair away from her face. "Don't be. I'm not. You needed to know."

She caught his hand, raised it to her lips, and kissed his palm. When she raised her head again, the wonder and longing that filled his eyes shot through her with the force of an earthquake. She felt the fortress around her heart crack.

The chirping of her phone made them both jump.

"That's probably your boss," Peter said. "This morning's weather news isn't good."

Kate plucked her phone from the floor and scrolled through the notifications that filled the screen. Weather models now showed the cone of uncertainty narrowing, with Galveston square in the middle.

"It could be a direct hit," she whispered, conjuring mental images of destruction that made her wince.

Peter leaned forward and put his hand on her back. "As if we didn't have enough to worry about, right?"

She laughed despite the dread squeezing her heart. Then the snippet of the verse she'd tried to remember a few days earlier flitted through her mind.

"What was that you said to me a while back about fearing no evil?"

He smiled. "Psalm 23. The Lord Is My Shepherd. It says, 'Even though I walk through the valley of the shadow of death, I will fear no evil.'"

"For you are with me." She smiled at him as the rest of the verse rolled easily off her tongue.

He nodded and laced his fingers through hers. "He is. Always."

At 8 a.m., Kate strode through the front doors of city hall. She took the stairs to the second floor lobby two at a time. Television cameras covered every inch of floor space, and city officials milled about behind the podium. All of them looked worried. As she scanned the room, Kate spotted Peter slip in the back entrance and head to the knot of police officials gathered in the far corner. The mayor had called for all senior department leaders to attend the news conference. That made it easy for Peter to follow her to city hall without attracting attention.

He insisted on making sure she wasn't alone. That would have been hard enough on a normal day, but with the entire city scrambling to prepare for a major hurricane, it seemed impossible. He couldn't do his job and follow her around while she did hers. She shuddered as she recalled the tone of his voice when he told her he wasn't worried about the chief. She didn't doubt he would quit if Lugar ordered him to stay away from her.

The thought of coming face-to-face with Tommy Gage paralyzed her with fear, but she would never forgive herself if Peter gave up his job to protect her.

She forced thoughts of Gage to the back of her mind and concentrated on finding a place to stand in the scrum of reporters. Ignoring protests from cameramen and a few other reporters, she squeezed herself into a spot in the middle of the lobby. Moments later, Mayor Matthew Hanes walked to the podium.

"Good morning," he said, with a gravity that oppressed his characteristic energy. "As you all know, Hurricane Julio strengthened overnight and took another turn to the north. It now looks like Galveston may bear the brunt of this storm's wrath. I cannot stress enough how serious this situation is. On the advice of the National Weather Service and our own emergency management officials, I am urging everyone to seek shelter off the island."

A murmur undulated across the room as the assembled reporters took in the news.

"We will have buses at the community center in a few hours to help evacuate anyone who wants to go but doesn't have reliable transportation. They will make as many trips as necessary to get everyone to safety."

Hanes turned to the crowd behind him and motioned to the police chief to join him.

"Our officers will fan out across the island," Lugar said after the mayor's introduction. "We will go through every neighborhood looking for anyone who needs help. Please check on your friends and neighbors. If you know someone who needs assistance, call the police department and we will send an officer over."

Kate pictured police cars patrolling every street. If Gage was out there, he'd surely lie low. From across the room, Peter caught her eye and flashed her the briefest of smiles. After Lugar, Stephen Rush took the podium. Next to him, Eddie Vasquez held a foam board filled with the flood study drawing he'd shown her the day before.

"This drawing shows the possible inundation of a major hurricane making landfall on the island at high tide," Rush said. The warning in his voice sent a shiver of dread down Kate's back. "This is not an exaggeration. We don't know how high the water could get in these areas, but we can say with a fair degree of certainty that a significant amount of water will wash over this island. You do not want to be here when that happens."

The rest of the news conference passed in a blur. Kate scribbled furiously, filling four pages in her notebook with details about the evacuation and storm preparations. When Hanes finally stepped away from the microphone, her whole body hummed as though she'd downed five shots of espresso. When her phone buzzed in her pocket, she fumbled and almost dropped it. A text message from Peter flashed across the screen. *Wait for me in the parking lot.*

As she headed for the door, she caught sight of Lugar. He was headed straight for Peter with a scowl darkening his already surly face.

Peter steeled himself as his boss marched toward him with a look that should have made him tremble. But he'd sensed it coming, and he was prepared to face the man's wrath. He'd certainly had plenty of warning.

"Johnson," Lugar barked. Several of the officers standing nearby jumped and hustled to flee the impending confrontation. "Where were you last night?"

Peter debated how to respond, but Lugar didn't give him a chance.

"Never mind. I know where you were. The officer patrolling around Ms. Bennett's apartment, at your request, spotted your car. I gather you were there all night."

Peter gave a curt nod. "I know you're not convinced Tommy Gage is still on the island, but with all due respect, I think you're wrong. And if he's here, Kate is in danger. Why else would he stay if not in hopes of getting at her?"

"That should not be your concern!" Lugar thundered, balling his meaty hands into fists at his side.

"Maybe not in your mind," Peter said evenly. "But it is, nevertheless. And I can't change that."

Lugar's eyes bulged. "Well, you'd better change it if you want to keep your job."

Peter nodded. "I understand, sir."

Lugar swore. "I don't think you do," he growled. "You're lucky there's a hurricane headed straight for us or I'd fire you on the spot for insubordination. As it is, I need all hands on deck. But when this is over, you have a choice to make."

Peter nodded again. Even though he'd anticipated what the chief would say, the finality of his ultimatum still struck him like a baseball bat to the chest.

Lugar swore again, more loudly this time. "You're one of my best detectives. You could have my job one day! And you're willing to throw it all away. I'll never understand that."

Before Peter had a chance to respond, Lugar brushed past him and stalked down the hall, continuing to mutter under his breath as he went.

Peter followed Kate back to the newspaper and watched her walk up the front steps and disappear inside the building. He'd managed to deflect her questions about his conversation with the chief, mostly because she'd been anxious to get back and write her story. But he could tell by the worry in her eyes that she suspected the worst. No matter what the chief said, he'd planned to shadow her all day. But after the mayor's news conference, he realized how impractical that would be. She had to cover the evacuation, and he had to attend storm response meetings. He didn't like leaving her alone, but he'd conceded to her going to the community center with photographer Doug Cowel in the afternoon. It wasn't far from the newspaper office, and plenty of officers would be on hand to help with crowd control. He figured she'd be safe enough for a few hours. He promised to meet her at the end of the day to follow her home.

The next few hours passed in a flurry of planning that left his mind numb. When they broke for lunch, Mark Jarrell pulled him aside.

"I heard about the fibers at your crime scene," the lieutenant said. "Anything that doesn't pertain to hurricane prep work is on hold for now, including our detail on Gage's girlfriend. If anyone asks, we did not have this conversation. But if I were you, I'd drop in for a visit and see how she's doing."

Peter frowned and looked around to make sure no one was listening.

"Did the officers report anything suspicious?"

Jarrell shook his head. "No, but that doesn't mean there's nothing suspicious going on. Gage has managed to evade capture this long, so we know he's being careful. We may never catch him unless someone gives him up. And she's our best shot."

Peter nodded and clapped the lieutenant on the shoulder. Then he headed for the parking lot. Twenty minutes later, he stood at the edge of the Pelican's Landing deck, scanning the tables for Aleah Price. The girl who'd greeted him the day before spotted him and sauntered over, her lips curled in petulant annoyance.

"If you're here to see Aleah, you're out of luck," she said. "She didn't show up for work this morning, so I'm having to pick up her tables."

The hair on the back of Peter's neck bristled. "Did you call her?"

"Yeah, no answer. If she was going to skip out, she should at least have the decency to give me a heads up."

Unless she couldn't, Peter thought as he spun on his heel and jogged back to his car. It took him less than 10 minutes to get to Aleah's block. He parked the car around the corner and approached the long driveway on foot. Staying close to the tall oleanders lining the pavement, he eased his gun out of its holster. He thought about calling for backup, but he didn't know what he was walking into. He decided the element of surprise could prove more valuable than extra firepower.

He paused where the driveway widened into a parking pad in front of Price's garage apartment. Her car sat in its normal spot. The doors to the garage appeared to be shut tight, as did her front door. He eased into a crouch behind the car and strained to catch any unusual sound. Nothing. In the utter silence he could almost hear the thrumming of his nerves. When he counted to ten and nothing happened, he edged his way around the car and put his back to the house. As he tip-toed up the steps, he prayed he wasn't walking into something he couldn't walk out of.

When he reached the door, he tried peeking through the blinds covering the front window. But just like before, they were closed tighter than hurricane shutters. He took a deep breath and knocked.

No answer.

"Aleah, this is Detective Johnson with the Galveston Police Department," he said, raising his voice to just below a shout. He knocked again.

Still no answer.

Sliding away from the opening, he shifted his weight and reached out his free hand to try the knob. It turned easily.

He took another deep breath and swung the door open, spinning to cover the room with his gun. An eerie stillness whispered out the door. He peered into the small living room. A half-eaten bowl of popcorn sat on the floor by the couch. Dirty dishes covered the small counter in the kitchen. But nothing looked out of the ordinary.

Tightening his grip on his gun, he moved toward the door to what he assumed was the bedroom. It stood slightly ajar, just enough for him to peer inside. Clothes and shoes covered the floor. The covers on the bed mounded in the middle, but he couldn't tell if they were hiding pillows or something else. His pulse sounded like a bass drum in his ears.

He worked his way toward the headboard, his gun trained on the pile of blankets. From one edge, a swatch of black hair spilled out. His hammering pulse skipped a beat. Could she just be asleep?

"Aleah," he bellowed. The mound didn't stir.

He grasped the edge of the top blanket in his left hand and peeled it back an inch at a time.

The girl's eyes appeared first, wide open but staring at nothing. Her slack mouth made it look as though she were trying to say something. But he knew before he spotted the trail of dull red running down her side that she would never say anything again.

The brown handle of a thick knife protruded from the middle of her chest. As he looked down at Tommy Gage's handiwork, an oppressive fear wrapped icy fingers around the back of his neck. Aleah Price could have been Gage's ticket off the island, especially with an evacuation underway. Instead, he'd killed her.

Peter closed his eyes and whispered a prayer for mercy.

Chapter 16

Kate's eyes widened with surprise as Doug Cowel pulled his aging Volvo into the parking lot of the community center. Twenty-four hours earlier, it had been almost empty. Now, television news vans dotted the perimeter and crowds of people milled about. The promised buses were nowhere in sight.

Cowel let out a low whistle. "There must be two hundred people here," he said.

"At least," Kate breathed.

Kate scanned the crowd for a familiar face and spotted the woman she'd talked to the day before in the community center office. She had a soft-sided cooler slung over her shoulder. As she walked from one cluster of people to the next, she pulled bottles of water from its zippered opening. They vanished into thirsty hands as soon as they emerged.

Kate trotted toward her and waved when she got close.

"What a difference a day makes!" she said, dodging to one side to avoid being trampled by another thirsty evacuee.

"That's for sure," the woman said, handing off a bottle. "They started showing up about an hour after this morning's news conference. But the buses won't be here for at least another 30 minutes."

"Can't they wait inside?"

"It's full already," the woman said, shaking her head. "We tried to encourage people to leave the lobby for the elderly and anyone with health conditions, but you know how people are. It's every man for himself."

Kate grimaced as she threaded her way through the throng, looking for someone who might have an interesting story. She was so engrossed in people watching that she didn't notice the hand reaching out toward her until strong fingers encircled her arm. Yelping in surprise, she tugged backward, but the hand only tightened its grip. Panic exploded in her brain and all she could think about was getting away.

"Let go!" she yelled, trashing her arm wildly. Without warning, the hand released its grip. Her momentum carried her backward, and she stumbled into several people behind her, who grumbled loudly in protest.

Before she could apologize, the familiar blue of a police uniform emerged from the crowd and Dylan Conner reached out to steady her. The rush of relief made her dizzy.

"Everything okay?" Conner asked, guiding her away from the irritated evacuees.

"I'm not sure," she stammered, trying to steady her ragged breathing. "Someone reached out and grabbed my arm. I just panicked."

The young officer's sun-bleached brows scrunched together as he scanned the crowd. She followed his gaze, searching for anyone she might recognize. After a few moments, he turned back to her.

"I don't see anyone who looks unusual," he said. "But why don't I walk with you for a bit, just in case? If you need help convincing people to talk, I'll try to look intimidating."

Despite the adrenaline still sending shock waves through her body, Kate cracked a shaky smile.

"It was probably just someone trying to get my attention," she said, trying to sound more confident than she felt. "Did Peter know you were going to be here?"

Conner nodded. "He asked me to keep an eye out for you. Officially, I'm here to make sure the evacuees stay calm and everything goes smoothly. Given your tendency to find trouble, I don't think I'm disobeying orders."

Kate tried to look offended, but she was too relieved to protest. For the next hour, Conner shadowed her as she interviewed people frantic to get out of Hurricane Julio's path. Many lived in the city's public housing projects. Some didn't have reliable transportation or money to book a hotel room for a night, let alone three or four. One older woman sat on the curb with a little boy of about three perched in her lap.

"I never left before this," she said. "But I'm raising my grandson now, and I don't want to worry about him if things get really bad."

Next to them sat a battered suitcase and four grocery bags filled with clothing. The little boy clutched a threadbare stuffed bunny.

"Is this all you're taking with you?" Kate asked, wondering about the things the family must have left behind.

"It's all I could carry," the woman said with a resigned sigh. "I hope we'll have something to come back to when this is all over. Lord help us if not."

Two hours later, Kate collapsed into the only empty chair at the conference room table in the managing editor's office. Mattingly had called an all-hands meeting, but they had to wait for Kate to finish her story first. She slouched down and tried to ignore the annoyed looks boring into her from around the table. She'd gotten her copy to Mattingly as fast as she could. The weight of the day's events lay across her shoulders like a lead blanket.

Mattingly smacked his keyboard with unnecessary force. Kate imagined her story shooting through the ether onto the newspaper website as though fired out of a starter's pistol.

"Right. It looks like we've got some hurricane coverage to plan," he said.

A crackle of excitement zipped around the table. Kate felt its tingle from a distance. But even the anticipation of covering a major story couldn't ease the anxiety she still felt after her scare at the evacuation site.

Mattingly took his seat at the head of the table. "Bennett and Denison will stay on the island, along with Cowel," he said. "Everyone else will head to the mainland."

"You don't expect us to go tomorrow, do you?" Delilah Peters didn't bother trying to hide her annoyance at being sent off the island.

"Friday morning," Mattingly said. "Tomorrow you need to take time to get ready. Plan for the worst. Total destruction. It may not be that bad, but you won't have time to scramble at the last minute. I need you absolutely focused on work by Friday. No worrying about what may happen at home."

Kate pictured her second-story loft with a pang. She hadn't realized how much it had become her home until she faced the prospect of losing it. Even with the worst-case scenario she'd seen on the maps in Vasquez's office, she doubted water would get that high. But she had no idea what damage wind and flying debris might do.

"Where will we stay?" Business reporter Jessica Linton's whiny voice sounded genuinely alarmed.

"Still working that out. Somewhere north of Houston. Hopefully, that will be far enough away that you won't lose power. If not, you'll all have to head up to our sister paper in New Braunfels. They're making plans to accommodate us, just in case."

"Do you really think it will be that bad?" Jessica's voice wavered just slightly.

"Who knows? But I'm not taking any chances."

"I'm sure the national media won't either," Delilah said. "After what happened last year in Florida, they're going to be all over this."

"Right, and I don't want us to give them an inch," Mattingly growled. "This is our story, our town. We have to make sure we're on top of every part of this. Events like this make people realize how much they rely on their local newspaper. Let's make sure we remind them of that with every line we print."

"I assume you want me to cover law enforcement while Kate handles the city officials?" Ben asked.

"Yes, but I want you to work together and make the most of all available sources." Mattingly looked pointedly at Kate. "I want anything we can get an exclusive on."

Kate's face burned. Mattingly didn't miss an opportunity to chastise her about Peter, but he had no problem demanding she use him when it suited the newspaper's purposes.

"We'll have plenty of chances to get information from people we wouldn't normally have easy access to," Ben said. "Every police officer, firefighter, work crew, and city department head is going to be hunkered down at the convention center. It's the safest spot on the island, and they're going to want people to move quickly as soon as this thing blows through."

The massive convention center sat atop the site of a Civil War-era fort behind the seawall. The building's underground ballrooms could withstand just about any barrage, man-made or otherwise.

"As long as you have power and an internet connection, I want you filing stories every few hours," Mattingly said. "Hunter will probably edit most of them."

"Where will you be?" Kate asked.

"Here. We've got a generator on the way to keep us up and running, at least with emergency power. We won't be able to run the presses, but no one's going to read printed papers, at least not for a few days."

"You know, in Florida, they cut off access to the hardest hit areas," Delilah said. "That could easily happen here if the damage is bad enough. You need to plan to be cut off from the mainland for a while."

Nobody said anything for several heartbeats as the reality of what that could mean for the island sank in. Kate swallowed against the lump that filled her throat. She pictured the mounds of debris left by last year's storm in Florida and tears pricked the back of her eyes. She couldn't bear the thought of the same scenes of destruction playing out across the island.

Mattingly cleared his throat. "You've all got your assignments, so get out of here. Enjoy the rest of the evening. I have a feeling this may be the last night of peace we have for quite a while."

Peter's stomach twisted as he watched the coroner do his initial assessment of the body. He had conquered his revulsion of death after years of working murder investigations, but this case was too personal for him to be objective. Every time his eyes fell on Aleah Price's lifeless body, he pictured Kate lying there instead.

His stomach lurched again, and he closed his eyes to block out the terrifying images. Mumbling an apology, he hurried into the living room and almost careened into Jarrell.

"What do we got?" the lieutenant asked, nodding his head toward the bedroom.

Peter wrestled his fear for Kate into the back of his mind and focused on giving as succinct a report as possible. "She probably died yesterday, before midnight. I don't really see signs of a struggle, but it's a little hard to tell. I'm guessing he was here for a while, at least long enough to get some food. I assume she let him in willingly."

Jarrell shook his head and then shrugged. "We tried to warn her he was dangerous."

"I just don't know why he would kill her. Did he think she might turn him in?"

"Seems unlikely, but I guess it's possible."

The roiling dread he'd been fighting off for the last few hours muscled its way back into his consciousness. All he could think about was Kate.

"So, what's his next move?" he murmured, more to himself than Jarrell.

The lieutenant blew out a breath. "That's the million dollar question. And with this storm barreling down on us, I'm not sure we'll have time to answer it."

"Until he hurts someone else, you mean." Black spots danced at the edges of Peter's vision.

"I hope not. But you need to be ready."

Peter simply nodded. His tongue felt like it was stuck to the top of his mouth. Tommy Gage had the upper hand from the moment he charged out of the jail. He'd killed two people already. If he was determined to hurt Kate, could Peter stop him? A sense of helplessness clawed at the center of his soul.

"I need to go," he said, charging toward the front door.

Thirty minutes later, he sat in the newspaper parking lot, tapping a nervous rhythm on his steering wheel as he waited for Kate to emerge from the building. When she finally pushed open the front door and stood blinking in the sun, he had to fight the urge to run up the steps and wrap his arms around her. She looked so vulnerable standing there all alone.

He forced himself to be patient as she trudged toward him. Her pale face and frightened eyes suggested she'd heard about the murder already. He stepped out of the car to meet her.

"Ben just got a call from Jarrell," she said, looking up at him with a mixture of horror and fear. Her voice sounded like sandpaper over rough wood.

He put his hands on her shoulders and held her gaze. If only he had comforting answers for every question he saw there. He kicked himself for not calling to tell her before she heard it from someone else.

"I'm sorry I didn't tell you myself." He took a deep breath and sent up a silent prayer for protection. "I know there's no point in telling you not to worry. But whatever happens, we'll face it together. And we're not alone."

"In the valley of the shadow of death?" The corners of Kate's mouth pulled into a wan smile. "We may not be alone, but I still don't like walking through it."

"Me neither." He pulled her into a tight hug and then released her. "Let's get back to your place. I'm sure the dogs are ready for a walk."

"What about my car?"

"Leave it. We'll come back and get it tomorrow."

Kate kept her face turned toward her window as they rode downtown in silence. Peter stopped himself several times from asking her what she was thinking. He wanted to fight every battle for her, but the war in her own heart and mind was a solitary conflict.

He parked on the street near the entrance to her building, scanning the sidewalks on either side. He took her hand as they crossed the street and gave it a quick squeeze.

"Just keep behind me as we go inside," he said, drawing his gun. He eased open the building's front door and quickly swept the lobby. They crept up the stairs against the wall. Peter strained to catch any sound that seemed out of place. Tension hummed through every nerve. When they got to her landing, he motioned for Kate to hand him the keys. He heard nothing from the other side of the door, until he slid the key into the lock. A chorus of barking erupted, and he sighed in relief. With the dogs on guard, he knew no one had gotten in.

A flurry of wagging tails and wet noses greeted them when they pushed open the door.

"Good boys," he said, scratching behind their ears in turn. "You're the best security system money can buy."

Kate dropped her messenger bag next to the kitchen table and headed for the couch.

"Sorry, but we've got to walk the dogs first," Peter said. Kate groaned and looked like she might protest, but she dragged herself back toward him without saying a word.

As anxious as the dogs were to get outside, they waited patiently for Peter to clip the leashes to their collars and guide them out the door and down the stairs. Once they hit the sidewalk, they pulled eagerly, noses to the ground to take in each new smell. Kate lagged a few steps behind and Peter reached back to snag her hand. She frowned but didn't pull away.

They'd always been careful in public to keep up a platonic facade. But he no longer cared who saw them together. He needed the comfort of her hand in his as they walked through the streets, exposed to potential danger.

The dogs pulled them toward the Strand. Few people dotted the streets, but several store owners had already started making storm preparations. Outside an

Italian restaurant where they'd eaten several times, two workers struggled with a wide sheet of plywood. Their sweat-soaked shirts clung to their backs as they wrestled it up to the window. A few doors down, another store owner already had a wall of sandbags against her building.

Kate's fingers tightened around his.

"How much of this will still be here on Sunday?" she said, her voice barely above a whisper.

He'd been so absorbed with worrying about Tommy Gage that he'd given little thought to the storm damage. But as they walked back toward Kate's building, he let his mind wander over all the places he'd come to love, starting with the mud-colored beaches. He always thought of Africa as home, but Galveston ranked a close second.

When they got to the apartment, the dogs flopped down on their beds by the door and Kate and Peter collapsed onto the couch. He had just persuaded the muscles in his neck and shoulders to relax when the shrill whistle of her cell phone made them both jump.

Kate slid the device from her back pocket, glanced at the screen, and sighed.

"Hey, Dad," she said, pressing the phone to her ear with an apologetic glance at Peter.

He smiled encouragingly and then leaned his head back and closed his eyes. He listened as she gave her father a brief account of the day's events. The strain in her voice revealed the fear she tried to mask with bravado.

"I'm fine, Dad. Really. I'm well protected."

Peter could hear her father's muffled reply, but couldn't make out the words.

"What?" Kate snapped. It always amazed him how much annoyance she could stuff into such a small word. He smiled to himself.

"Yes. He's sitting right next to me."

Peter opened his eyes a crack and glanced over at her.

"Seriously?" she asked, her eyes narrowing. Then she huffed out an exaggerated sigh and held the phone out to him. "He says he wants to talk to you."

Peter sat up and took the phone. Tension threaded its way back across his shoulders. Even though they'd had a very cordial chat earlier in the week, he still sensed the importance of making a good impression.

"Yes, sir," he said, pressing the phone to his ear.

"Peter, I want you to shoot straight with me," the older man said. "Katie says there's no need to worry, but I don't trust her to tell me the truth. How much danger is she really in?"

Peter weighed his words. "It's definitely a serious situation. I can't say with absolute certainty, but I assume Tommy Gage has stayed on the island because there's something here he wants. I can't think what that would be, other than Kate or me."

"I know she doesn't want to leave, but do I need to come down there and make her go? I could be there by midnight."

Peter looked over at Kate. She stared back, flashes of warning filling her eyes. As much as she would hate him for it, he wouldn't hesitate to take her dad up on the offer if he thought she would really be safe. But if Gage somehow found out she'd left the island and tried to follow her, she'd have no one to protect her.

"No sir, I don't think that's necessary," he said. "With the storm coming in, we'll have every member of the police force on the streets. I think she'll be as safe here as anywhere. I'm going to stay with her and make sure she's never alone."

"If you're sure," her dad said. Doubt and worry filled his voice.

Peter stood up and walked to the window, away from Kate's piercing gaze. "Believe me, if I thought that was best, I would do whatever I could to make it happen."

"I believe you. It's just, she's all I've got." The older man's voice cracked, and Peter's throat tightened.

"I know," he said. He glanced at Kate, and his breath caught in his throat. "I would give my life to protect her. I can promise you that."

WEATHER BULLETIN

Hurricane Julio intermediate advisory number 42

NWS/TPC National Hurricane Center, Miami FL
300 AM CDT - Thursday, August 31
... Julio is now a Category 3 storm ...
Maximum sustained winds are now near 115 mph ... with higher gusts. Julio is a Category 3 hurricane on the Saffir-Simpson scale.

At 300 a.m. CDT ... the center of Hurricane Julio was located about 580 miles east-southeast of Corpus Christi, Texas and about 470 miles east-southeast of Galveston, Texas.

Julio is moving toward the west-northwest near 10 mph. A general west-north-westward motion is expected over the next 24 hours.

The center of Julio should be very near the coast by late Friday. But because Julio is a very large tropical cyclone, weather will deteriorate along the coastline long before the center reaches land.

Coastal storm surge flooding of up to 20 ft above normal tide levels ... along with large and dangerous battering waves can be expected near and to the east of where the center of Julio makes landfall.

Julio is expected to produce rainfall amounts of up to 5 to 10 inches along the central and upper Texas coast and over portions of southwestern Louisiana. Isolated amounts of 15 inches are possible.

Chapter 17

The next morning, Peter dropped Kate off at the newspaper office with a promise to return in a few hours. As he drove toward the police station, he mulled over his conversation with her father. She'd been quiet afterward, but not distant. His vow to protect her couldn't have come as a surprise. Still, hearing him say it out loud, let alone to someone else, probably made it more real. It would be impossible for her to doubt his commitment now. He'd agonized over what thoughts might be churning behind the eyes she kept averted, but he'd forced himself not to ask. He knew she needed time to process her own feelings. Her silence had started to grow heavy by the time they finished dinner and headed for the couch. But then she'd curled up beside him. Her nearness spoke more clearly than any answer she might have given to his questions. He could have sat with her like that all night.

By the time he got to the station, ranking officers already filled the conference room. Lieutenant Jarrell nodded to him from the other side, and Peter made his way around the table to stand with him against the far wall.

"The coroner gave us a preliminary time of death for Aleah Price," Jarrell said quietly. "Between 4 a.m. and 7 a.m. yesterday."

Peter did a little quick math. "Less than 24 hours after Bill Presley, and about five hours before I found her," he said. "Did you find any other clues in the apartment?"

"Still processing."

Before Jarrell could say any more, the police chief strode through the door. He nodded to the men and women gathered around the room and took his seat at the head of the table.

"I'm sure you've all seen the latest weather update," Lugar said. "This storm keeps getting stronger the closer it gets. Fortunately, it looks like a lot of people are heeding the mayor's call to evacuate. Our job in the next 24 hours is to talk to as many of the holdouts as we can and persuade them to leave, too. I want this island as empty as possible when this monster comes ashore tomorrow night."

Lugar passed around printouts of patrol assignments for the next 24 hours, fielding questions as the information percolated around the room.

"I want everyone at the conference center by noon tomorrow," Lugar said. "We'll continue to patrol in shifts after that, for as long as we can. But when the conditions get too bad, we'll pull everyone in. Whoever's left on the island after that will be on their own."

A somber silence hung in the air for several moments. Peter glanced around and caught the chief staring at him.

He shifted uncomfortably under the older man's penetrating gaze and wondered if he was in for another lecture after the meeting. Lugar cleared his throat.

"As most of you know by now, it appears that our escaped prisoner is also still on the island," he said. "Lieutenant Jarrell's team is investigating the murder of Aleah Price, but we believe Tommy Gage is likely responsible."

A murmur rippled through the officers, and Peter sighed with relief. At least Lugar had finally admitted the obvious.

"I want every officer out on patrol to be on their guard," the chief said. "We don't know what Gage might do with so many people leaving the island. It might make it easier for him to hide. But he might be easier to catch. He'll be exposed to the storm's wrath just like everyone else."

Lugar dismissed the meeting with a wave of his hand, but fixed Peter with a steely look. As he neared the door, the chief motioned for him to wait. After the room emptied, Lugar squared his shoulders and crossed his arms.

"Since it's no good telling you to stay away from Kate Bennett at this point, you have my permission to keep an eye on her."

A wide smile spread across Peter's face, and gratitude filled his heart.

"Thank you, sir."

Lugar sighed. "I'm assuming the worst about Gage's intentions, as I'm sure you are. Believe it or not, I don't want to see him hurt anyone else on my watch, even your friend at the *Gazette*."

Peter started to nod, but stilled when Lugar held up a warning hand.

"This is a temporary concession. Everything I said before about your relationship with a member of the media stands. It's untenable. And after this is all over, we'll still have that to reckon with."

Peter nodded slowly. "About that, sir."

Lugar shook his head vigorously. "Not now," he growled. "We'll have time for that later. Right now, we just need to focus on keeping everyone on this island alive."

Kate stared out the window of Peter's car as they drove toward the Bayou Shores neighborhood. A steady stream of cars passed them, headed for the causeway. She obviously wasn't the only one alarmed by the morning's weather report. The twenty-foot storm surge warning conjured up mental images of Florida. She'd spent the last few hours trying not to layer them over the map of the island.

"Lots of people who planned to stay yesterday are leaving now," Peter said. "I'm sure these people you met will go, too."

Kate thought about Carl Neal's emphatic refusal to abandon his home. "I hope you're right," she said. "If not, maybe you can talk some sense into them."

Peter chuckled. "Those are my orders. I'll do my best."

The street that had rested quietly in the afternoon heat less than two days before now hummed with activity. Cars filled driveways, and homeowners ferried sheets of plywood across lush green lawns. Kate scanned each house as Peter threaded their way through cars parked along both sides of the street. He squeezed into an empty spot several houses down from the Neal's address. She squinted through the bright sunlight and spotted Carl perched on a ladder leaned up against the front of his house.

"That's where I'm headed," she said, pointing down the street.

"I'll just check in with a few of the neighbors first," Peter said. "That will give you a chance to talk to him before I make my pitch."

Kate smiled to herself as she walked down the sidewalk. If anyone could persuade the Neals to leave, it was Peter. Carl was just coming down from the ladder when she walked across his driveway.

"Looks like you're expecting a storm or something," she said with a grin.

He laughed. "I heard we might be getting some bad weather."

"Have you and Gigi decided to leave?" Kate tried unsuccessfully to keep the hope out of her voice.

"Not us! I told you the other day, we're staying put."

Kate's pulse kicked up a notch. "Did you see the storm surge predictions?"

Carl waved his hand dismissively. "Yeah, but those weather guys always exaggerate. They have to or they'll get blamed for not giving enough warning. But it won't be that bad. Nothing we can't handle."

Kate looked across the street at the water. Although the sky overhead remained deceptively cloudless, the surface of the bayou rippled and churned. Every now and then, white foam topped a wave, like a tiny monster bearing its teeth.

"I wish you would reconsider," she said. "If they're wrong, you'll have to spend one night at a hotel. That's the worst that could happen. But if they're right and you stay, you could be trapped in your house."

Carl cocked his head and looked at her intently. "You're really worried about us."

"I'm worried about everyone who won't leave!"

"We're going to be just fine. Come on, let me show you around back. I've got a stack of sandbags to put around the doors and two big coolers I'm going to fill with ice."

Kate followed him up the driveway and around the back of the house. He was just pointing out the makeshift outdoor kitchen when Gigi shuffled through the back door. She nodded and smiled, crushing Kate's hopes that she might be less enthusiastic about staying than her husband.

"We ready," she said, pointing to the grill and its extra bottle of propane.

"Unless it's all under water," Kate said. "That's a real possibility."

"If we get that much water, and that's a big if, it will drain off," Carl said. "Then I'll fire this baby up, and we'll grill some chicken."

Kate started to respond when she heard Peter yelling her name. She walked back to the driveway in time to see him sprinting toward her. Fear spiked through her body and tightened like a vice around her heart.

"What's wrong?" Her thudding pulse filled her ears, muffling the sound of her own voice.

Peter slowed his stride and came to a stop, bending at the waist to rest his hands on his knees.

"You disappeared," he gasped. "I thought I'd lost you."

His stricken look cut her like a knife in the chest. Kate sucked in a breath.

"I'm sorry," she stammered. "Mr. Neal wanted to show me his preparations."

"Everything okay?" Carl Neal's voice behind her held a hint of suspicion. Kate glanced over her shoulder to see him eyeing Peter warily.

"Yes, it's fine," Kate said, trying to bluster through the embarrassment that flushed her cheeks. "This is Detective Peter Johnson with the Galveston Police Department. I'm sort of riding along with him while he's out talking to people about the storm. He got worried when he lost sight of me."

Peter had recovered enough to straighten and extend his hand. Carl took it but didn't look convinced.

"Has the mayor issued a mandatory evacuation order that I'm not aware of?" he asked, crossing his arms.

"No, nothing like that," Peter said, still slightly out of breath. "We're just making sure that everyone is aware of the danger. We're here to help if you need us."

"I think we've got everything under control," Carl said. "We're staying put. But I'm not worried. I've been through my share of storms, and I know what to do."

Peter nodded. "I understand. But this storm won't be like the ones you remember. Those were wind storms. Julio's biggest threat is water."

"I was just showing Ms. Bennett my stash of sandbags," he said, pointing to the back of the house. "I have enough to go halfway up both doors."

"What if that's not enough?" Kate blurted. "During that storm in Florida, people ended up on their roofs."

Carl huffed in exasperation, but Kate caught a hint of concern as it flitted across his wife's face.

"We have a ladder to get into the attic if we have to," he said. "But I'm telling you, the water won't get that high."

Peter reached into his pocket and pulled out a business card. "Keep this, just in case. It's got my cell number on it. Dispatch may be overwhelmed by this time tomorrow. We'll be patrolling as long as we can."

Carl hesitated but finally reached out and took the card. "I appreciate it. If you get tired of whatever rations the police department has socked away, come by for some grilled chicken on Sunday."

Kate shook her head in disbelief as the two men shook hands. She couldn't help making one last appeal.

"Even though the city's not opening any shelters on the island, the convention center is a refuge of last resort," she said. "If it gets really bad, that's where you should go. It's the safest spot on the island."

Carl smiled. "I'll keep that in mind."

Kate fought the urge to continue to argue. He clearly had no intention of reconsidering.

"Good luck," she said, feeling the inadequacy of her words as they tripped off her tongue.

"You, too," he said with a wink. "If you're out there covering this thing, you're going to need it more than I will."

For the next hour, Kate and Peter wound their way through the neighborhood, stopping at each house they passed. Most people planned to leave that night, although a few said they would head out in the morning. Only three of the people they talked to shared Carl Neal's stubborn confidence. Peter noted down the addresses, handed out his card, and urged them to call if things got worse than they expected.

As they walked back to the car, Kate watched him out of the corner of her eye. She'd witnessed him doing his job for more than two years, but never at such close range. He'd learned to be a good detective, but he was a natural protector. She realized with a pang that her inclination to independence would always be at war with his desire to shield her—and everyone else—from harm.

"I'm sorry I gave you such a scare," she said, wincing at the memory of his panicked face as he pelted up Carl Neal's driveway.

He stopped and gazed at her for what felt like an eternity. Then the corner of his mouth lifted in a lop-sided smile.

"I'll just be glad when this is all over. I don't think my heart can take much more."

They stopped for lunch at a sandwich shop downtown. While they ate, Kate worked on her story. Across the table, Peter made a steady stream of phone calls she tried to ignore, with limited success. The first two seemed to involve evidence from the Presley murder. The third centered on getting his three pets evacuated safely. At the last one, she abandoned any pretense of writing and listened.

"Hey, Mom," he said, squinting into the distance. "I'm sorry I missed your calls these last few days. It's been crazy around here getting ready for this storm. I guess you're at therapy with Dad now. I'll try you again in a few hours. But don't worry. Everything's fine. I'll talk to you soon."

Kate watched as resignation chased sorrow across his face. They vanished so quickly Kate thought she might have imagined them, if it weren't for what she now knew about his past. He caught her watching him and sighed.

"Thursdays are therapy days," he said. "Dad still needs regular sessions to help with the scarring. I should have remembered that before I called."

Kate swallowed against the knot forming in her throat. She reached across the table and took his hand. She wanted to remind him that what happened to his father was not his fault, but she knew words only had so much power against convictions lodged deep in the heart.

"Did you find someone to take the dogs?" she asked.

"Shelly Archer, the animal shelter director. They'll be in good hands. We'll drop them off tomorrow on the way to the convention center. I don't want to be without them tonight."

She nodded, but before she could respond, her phone buzzed.

"It's Eddie Vasquez," she said, swiping her thumb across the screen to read the text message. "He wants me to come down to the lift station and see the preparations they're making. He probably wants to show me his latest flooding predictions, too." She shuddered.

"Sounds good. I can find out when he plans to pull all his crews off the street, so we have it in our logs."

The city's main water pumping station operated out of a 100-year-old building about seven blocks from the port. Kate had written a story about the historic site the year before, when the city's historical commission protested expansion plans. Kate always thought its classical brick facade made it look more like a college classroom building than a vital link in the city's infrastructure.

Vasquez waved from the front steps as they pulled into the parking lot. A trailer parked on the emerald grass in front of the building sagged under a mound of sandbags. Vasquez barked orders at a half-dozen men ferrying the burlap sacks to a makeshift dam rising around the side of the building that faced the port.

"Shouldn't those be over there?" Kate called, pointing toward the south side. "The storm's coming from the gulf."

Vasquez shook his head. "That's what the seawall's for. I'm worried about water washing over us from the back side of the island."

Goosebumps rippled over Kate's arms. Vasquez made it sound like the storm was sneaking up on them where they least expected it.

"Come look at my latest maps," he said. "This thing just keeps getting worse."

"I told you," Kate muttered as they trudged up the steps. Peter chuckled, a comforting sound amid the rising tide of bad news.

Inside the building, another crew was busy packing sandbags around a massive pump. Vasquez surveyed their progress, his mouth pressed into a thin line.

"Officially, I'm supposed to tell you about all the prep work we're doing here to make sure we can still pump fresh water to the island in forty-eight hours," he said. "Unofficially—and off the record—none of this is going to make any difference. Detective, you can just pretend you didn't hear that."

"What do you mean?" Kate asked.

"Take a look at this." Vasquez slipped a printed map from under a stack of papers piled on a table by the door. "This is the latest weather service data plugged into our flood projection model."

Kate stared at the map, a storm of alarm swirling in her chest.

"That shows water covering more than half the island," she whispered.

Vasquez nodded. "Sandbags aren't going to do any good if this model is right."

"When do you think we'll start seeing it cover the streets closest to the water?" Peter asked.

"By this time tomorrow, if not sooner."

"I'll be sure we prioritize the neighborhoods that are likely to flood first," Peter said.

Kate thought about Carl Neal and his insistence that he had nothing to fear.

"What about the people who refuse to leave?" she asked. "What can we do to help them?"

"Be sure your next story makes it really clear how serious this is," Vasquez said. "And pray. That may be the only thing that can help these people now."

Chapter 18

Peter mulled over Vasquez's map as they drove back toward his house. If the projections were right, its eight-foot elevation and proximity to the seawall would protect it from the worst of Julio's wrath. He briefly considered moving Kate there for the night, but dismissed the idea as quickly as it came. Her apartment, with its single point of entry, would be much easier to defend if Tommy Gage decided to seep out of the shadows.

He was so focused on potential threats that he didn't notice the route he'd taken. As though his thoughts of Gage had drawn him toward the scene of the first murder, Peter realized with surprise that they were driving by the old orphanage.

"I don't guess anyone's going to board up the windows," Kate said, turning her face toward the building as they rolled past. "That's so sad. All of Bill Presley's dreams could just wash away."

"It'll probably be okay. Didn't they fortify it after the 1900 storm? And hasn't it survived every storm since?"

"Yeah, but the way Vasquez makes it sound, nothing's going to survive Julio."

"We will," Peter said, offering a reassuring smile. Kate smiled back, but her hands twisted together in her lap.

When they pulled up outside his old row house, Peter scanned the street for any signs of trouble. He hated to take her with him while he cleared the rooms, but he refused to leave her alone in the car.

"Stay right behind me," he said, sliding his gun out of its holster. "I just want to make sure we don't have any surprises." Kate nodded, the slight pinching at the corners of her mouth her only sign of fear.

It took just a few minutes to sweep through the small space. Peter spotted nothing out of place. His grouchy tabby cat, perched on top of a low bookcase, howled her displeasure at being left alone for so long.

"Sorry, old girl," he said, scooping her into his arms and scratching under her chin. "You're going to be even more mad at me here in an hour or so."

While Kate settled down on the couch to finish her story, Peter went back outside to complete his own storm preparations. He pulled several sheets of plywood and a drill from the storage space under the house and set to work. As he went from window to window, he thought about the first time he'd walked through the house with his real estate agent. It had needed some TLC, but the location and size were perfect. Now he wondered how much longer he could stay there. So much depended on the conversation he knew Kate still wasn't ready to have.

An hour later, he had all the windows covered. It took him another thirty minutes to gather up his tools and move them upstairs. He fished out the cat carrier last.

Kate had put away her laptop and watched him expectantly. He was just about to suggest they get moving when his phone rang. His favorite photo of his mom filled the screen.

"Hey, Mom," he said, perching on the edge of his recliner.

"Peter! Thank goodness you're okay. I was starting to worry."

He squirmed as his conscience stabbed his heart. "Sorry. It's just been a little crazy here, between work and this storm."

"We've been following the developments in the news, and praying. How's Kate holding up?"

He glanced at her, wondering how she would react to her name coming up so early in his conversation.

"She's hanging in there," he said. "It's hard to have dueling dangers hanging over your head."

Kate's eyes were locked on his face, but he couldn't tell what she was thinking.

"We're praying for a breakthrough, for both of you," his mom said.

The focus of her prayers had nothing to do with the storm, or Tommy Gage, although he knew she was appealing for their safety as well. She'd started praying for Kate as soon as they got back from Cuba last year. Sometimes he wanted to ask her to stop. She prayed for God to turn Kate's heart by any means necessary. He could think of a few things he would take off the table, including her physical well-being. But his mom took a no-holds-barred approach to salvation.

"You might not hear from me again for several days," he said. "I don't know what kind of cell reception we'll have after the storm. By this time tomorrow, we should start feeling the effects of the first bands."

"That's okay. We'll keep watching the news and reading the reports. As long as we see Kate's byline, we'll assume you're safe as well."

He smiled at his mom's practicality. "How's Dad?"

"About the same. Therapy wore him out today, so he went to lie down. But he told me to tell you to read Psalm 18."

Peter tried to recall what the verses said but drew a blank. "Okay. I'll look it up tonight."

"Take care of yourself, and call as soon as you can."

"I will, Mom. I love you."

"I love you, too, Peter. Remember, just because something's out of your control doesn't mean it's out of control."

He sighed as he disconnected the call. His mother's faith never wavered, even when she lost almost everything she valued in this life. He glanced up to find Kate's eyes still fixed on his face.

"Your mom knows about me?" she asked, the surprise in her voice tinged with concern.

He stifled another sigh. "I'm pretty sure Elian called my parents before our plane even left Havana. I couldn't exactly deny your existence."

Kate looked down at her hands, weaving her fingers together into a tight knot.

"She reads all your stories," he offered. "She's a big fan."

Kate rolled her eyes, but a smile tugged at her lips.

Forty-five minutes later, they pulled into the newspaper parking lot. Kate gazed up at the building, solid and stark as a fortress. Its ugly facade couldn't have been more different from the *Gazette*'s original offices in one of the Victorian-era brick buildings downtown. But it definitely looked like it could withstand a storm.

As they walked up the front steps, Kate spotted movement on the roof. She shielded her eyes against the late afternoon sun and spotted Doug Cowel, a camera protruding from his face. He stopped shooting and waved as they approached.

"You should come up here and see this," he called.

Kate glanced at Peter and shrugged. She led him inside and up the stairs into the dusty "morgue," where the archive of old newspapers sat yellowing in big binders. In the far corner of the room, a ladder dangled from the ceiling. She hesitated before putting her foot on the bottom rung.

"This better be worth it," she muttered as she started to climb. Behind her, Peter chuckled.

The setting sun hit them full in the face as they emerged from the hatch and stepped onto the flat roof. Ahead of them, the causeway stretched up and out toward the mainland. A steady stream of red taillights crawled slowly north as far as Kate could see. The lanes coming onto the island sat empty.

"It's been like this for hours," Cowel said. "I can't believe there's anyone left on the island."

"We know of a few," Kate said. "I hope they change their minds before tomorrow."

"If they don't, they're in for a wild ride," Cowel said. His camera shutter exploded as he took several more shots. "Is your last story in? Mattingly says we might go to press early tonight."

"Yep. It's all set. I just came by to get any last instructions from the boss."

"Don't do anything stupid, and start sending stuff as soon as you can. That's what he told me."

Kate laughed. "That sounds like Mattingly. I guess I'll see you tomorrow at the convention center."

Cowel saluted, then flashed a knowing grin at Peter. "See you tomorrow, detective. It'll be nice to have a law enforcement escort."

Kate glared at the photographer, but Peter only laughed. The sound echoed through the hatch as she climbed back down the ladder, a repeating reminder of how exposed her personal life had become.

The chatter that normally engulfed the copy desk stopped as though someone hit an invisible mute button when Kate and Peter walked into the newsroom.

"Great story tonight," a woman with a shock of red hair called as they walked by. "That couple you talked to must be crazy."

Kate shrugged. "I don't think they are. That's what makes their refusal to leave so hard to understand."

"Magical thinking," the copy editor said, brandishing her pencil like a wand. "It's an epidemic around here."

"Bennett!" Mattingly's voice boomed through his open door like a foghorn. "What are you doing here?"

Kate stuck her head through the opening. "I just thought I'd stop by and see if you had any last words for me."

"Don't do anything stupid, and start sending me stories as soon as you can."

"That's what Cowel said you told him. Anything else?"

Mattingly huffed. "I assume you're not here alone?"

"No. Detective Johnson's with me."

Peter stepped through the doorway, and held out his hand to the managing editor. Mattingly shook it grudgingly.

"Under normal circumstances, detective, this would be unacceptable," he said. "As it is, I'm glad you're watching Bennett's back. Try to keep her out of trouble."

Peter tried to hide his smile as he stepped back toward the door, leaving Kate to face her boss alone. Mattingly regarded her from under his bushy eyebrows.

"Take care of yourself," he said gruffly. "Covering a natural disaster is tough. But I know you've got other things to worry about, too. Just be careful."

"I'm always careful," she said, a little more sharply than she intended. "I came back from Cuba, didn't I?"

"Just when I'd almost forgotten," Mattingly grumbled. "That was bad. This could be worse."

The now familiar stirring of alarm swirled in Kate's chest. She nodded and turned to leave.

"Oh, I almost forgot," Mattingly said. "I want you to take this. It's a satellite phone. Cowel's got one, too. I should probably give this one to Denison, but something tells me you might need it more than he will. If we lose cell service, you should still be able to get a call through on this."

She took the bulky device and tucked it under her arm. "Thanks. Here's hoping I won't need it."

Kate felt ready to drop by the time they made it back to her apartment, settled the very annoyed cat in the bathroom, and took the dogs for their evening walk. They took turns cleaning up and then piled everything perishable on the kitchen table. She knew anything they didn't eat would go bad once the power went out, but it didn't make for a very appetizing meal.

They took their plates to the couch so they could watch the setting sun paint the sky while they ate. The wide strips of orange and red seemed to carry an urgent warning. An eerie silence filled the streets below.

Kate picked at her food for a while before giving up. She set her plate on the floor and walked over to her favorite spot on the windowsill. Folding herself against the unyielding brick, she closed her eyes. She felt like she'd been swimming in an endless sea for the last week, struggling to keep her head above water. Each revelation about Tommy Gage or Hurricane Julio crested over her head, threatening to drag her under. Her will to keep fighting the churning and tossing grew weaker with every wave. And land was nowhere in sight.

In 24 hours, the waves would wash over them in reality.

Kate had spent her life carefully orchestrating every step to keep from stumbling. But she had no power to change where her path led now. She'd walked through the valley of the shadow of death once. She never wanted to do it again. That's why she'd kept Peter at arm's length for so long. If she didn't love something, she couldn't lose it.

But somewhere over the course of the last year, she'd lost that battle. She knew it. She just wasn't sure she had the strength to admit it.

She opened her eyes a crack and looked down at the empty street below. How many times had she sat in this very spot wrestling with her hopes and fears? On her best days, she allowed her dreams to flow unhindered. In them, she embraced life with an open heart, loving freely. On her worst days, she clung to the safety of her walled fortress and watched as every dream dashed to pieces against its impenetrable walls.

She'd learned to let down her guard temporarily, but never to fully surrender. Until she did, she would stay trapped. She put her hands over her face as the familiar vortex of torment pulled at her soul.

"Kate," Peter whispered.

She grasped the sound of his voice like an anchor and held on for dear life. When she opened her eyes, he was kneeling at her side, his face contorted with worry. She reached out and touched his cheek. Why couldn't she just let go?

"Sorry," she murmured. "I was just thinking about everything."

"You don't just mean the storm."

She shrugged, kicking herself for getting involved with someone trained to uncover things people wanted to hide.

"The storm. Tommy Gage. All of it."

"Us?" The pain in his eyes cut like a knife.

She forced herself to hold his gaze until her lower lip trembled. She turned away and looked out the window again.

"I don't know why I thought we could just carry on like this forever," she said. "What happens when this is all over? If Lugar hasn't given you an ultimatum yet, he will eventually."

"I already told you I'm not worried about that."

"But I am!"

"Kate." He said her name like an appeal. It hung in the air between them until she finally turned back to look at him. "Do you trust me?"

Tears pricked the back of her eyes. "It's not you I don't trust," she whispered. "It's me."

What if she could never break out of the prison she'd built around her heart?

Before she realized what he was doing, Peter slid one hand behind her back and the other under her knees. He lifted her into his arms and carried her back to the couch. He set her down first then settled in beside her, wrapping his arm around her shoulders and pulling her close. She wanted to resist, but she drew too much comfort from his nearness.

"Well, I trust you," he said. "And I trust God. We're not walking through this alone."

After a long pause, she squeezed her eyes shut and asked the question that had eaten at her for the last year.

"How can you trust something you can't see or prove?"

He thought about it so long she thought he might not answer.

"You can't," he finally said. "Not unless you surrender."

WEATHER BULLETIN

Hurricane Julio intermediate advisory number 50

NWS/TPC National Hurricane Center, Miami FL

600 AM CDT - Friday, September 1

... Julio strengthens as it bears down on Galveston Island and the upper Texas coast ...

... Rising water levels and battering waves now affecting the area ...

Reports from an Air Force Reserve hurricane hunter aircraft indicate that maximum sustained winds have increased to near 120 mph ... with higher gusts. Julio is a strong Category 3 hurricane on the Saffir-Simpson scale. Some additional strengthening is forecast during the next 24 hours.

At 600 a.m. CDT ... Julio is moving toward the west-northwest near 12 mph. A turn toward the northwest is expected later today ... with a turn toward the north expected on Saturday. On the forecast track, the center of Julio will be very near the upper Texas coast by late today.

Weather will begin to deteriorate along the coastline soon.

Coastal storm surge flooding of up to 20 feet above normal tide levels, along with large and dangerous battering waves can be expected near and to the east of where Julio makes landfall. Surge flooding of up to 25 feet and possibly higher could occur at the heads of bays.

Water levels have already risen by 4 to 6 feet above normal along much of the northwestern Gulf Coast.

Do not venture outside during the eye of the storm. The strongest winds and highest surge will likely occur near or just after the eye makes landfall.

Chapter 19

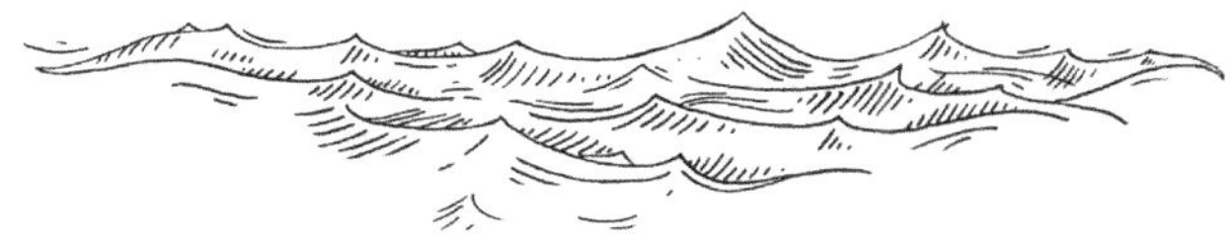

"Kate, wake up. It's time to go."

Kate groaned in confusion. She struggled to sit up and open her eyes. The pale gray of very early morning leaked through the curtains. From nearby, one of the dogs let out a low whine.

"What's the matter?" she asked, rubbing her hands over her face. "Isn't it too early to leave?"

"The water's almost to the curb already," Peter said. "If we don't leave soon, we could get trapped down here."

Kate shot out of bed and ran to the window. The pre-dawn gloom still clinging to the buildings made it hard to see the water, but as she peered down, a gust of wind rippled the surface. The water lapped nearly halfway up the tires of Peter's car.

"Oh my gosh, Peter," she breathed, shock rooting her in place.

"I know," he said, coming up behind her and putting his hands on her shoulders. "But there's no time to think about it. We have to move."

Without another word, Kate flew to her wardrobe and pulled out her backpack. In a few minutes, she'd stuffed everything she needed inside. Five minutes later, she sat down at the kitchen table to tie her shoes.

"Ready?" he asked as she stood to her feet.

She took one last look around her apartment, fighting back the swell of heartache that crested unexpectedly.

"Don't worry," Peter said. "This building has endured a dozen or more storms. It will still be here when we get back."

She nodded, slung the backpack over her shoulder, and picked up the cat carrier. Peter clipped the leashes to the dogs' collars and opened the door.

"Should we warn the neighbors?" she asked as they stepped into the hallway.

"I'm pretty sure they're already gone," he said, struggling to restrain the anxious dogs.

When they pushed through the lobby door, a blustery wind swirled Kate's hair around her face. The water had risen another few inches since she first looked out the window. Before long, it would spill over the high curb.

Kate glanced around while Peter unlocked the car and threw their bags in the back seat. Another car, its headlights glinting off the water, drove by on the next block. It was the only other sign of life she saw.

Peter drove slowly up the street, pushing water as they went. Kate glanced at her watch.

"It's still 18 hours before landfall," she said. "If the water's already this high, how high will it be by tonight?"

Peter reached over and squeezed her hand. "This may end up being worse even than Eddie Vasquez predicted."

Kate wondered whether water already filled the street in front of Carl and Gigi Neal's house. She stuffed her fear for them into a mental box and slammed it shut. It was the only way she could continue to function.

By the time they got a few blocks from Kate's building, they were out of the flooding and Peter gunned the engine. They sped down Broadway toward the animal shelter. A big box trailer sat in the parking lot, its back doors open to reveal rows of cages. Shelly Archer stood between the trailer and the building, directing staff as they loaded up the animals. Incessant barking filled the air. Two days ago, Kate might have considered the animal evacuation overkill. Today, she watched it with relief.

Peter gave both dogs a quick hug before handing their leashes and the cat carrier to the animal shelter director.

"Be careful," she said as a shot of wind tore around the building. "Seems like this storm is picking up fast. We should be out of here in the next thirty minutes."

"Call us if you want an escort over the causeway," Peter said, glancing toward the bridge. "You should still be okay, but I have a feeling we'll close it before too much longer."

Kate blinked in surprise. She hadn't thought about the wind being so strong they would have to close the island's only link to the mainland.

Peter offered her a reassuring smile as he climbed back into the car and drove toward the convention center. They met a few cars headed off the island. Some pulled trailers that probably contained as much furniture and other valuables as the family could cram in. Otherwise, the streets were empty.

Along with the wind, a heavy blanket of clouds had rolled in overnight. They pressed down on the island, giving Kate a sense of claustrophobia. Peter switched on the car's headlights. The palm trees that marched down Broadway in single file swayed in the wind as they drove past.

Several police officers stood at the entrance to the convention center parking garage, directing traffic. Peter pulled around them and parked in the surface lot.

"I doubt we'll be here long," he said. "I'm just going to check in and see where they want me out patrolling."

"I'm going to talk to Vasquez," Kate said, climbing out of the car. "If he's got crews going out, I may want to hitch a ride with one of them."

Peter frowned. "If you decide to do that, I'm coming with you."

Kate hesitated. "I don't want to get you in any more trouble with the police chief than you already are. Surely, if I'm with Vasquez and other members of his crew, I'd be safe enough."

"Not for me," he said.

All the arguments that sprang to life in her mind died before they crossed her lips. Her independent streak seemed so petty in light of the danger swirling around them. She knew Peter would give anything, even his own life, to keep her safe. How could she argue against that?

She followed him into the back of the convention center, leaving a slight distance between them. She hoped that might tamp down the inevitable whispering their constant togetherness would generate. Police officers filled the hallway, chatting and swigging bottles of water. Peter stopped to shake hands with several of the men.

"What's going on?" he asked.

"First shift should be coming in soon," said one of the men. "We're waiting on the mayor and the chief to agree on when to have us come back once the storm gets worse."

Kate peered around the crowd in the hallway and through the door of the first conference room. The murmur of raised voices filtered into the hallway.

"Let's go check it out," she said, heading for the door. "You first. I'll slip in behind you. Maybe no one will notice I'm there."

Peter shot her an exasperated look, and she shooed him into the room. Mayor Matthew Hanes stood in the middle of the room, hands on hips. He looked angrily between emergency management coordinator Stephen Rush and the police chief. Kate spotted Eddie Vasquez behind Rush. He had his arms crossed, and a fierce scowl creased his normally cheery face.

"People had plenty of time to leave," Hanes shouted. "We'll do what we can to help those who changed their minds. But I am not risking city property, or our employees, for people too stupid to do the right thing."

"I'm not suggesting we put anyone at risk," Rush growled. "But you only want our crews out in the streets for a few more hours. I'm saying that's not enough time.

Let our people do their jobs until it really is too dangerous. Then we'll pull them in."

Lugar held up his hands. "I'm with Rush on this one. I want all my officers to take every possible precaution. But our job is to serve and protect. We can't do that sitting around here."

"Look, chief, with all due respect, I'm the one who needs to call the shots here," Hanes sneered. "Thanks to the emergency declaration I signed this morning, I've got the power to do whatever I think is best under the circumstances."

Lugar's face flushed crimson. Kate held her breath for the inevitable explosion, but he managed to wrestle his anger under control.

"My men are not going to stand for abandoning this community when it needs them most," he snapped. "These are their neighbors and friends. They want to do everything they can to help for as long as they can."

"And what happens if one of them gets stuck in floodwater, or a tree comes down on one of their cars?" Hanes roared. "We cannot risk having to send a rescue crew out to rescue the rescuers. How's that going to look on tonight's news?"

At the mention of news, Ashleigh Tarver's head snapped up. As if drawn to Kate's presence, she turned and looked right at her. As soon as their eyes met, Ashleigh's mouth puckered as though she were sucking on a fat straw. She waved at the mayor frantically and pointed with wide eyes in Kate's direction. Kate thought about trying to duck out of sight but decided to stand her ground. When Hanes saw her, his already angry face contorted with rage.

"You!" he bellowed. "How did you sneak in here? I should have you arrested."

Peter's face showed no emotion, but his jaw muscle twitched. Lugar glanced their way and his eyes narrowed. Kate braced for him to spew his own vitriol.

"Maybe it's not such a bad thing to have a member of the media present," he said, fixing his eyes on Hanes. "What would the public think if they knew you were trying to pull police off the streets too soon? If none of my officers are visible, looters will have a field day."

"Fine," Hanes spat. "But I'm going to let you be the one to go in front of the TV cameras if something goes wrong."

Hanes turned on his heel and stalked off, fixing Kate with a murderous look as he strode past. As soon as he was out of sight, Kate trotted over to Rush and Vasquez.

"I had no idea this storm would come with a lightning show," she quipped, hoping to break the lingering tension.

"For once, I think we were all glad to see you," Vasquez retorted with a wink.

Peter tensed as Lugar headed right for him, his mouth set in a grim line.

"For once, your timing was perfect, detective."

"We really weren't trying to cause any trouble. We just walked in."

"Well, I suggest you stay out of the mayor's way for a while."

Peter nodded. "Is there anything in particular I can do to help?"

Lugar thought for a moment. "The first shift should be coming in now, and I'm about to send the next shift out. Why don't you check in with dispatch and see if they've had any calls come in that need immediate attention."

Peter glanced at Kate. She had her notebook out, scribbling down something Vasquez and Rush were saying. He decided not to interrupt, especially since the chief probably didn't want her hanging around the call center. As long as she stayed in the building, he was sure she was safe.

In the next room, four dispatchers sat around tables, staring with practiced calm at their glowing computer screens. Each woman wore a headset connected to a phone sitting by their right elbow. He caught the eye of the one closest to him and she waved him over.

"The chief asked me to check in and see if you had any calls that needed immediate attention. Second shift is a bit delayed getting out."

"No open calls at the moment," she said. "But we have had several calls from the same address where no one says anything. At first I thought it might be a prankster. But the last time I listened for a bit longer, and it seemed like someone might have been keeping the line open on purpose. But I couldn't hear anything. Ordinarily l would have called it out as a welfare check."

"I can swing by and check it out," he said, pulling his phone from his pocket. "What's the address?"

"2807 Church Street."

Something about the address sounded familiar, but Peter couldn't place it.

"The streets downtown were already starting to fill with water before dawn. Maybe it's someone who's watching the water rise and getting nervous. Based on what I saw this morning, that area is definitely going to be under water before long."

The woman nodded, the briefest hint of worry flitting across her normally placid face.

"I've heard a lot of things at the other end of these lines over the years. But this is going to be a long night."

"Hang in there," Peter said. "We'll do everything we can."

"Everything else is out of our control," she said.

The uncanny echo of his mother's words filled Peter's mind. In most other situations, he had no trouble admitting his own limitations. And as he'd told Kate the night before, surrender was both the gateway and the foundation to faith. But with a killer lurking and massive hurricane about to barrel over them at full speed, surrender somehow felt like failure.

When Peter returned to the conference room, Kate wasn't there. A jolt of panic shot through his chest, leaving him breathless. He dashed back into the hallway and looked around, trying not to look as frantic as he felt.

"She's on the balcony, detective," an officer standing nearby called with a smirk. "I saw her head out there with Vasquez and Rush a few minutes ago."

"Thanks," Peter muttered, embarrassed to be caught looking like a frightened child.

The convention center balcony was built to serve as a viewing platform for local officials to watch the annual Mardi Gras parades. Since it looked out over the gulf, it made a great spot to take in Julio's building wrath. Kate stood at the edge of the decorative iron railing with Vasquez, her hand shading her eyes from the wind.

Peter stepped out to stand next to her. The muddy brown waves of the gulf churned and frothed, crashing onto the beach with increasing force. About half a dozen people stood on the seawall, watching the display of nature's power. In front of the convention center, Peter counted seven television crews doing live shots.

"That's CNN," Kate said, pointing to the one in the middle. "Over there is The Weather Channel."

"I've already given interviews to *The New York Times* and *The Wall Street Journal*," Vasquez said, flashing Kate a grin. "I told them I was a pro at giving interviews, thanks to our relentless local news media."

Kate rolled her eyes. "Glad I could help."

"I just got another update from the National Weather Service," Rush said, holding up his phone. "Wind speed's increased by two miles per hour. We need to get those people off the seawall."

"We can send a couple officers out to talk to them," Peter said. "The wind won't be the only problem before long. Look at the waves hitting the end of the fishing pier."

Wave after wave battered the long pier that stretched about fifty yards out from the beach. As they watched, it shuddered. Vasquez let out a low whistle.

"It won't take much more of that," he said.

"And when it breaks apart, all that debris is going to wash this way," Peter said.

"I'm going to go see if I can get those television reporters to encourage people to stay away," Rush said, ducking back into the building.

"Are you headed out?" Kate asked, turning toward him. Her hair flew around her face, giving her a wild, untamed look.

He nodded. "Dispatch had an address they wanted me to check out. It's probably nothing, but we can swing by while we're making the rounds."

"Maybe I'll get an exclusive on a dramatic rescue," she said, flashing him a smile.

"Or maybe we'll have a nice, uneventful drive and come back here to wait out this monster," he said. "That sounds like a much better idea."

Chapter 20

The wind whipped Kate's face as they stepped out the back door of the convention center. In the short time they'd been inside, it had already kicked up a notch. A long line of city vehicles had formed at the entrance to the parking garage. The police officers directing traffic barked orders and waved their arms like an airport ground crew to keep the line moving. Police vehicles, ambulances, and fire trucks filled the surface lot.

The background hum of the surf, normally a soothing ebb and flow, now roared like a bear caught in a trap. Kate felt every wave as it exploded at the base of the seawall. She could almost sense the island tremble. When they scrambled into the car and closed the doors, the silence seemed unnaturally loud.

Peter stared out at the chaos unfolding around them for several moments before firing up the engine.

"Where to?" Kate asked.

"We'll head back toward downtown first," he said. "I want to see how high the water is now. I bet some people closer to Broadway who didn't think they needed to leave are going to get caught by surprise."

"What about that call dispatch wanted you to check out?"

"It's in that direction. I'm guessing that may be why they've been calling."

Peter switched on the headlights as he pulled out of the parking lot. It was only mid-morning, but the storm's encroaching gloom had the feel of twilight. As they drove down the empty street, debris picked up from nearby neighborhoods skittered across the pavement in front of them. Kate peered out the windshield at the palm trees gyrating in the wind. A dead frond tore loose as though plucked by an invisible hand. It bounced when it hit the street, and Peter swerved to miss it.

As they neared Broadway, a city dump truck lumbered by. In the back sat two men clutching trash bags in their laps.

"Looks like they're already making some high-water rescues," Peter said.

Before Kate could respond, his cell phone rang.

"Detective Johnson," he said in the professional voice that sounded both familiar and foreign. "Yes, sir, we're still out patrolling. In fact, I'm not far from you right now."

Kate strained to hear the voice on the other end of the line but could only make out an indistinct murmuring.

"I'll be happy to come get you," Peter said. "Kate Bennett's with me. I know she'll be relieved to see you."

He flashed her a smile, and she raised her eyebrows questioningly.

"Okay, we'll be there as soon as we can," he said, ending the call and dropping his phone in his lap. "Looks like you're going to get to witness a rescue after all, although I don't know how dramatic it will be. Carl Neal decided he doesn't want to stick it out at home after all."

Kate grinned, relief giving her a boost of energy. "About time. This is going to make a great story."

Peter laughed. "I'm sure he'll be happy to hear it."

A sudden gust of wind rocked the car, and Kate instinctively reached for the dashboard.

"I'm glad he called now," Peter said. "The storm's really picking up. I don't know how much longer we'll be able to stay out."

As if on cue, the police scanner crackled to life. "All units be advised: the causeway is now closed to traffic. The city is opening a shelter of last resort at Ball High School. Anyone picked up from now on needs to be taken there. Continue to patrol for now, but plan to come in earlier than expected."

Kate's pulse quickened. "Surely they won't pull all the rescue teams off the streets just when they opened a shelter, not if people are still calling for help."

Peter glanced at her, his mouth set in a grim line. "We're not out of time yet," he said. But the urgency in his voice told her it probably wouldn't be long before they were.

He stepped on the gas and the car lurched toward Bayou Shore Drive. After two blocks, water started to fill the gutters and creep toward the center of the street. In another two blocks, Peter pulled the car to a stop. A narrow strip of pavement stretched out in front of them. But water completely covered the intersection ahead.

"We can't go any further," he said. "The water is coming too fast."

Kate peered out the window, her alarm rising as fast as the water outside. Peter put the car in reverse and backed up to the next block.

"That should buy us enough time to go in and get them out," he said, killing the engine and opening his door. "We're going to have to wade. Are you ready?"

Kate nodded and stepped out into the wind. She tucked her notebook into her back pocket and twisted her hair into a knot at the base of her neck, using her pen to hold it in place. They walked down the center of the street on dry ground for about a block. Kate inspected each house they passed, looking for any signs of life behind the shuttered windows. They were still a block away from the Neal's street when water started to lap around their feet. Kate shivered at the unexpected cold working its way toward her ankles. By the time they had sloshed their way to Bayou Shore Drive, it swirled around her knees.

Peter reached out to her. She hesitated only a moment before grasping his hand. It no longer seemed important who saw them together or what they thought about it.

"The current's really strong," she said, tightening her grip. "I'm not sure why that's surprising."

"That's why so many people get in trouble," Peter said, pulling her closer. "This water has a lot more power than we realize."

When they turned the corner, Kate spotted Carl Neal standing on his front porch. Water already covered his shoes.

"It must be in their house already," Kate said. "It's still hours before landfall. Thank God he changed his mind."

Peter cupped his hands to his mouth and yelled to get Carl's attention. He turned slowly and raised his hand in a dejected salute of acknowledgement. He took one more look at his front yard and disappeared through the front door.

Kate and Peter slogged their way up the street. With every step, she expected the Neals to come out to meet them, but they made it to the front steps without another sign of the couple.

"Mr. Neal?" Peter called. "Are you ready? We need to get moving before the water rises much higher."

"We're just about ready," Carl yelled.

Kate followed Peter up the steps, glad to be out of the tugging current for at least a few minutes. The tidy living room she'd seen just a few days before was now in disarray. The couch, chairs, and coffee table sat on concrete blocks, dry for now. But it was clear the water would soon start creeping up their legs. Kate gazed around the room, wondering how high it would eventually climb. As she stood looking around, Gigi Neal bustled into the room, her arms full of a stack of clothes she deposited into two duffel bags sitting open on the couch. She turned to go back down the hallway and bumped into her husband.

"That's enough," he said, more sternly than Kate thought was necessary.

"But my mother's jewelry!" Gigi protested, stepping around him and charging down the hall.

Carl groaned. "I'm sorry. We're almost ready."

"I know it's hard to know what to take and what to leave behind," Peter said. "But that water won't wait."

Carl nodded and turned to go after his wife, but she ran back into the room with her arms full.

"I found a few more things," she said apologetically. "Just a few more."

Carl helped her squeeze them into the bags and then tugged the zippers closed.

"That's it," he said. "Nothing else. We have to go."

Carl slung one bag over his shoulder, and Peter reached out to take the other. Kate threaded her arm through the older woman's and smiled encouragingly.

"The current's pretty strong," she said. "It helps if we hold on to each other."

Gigi nodded and began to slosh toward the door. Her sudden cry of anguish made Kate jump. Yanking her arm away, Gigi hurled herself at the wall covered in photos.

"Oh, no! We can't leave these," she cried, reaching out her hand to take a heavy frame off the wall.

"Gigi, no," Carl said, the commanding edge gone from his voice. Gently, he put his hands on his wife's shoulders. "There's no room, and there's no time."

"But it's our whole life," she said, putting her hand to her mouth to hold back a sob. "All our memories."

Carl turned his wife around to face him and smiled down at her. "It's not our whole life. That's in here." He put his hand over his heart. "These are just reminders of what we have stored away."

She gazed up at him as though she couldn't process what he was saying. Then her face contorted, and she collapsed against him. Kate's chest tightened as she watched Carl wrap his arms around his wife and murmur comforting words over the top of her head. She glanced at Peter. He took in the scene for a moment and then turned away. But not before Kate caught a fleeting look of longing in his eyes.

Peter began shuffling toward the door again, and Carl gently turned his wife to follow. But as they passed a photo of the family all together, Gigi's hand shot out and lifted it from its hanger. She hugged the frame to her chest as her husband led her out the front door.

The wind caught Kate by surprise after their brief respite inside. It nearly knocked her off balance as she reached the bottom step and felt around with her foot in the swirling water for a solid place to stand.

"Let's head for the street," Peter called. "We'll be less likely to trip over something there."

He waited for the Neals to pass him and reached out his hand to Kate.

"Be careful," he said, squeezing her fingers. "There's no telling what this water's washed up already."

Even though they'd been inside for less than fifteen minutes, the current already felt significantly stronger. Gigi stumbled, and Carl caught her before she fell face-first into the water.

"We need to keep moving," Peter called, urgency stretching his voice tight. "But I'm going to call for a pickup."

A few minutes later, a high water rescue vehicle rolled to a stop at the intersection about 20 yards away. Peter waved to get the driver's attention and two men jumped down from the bed of the truck and waded toward them. Kate sighed with relief.

"I'm glad you weren't far," Peter said when the two men got close enough to hear him over the wind. "Feels like we're walking in quicksand."

"It's a good thing you called us," the younger of the two men said as he took Carl's bag. "We were about to head across 61st Street. We're getting a bunch of calls from out there."

Kate's pulse quickened. "Any you can't reach yet?" she asked.

The man shook his head. "Not yet, but it won't be long."

A shiver of dread zipped down her back. She couldn't imagine having to battle this water alone, all night.

"That your car we passed?" the man asked Peter as he helped Carl and Gigi into the back of the towering truck.

"Yep," Peter said, passing the couple's second bag up to Carl. "I hope it's still dry."

"It is, but I wouldn't hang around here for much longer."

"We're leaving," Peter said. He swung himself over the tailgate and reached back for Kate. Before she could decide how to scramble aboard, he had lifted her up and set her next to Gigi. The two workers clambered up behind her.

The truck lurched forward, and Gigi leaned her head on her husband's shoulder, tears trickling down her cheeks. Carl put his arm around her. Peter knelt down in front of them.

"I know this is hard, but you're safe now," he said. "And in a few months, this will just be another adventure you can put on your wall."

Gigi sniffed and nodded. Warmth spread through Kate's chest as she watched Peter's compassion at work.

"Thanks for coming so quickly," Carl said, clearing his throat. "I never should have tried to stay."

Peter nodded and clapped him on the shoulder. Before he could say anything else, the truck lurched to a stop.

"I guess this is where we get off," Kate said, turning to Carl. "I'm really glad you're safe. I'll try to check in on you tomorrow."

"Take care of yourself," Carl called as she scooted toward the tailgate. "I have a feeling it's going to be a nasty night."

Peter watched the truck lumber down the street before unlocking the car and helping Kate inside. He fished a few towels from the trunk and slid behind the wheel. Kate looked at him in amazement.

"You thought to bring towels?"

He laughed. "It seemed like they might come in handy."

They squeezed the water out of their pants legs and listened to the steady stream of calls coming across the police radio. Most were rescue requests. Anxiety furrowed Kate's forehead.

"They'll never have time to get to them all," she whispered.

He put his hand over hers. "It's still early. And you saw how tall those rescue vehicles are. The water will have to get a lot higher before they have to come in."

She nodded and bit her lip. When his cell phone rang, he let go of her hand reluctantly. The number for one of the dispatch extensions flashed across the screen.

"We got another call from that house," the dispatcher said, not even bothering to return his greeting. "Have you had a chance to check it out yet?"

"No, we got sidetracked by another rescue," Peter said. "But we're about to head that way."

"Good. I was getting ready to send another unit out there, but you're probably the closest."

"Did you get any information from the caller this time?"

"No. Still no direct contact. But I could hear voices in the background and someone saying something about a baby."

Peter's pulse quickened. He had a hard time imagining anyone with a baby trying to ride out the storm, but people did things all the time that he couldn't explain.

"Okay, we'll go right now. The water's already pretty high over here, but hopefully it's not as bad in that direction. We're right by the water."

"Thanks, detective. Be careful."

Peter hung up and looked at Kate, who was watching him expectantly. He briefly debated taking her back to the convention center. Tommy Gage remained a threat, but right now, Hurricane Julio posed the biggest danger.

"Well, what's our next assignment?" she asked.

He sighed. Even if he had time to take her back, he'd never talk her into staying behind.

"We're going to that address dispatch wanted me to check out. There may be someone at the house with a baby."

Kate sucked in a breath. "What are you waiting for? Let's go."

Chapter 21

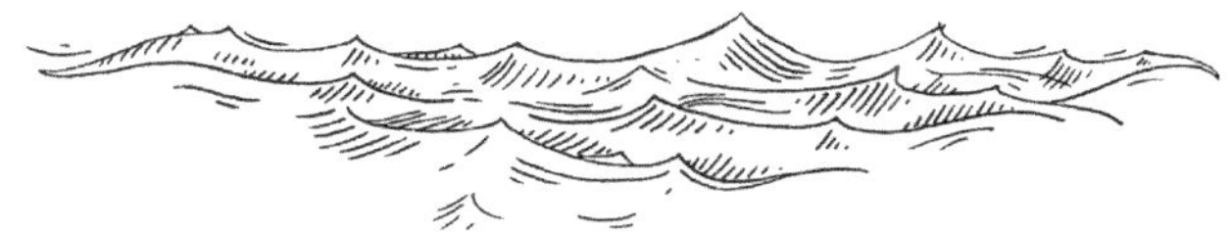

The gray clouds that blanketed the sky all morning had deepened into pewter. They towered overhead in bulbous formations that would have been beautiful, if not so ominous. Peter looked up at them through the windshield and a sense of foreboding squeezed his chest. It seemed like the world might collapse in on them.

He mashed the gas pedal to the floor, and the car rocketed down the deserted street. Ever since they'd left the convention center, a stray thought he couldn't pin down had scratched at the edge of his consciousness. Paired with the threatening sky, it fed his growing anxiety. He glanced at Kate. She was as safe, sitting next to him, as she could possibly be. What was he missing?

He slowed as they neared the intersection with Broadway. Palm fronds and trash already littered the city's main thoroughfare. He drove across, dodging as much of the debris as he could. The last thing they needed was a flat tire. Several blocks ahead, as the street neared the port, it started to shimmer and roll. Water. If the flooding had come that far already, it must now cover downtown.

Kate gasped and pointed out her window. "Look, there's someone over there. It looks like he's trying to flag us down."

Peter squinted into the distance until he spotted the man. He was waving his arms over his head. As they rolled closer, Peter realized the problem. The man's car, parked in a driveway that sloped away from the street, sat in at least three feet of water. The driver's side door stood open, as though the man had just stepped out of it when he realized it wouldn't start. Peter couldn't believe he'd even tried. Water covered half the hood and filled the interior.

Peter rolled down his window as the man trotted over to them.

"I need help starting my car," he said, huffing with the effort of making his way through the water. "I can't get it to turn over."

"The engine must be flooded by now," Peter said. "It's never going to start. Do you have another way out?"

The man shook his head. "No, man. This is my ride. I gotta get it started."

"It's never going to happen, even if we pushed it out of the water." Peter wavered between exasperation and compassion. "Do you have anyone with you?"

"Naw. They all left. It's just me."

"Let me call someone to come get you. They've opened a shelter at Ball High. You'll be safe there. It's only going to get worse out here."

The man shook his head. "I can't leave my car."

"It's gone. There's nothing you can do."

The man put his hands on his head and looked up at the sky.

"I'm going to call for a rescue vehicle," Peter said, reaching for his radio.

The man shook his head and waved them off. Peter watched as he waded back toward his flooded car.

"Can't we make him come with us?" Kate asked, her voice rising in frustration.

Peter sighed. "I can't force anyone to make the right decision," he said. "I just hope he realizes he needs help before it's too late. We'll come back and check on him before we go back to the convention center."

He put the car in reverse and backed slowly up the street. As he turned toward their intended destination, the nagging sense of unease that had plagued him for the last few hours churned into full-blown anxiety. He stopped the car and looked around, searching for some sign of impending danger.

"What's wrong?" Kate's eyes glittered with worry.

"I don't know. I just have this feeling."

Peter shook his head and took his foot off the brake, allowing the car to roll forward again. They were halfway through the next intersection when the amorphous warning crystallized into a clear image. A rundown row house with peeling paint and a shiny Dodge Charger sitting in the driveway. Peter's heart thudded so hard in his chest that he couldn't breathe for several beats.

"Peter?" Kate gripped his arm, her eyes now wild with fear.

"Rudy Williams," he whispered, willing himself to take a deep breath. "That's whose house these calls have been coming from."

Kate looked confused. "Who's that?"

"The guy who helped Gage escape." Every word felt like poison as it rolled off his tongue.

Kate stared at him, mouth half open. "Are you sure?" she finally stammered.

"Positive. I knew it sounded familiar when the dispatcher read it out, but Williams was the last thing on my mind. I just didn't make the connection."

"Did Williams get out?"

Peter shook his head. "He made a deal with the DA, but he couldn't have gotten out that quickly."

"So, who's been making the calls?"

"It's his mom's house. But his girlfriend lives there, too."

"Does she have a baby?" Kate's voice was so low he almost couldn't understand her.

He nodded slowly as the seriousness of the situation sank in. If the Williams women had decided to stay and now realized they needed help, why not just ask for it when dispatch answered their call? And why call more than once? Peter could think of only one scenario that fit the dispatcher's description.

"You don't think this is a coincidence, do you?" Kate whispered.

He shook his head, suddenly feeling like he might throw up. "Whoever made those calls couldn't talk openly," he said. "They must have hoped dispatch would hear enough to figure out something was wrong."

"You think Gage is there?" The slight tremble in Kate's voice wrung his heart.

"It makes sense. He needed somewhere to go after he killed Aleah Price. Maybe he thought they could help smuggle him off the island."

"But if they called 9-1-1, something didn't go as planned. Maybe they refused to help."

Peter reached for his radio. "I'm calling for backup. Then I'm taking you back to the convention center."

Kate pressed her lips together but didn't argue. When the dispatcher answered, Peter explained the situation as quickly as he could.

"I need at least two units on my location. No, make that three. Someone will need to take Ms. Bennett back to the convention center."

"Can't you take me?" Kate hissed as they waited for the dispatcher to put the call out.

"I can't send someone else in to face Tommy Gage while I run to safety." The image of the plane that carried him away from his old home scrolled across his memory. He'd taken the easy way out once. He wouldn't do it again. As long as he knew Kate was safe, he was willing to risk his life to face another man bent on revenge.

"Detective," the dispatcher's voice crackled over the radio. "All available units are on other calls. We've been slammed since you left. I can't get anyone to you anytime soon."

Peter slammed his palm into the steering wheel. "I'll head back to the convention center and pick up help there."

"10-4," the dispatcher said, and the radio went silent. He reached up to put the car in gear, but Kate put her hand on his arm.

"Peter," she whispered. "Those people are in danger. If you're right and Tommy Gage is there, he'll kill them without a second thought. Even the baby."

He tightened his grip on the steering wheel. Her words crackled through his brain like fire in a brush pile. He could feel the heat burning behind his eyes.

"It will take too much time to go back to the convention center. You can't risk their lives just to protect me."

"No!" the word flew from his lips like a cannonball. "I've spent the last week making sure he didn't come near you. Now you want me to take you right to him?"

Kate shook her head. "No, but I don't want anyone to die because of me. How could I live with myself?"

With one blow, Kate sent a crack tearing through his defense. He'd spent half his life burdened with guilt and regret. How could he sentence Kate to the same penance? And if he did, would she ever forgive him, or herself? He groaned with an agony that seeped from the depths of his soul. Surrender. That was his only option.

He threw his head back and squeezed his eyes shut.

"Please, God, not like this." His voice rose with every word. "Don't make me do this."

A gust of wind rocked the car. Peter's eyes flew open. Kate was staring at him, her own eyes wide and her face pale. His heart, beating fast just moments before, began to slow. He still trembled over what might lie ahead, but a stillness settled over his soul. It quieted his pleading and muted his anguish.

Kate slipped her hand under his fingers, loosening them from the steering wheel. He wrapped his hand around hers and brought it to his lips.

"It's going to be okay," she whispered. "We have to go."

He took a deep breath and nodded. With an effort that required every ounce of his strength, he lifted his foot from the brake pedal. The car rolled slowly forward.

Kate's stomach churned as they eased down the next block. Peter radioed dispatch again to let them know he was going to the Williams house. The dispatcher promised to send help as soon as she could. Kate had little experience praying, but she sent up a silent plea that help would come sooner than later.

Peter's raw appeal to God had torn through her heart and soul. She hadn't realized until that moment how much he wrestled to hold on to his faith. It wasn't an easy, knee-jerk response to a lifetime of conditioning. It was a daily decision to submit himself to something he believed was bigger, more meaningful, than his present reality. His faith was wild and dangerous and all-consuming. Like riding a surfboard into the eye of a hurricane.

When Peter pulled over and stopped the car, Kate peered out the window. Butterflies whirled in her chest.

"It's in the next block," Peter murmured. "I didn't want to announce our presence."

Kate nodded. He took her hand.

"I have no idea what we'll find when we get to the house," he said. "If things go bad, don't hesitate to run." His eyes bored into hers. "Don't hesitate."

She swallowed to ease the lump in her throat. She had no intention of leaving him behind, but she wasn't about to tell him that. He sighed, almost like he knew she would do whatever she thought best, no matter what he told her.

"I would leave you in the car if I thought you would stay," he said. "Or if I thought you'd be safe here. But I don't want to let you out of my sight."

"I'll do my best to stay out of trouble." She cracked a smile she hoped would ease the tension.

He smiled back, but it didn't mask the fear in his eyes.

Peter stepped out of the car and nearly fell back against the door as another gust of wind blew over them. No audible voice had responded to his cry to God, but he'd sensed an answer in the roaring fury around them. Not flee to safety, but trust Him in the storm. He felt like Job, bowed down before the demonstration of God's might. Who was he to question God's plans and purposes?

From the trunk, he pulled a tactical assault weapon. He already had his pistol strapped to his side, but he wrapped the holster for another around his thigh. Then he motioned for Kate to come closer. Pulling out his bullet-proof vest, he slid it over her head.

"What are you doing?" she protested. "I'm going to be behind you, remember? You're the one who needs this."

"Hopefully, neither of us will need it. But I'd feel much better if you were wearing it."

He slammed the trunk shut and sent a prayer for protection into the wind. Then he motioned Kate to follow.

He'd parked the car on dry ground, but they waded into water as soon as they crossed the intersection. It was only about ankle deep, but it was advancing quickly. He glanced back at the car. If he hadn't parked it far enough away, he'd just have to deal with the consequences. There was no going back now.

They kept to the same side of the street as the Williams house, picking their way carefully across yards obscured by muddy seawater. Peter could just make out the outline of the house in the distance, the shiny Charger still in the driveway. That confirmed the women hadn't left. Another gust of wind shot down the street and the screen door slammed against its frame.

Peter kept his eyes locked on the house as they moved along, searching for any signs of life. He could now see the glow of light around one of the side windows, but the front of the house remained eerily dark. He hoped that meant no one was expecting an ambush. When they reached the edge of the next door neighbor's yard, they crouched behind a trashcan.

"You okay?" he whispered.

Kate nodded and tugged at the neck of the vest. "This thing is so heavy."

He leaned forward and touched his lips to her forehead. Half a dozen things he wanted to tell her filled his mind, but he pushed them back. She only needed to know one thing, and by this point, he didn't need to say it.

"We're going to make our way behind the car," he said, slipping his backup pistol from the holster on his leg. "That will give us some protection in case we need it. Remember, if you have to run, do it. Don't look back."

She looked at him with wide eyes. "Peter," she said, her voice cracking.

"Whatever it is, save it for when this is all over." He took her hand and pulled her to her feet. "Let's move."

They ran full out until they reached the back of the Charger. Peter stayed in a crouch, half expecting a volley of bullets to erupt from the front door. But they made it without any sign that they'd been spotted. Peter took a moment to get his bearings and check for escape routes. They had walked in from the east, but the west end of the street appeared just as deserted.

"If you have to run and you can't make it back to the car, go that way," he whispered, pointing west. "If you do make it back to the car, the keys are in the console."

She nodded once, then turned back to look at the house. Peter took a deep breath and then stood, leaning over the back of the car so he wasn't completely exposed.

"Lashonta Williams," he yelled. "This is the Galveston Police Department. We're doing a welfare check on everyone who hasn't evacuated."

A thump and a muffled cry came from inside the house. Peter squeezed the grip on his gun but held his position.

"Mrs. Williams?" he yelled again. "Are you alright?"

More bumping in the house signaled movement.

"Stay down," he whispered. "I don't want whoever's in there to know you're here."

With a creak, the front door opened a crack.

"This is Lashonta Williams," a shaky voice declared. "I'm fine. I don't need no help."

"Can you step out on the porch, please? I'd like to see for myself that you're alright."

After some shuffling and murmuring, a heavyset woman in a red house dress stepped through the door. Her hair hung limp around her head and Peter could detect a darkening ring around one eye. Her mouth hung open slightly, as though she wanted to say something but couldn't. Peter stood up so she could see him better.

"Mrs. Williams?" he said. "Are you sure you're okay? It looks like you've got a black eye."

Her mouth moved, but no words came out. Her eyes darted to the side, as though listening to someone behind her.

"Who are you?" she finally croaked.

"Galveston Police," he said.

"I seen you before, haven't I?"

Peter took a deep breath and let it out slowly. "Yes, ma'am. I'm Detective Peter Johnson. I came to talk to you about your son, Rudy, last week."

The woman yelped as though someone slapped her, and Peter ducked back down. He glanced at Kate. A grimace contorted her face.

"He's in there," she whispered. "I can tell. Someone's telling her what to say, and now he knows you're here." She clamped her hand over her mouth as though she couldn't bear to say more.

"Mrs. Williams, are you alone?" Peter called, peering over the top of the Charger to catch her reaction.

Before she could answer, Peter heard shattering glass from somewhere in the house.

"Help!" a younger woman yelled. "He's got us trapped in here. And I've got a baby."

Mrs. Williams cried out as an invisible hand dragged her back inside and slammed the front door shut. Peter crouched back down behind the car, but he could hear a series of thumps coming from the house. At least they were all still alive. He squeezed the button on his radio to call dispatch.

"10-4, detective," the woman said after he relayed what they'd discovered. "We'll have units to your location as soon as possible."

He sighed with relief. "Kate, listen, he doesn't know you're here. You need to go back to the car and wait for backup. You can tell them my position so they know where not to shoot."

Before Kate could reply, the screen door banged open again and a baby's cry lofted across the yard.

"Detective Peter Johnson," a raspy, menacing voice called. "It's about time you finally caught up to me."

Chapter 22

Malevolence dripped from Tommy Gage's voice. All the hair on the back of Peter's neck stood on end. He motioned for Kate to stay down and eased up so he could see the house. Gage stood on the front porch, a baby clutched in one arm. A short, sharp knife glinted in his free hand. The baby kicked his legs and waved his arms, wailing at the top of his lungs. Gage didn't seem to notice.

"What did you do with the women?" Peter called, searching for any sign of blood on the knife.

Gage's lip curled in a wicked grin. "They're still alive, for now. Whether they stay that way is up to you." He looked down the street in both directions. "You came alone? That was not a smart move, detective."

"I've got backup on the way," Peter said, easing up so Gage could see him and the rifle slung across his chest. "They'll be here any minute."

"Well, then, I guess we'd better get down to business." Gage gave the baby a slight shake, and the child hiccuped in surprise before renewing his cries. "I've got three hostages and I want something in return."

"Forget it, Gage," Peter growled. "That's not how this works."

The baby let out a piercing scream as Gage pricked his leg with the knife. A small trickle of blood ran over his chubby knee and down his shin. Peter's fingers tightened around the grip of his gun as his stomach twisted in revulsion.

"I'm in charge here," Gage bellowed, his face flushing crimson. "I'll be the one telling you how this works. Unless you want to watch me slit this baby's throat, you'll get on your radio and tell whoever's coming they'd better bring Kate Bennett with them."

Peter heard Kate gasp, but he didn't take his eyes off Gage's face. Thanks to the wind, he was sure Gage couldn't have heard her. All he had to do was keep Gage occupied until backup arrived. Gage never had to know Kate was there until someone else could take her to safety. He kicked himself for not leaving her in the car.

"And what do you plan to do then?" Peter asked.

"That's a stupid question, detective. I plan to kill her."

Peter forced himself to take a breath. "You know I'm not going to just turn her over to you," he said.

Gage huffed out a mirthless laugh. "I guess you do really love her," he said. "My worthless lawyer insisted that was my best defense. I had my doubts, but it turns out he was right."

"I wouldn't hand anyone over to you, especially not when I know you plan to kill them."

"But I don't want just anyone. I want her."

"It's not going to happen, Gage."

The baby let out another shriek and flailed in Gage's tight grip. Blood spurted from his other leg. Peter's throat tightened.

"Make the call or this kid's gonna lose a finger."

A muffled sob wafted out of the house. "My baby," a woman moaned. "Don't let him hurt my baby."

"Alright, just relax," Peter said. "I'll call right now."

He squeezed the button on his handset, and the radio crackled to life. Pretending to glance at the dials, he snuck a look at Kate, still crouched at his feet. She had her eyes squeezed shut and her hands clamped over her ears.

"Dispatch, this is Detective Johnson," he said. "I need one of the units responding to the Williams address to find *Galveston Gazette* reporter Kate Bennett and bring her here."

"Repeat your last transmission," the dispatcher said, her usual monotone laced with confusion.

"We have a hostage situation in progress," Peter said. "Tommy Gage is at the Williams house. He has two women and a baby with him. He's threatening to kill them if we don't bring him Kate Bennett."

After a long silence, the radio crackled. "10-4 detective. I'll deliver the message."

"There," Peter said. "I did what you asked. All we can do now is wait. Why don't you give the baby back to his mother?"

"And give you a clean shot at me?" Gage laughed, as though genuinely amused. "Not a chance."

The baby's crying had quieted, probably due to sheer exhaustion. Peter could see with relief that the blood no longer dripped from the spots where Gage had nicked him.

"Do you know I dreamed about this day, detective? I played it over and over in my mind while I rotted in that jail cell. I've learned a thing or two since the last time we did this. You won't catch me by surprise this time."

"So what's the plan? Where are you going to go? They've closed the causeway."

Gage shrugged. "Doesn't matter to me. If I wanted to get away, I'd be long gone by now. I had plenty of opportunities. That's not what I'm after."

"You're after revenge," Peter said. "It won't change a thing, you know."

"Yes. It. Will." Gage yelled, making the baby whimper. "That woman is going to pay for what she did to me. She's got it coming."

"The role she played in your capture was purely an accident," Peter said. "She had no idea what was going on that day. No one did."

"That's right," Gage growled. "No one had any clue until she started snooping around. I could have spent the last two and a half years touring South America instead of being locked up in that jail. I'm not gonna spend the rest of my life behind bars."

Peter knew it was useless to try talking Gage out of anything. He just had to keep him distracted until someone else got there.

"What is taking so long?" Gage barked. "They should be here by now."

"Everyone's busy with the storm," Peter said. "Making rescues."

"That is not important! Get back on that radio and tell them I'm losing patience."

The baby started to wail again, and Peter heard another muffled sob. This time, it came from Kate.

"I can't get them here any faster," Peter said.

Gage's eyes narrowed. "You're stalling."

"I'm not. I promise. I want them here as fast as you do."

Gage continued as though Peter hadn't spoken. "You don't think I'm serious."

"I do. I absolutely do." Alarm rippled down Peter's back as he watched Gage's face pucker in fury. "Hurting that baby won't make them get here any faster," Peter said.

"Oh, yeah?" Gage bellowed. "What if it just makes me feel better? What about that?"

"Stop!" Peter yelled, but Gage had already taken two quick swipes at the baby's legs. Blood flowed freely, dripping off his toes. The baby's pitiful screams ripped through Peter's heart.

"Enough. Please, that's enough." It took Peter a moment to register that the wavering voice was coming from beside him. He watched in disbelief as Kate stood up and walked around him to stand in full view of Tommy Gage.

"I'm right here. Please don't hurt the baby anymore."

Kate trembled so violently her teeth chattered. She clamped her jaws shut in a vain attempt to keep Gage from seeing her terror. The last thing she had planned to do when she heard his voice slither over the flooded yard was surrender. But she would do anything to end the torture of an innocent baby.

A grin that reminded Kate of an evil clown spread across Gage's face.

"There you are," he whispered. Or was it the wind? Kate couldn't tell.

Peter's hand shot out and grabbed her arm. He tried to pull her back down to safety behind the car. But she anticipated his move and locked her knees where she stood. Although his tugging nearly knocked her off balance, she stood her ground.

"Kate!" he hissed, his eyes wide with fear.

"Don't," she said, lowering her voice so Gage couldn't hear. "I can't just sit here and do nothing. I could never forgive myself if he killed that baby."

Gage whooped victoriously, making Kate jump.

"You brought her right to me!" he yelled. "And here I thought this might actually require some effort. But you already did all the work."

Gage shifted the baby to cover his chest like a shield. Then he pointed at Kate with his knife.

"Come here. Now."

Kate swallowed back a wave of nausea. She looked down at Peter one last time. Tears filled her eyes.

"I'm so sorry," she whispered. She wanted to reach out and touch his cheek, but fear of Gage kept her hand at her side.

Peter looked at her in stunned silence, as though he could barely comprehend what was happening.

"Now!" Gage barked.

The baby started crying again, and Kate took a shaky step forward. Those wretched wails stirred a well of anger deep in her heart. It rose with every cry, and each step she took toward the house grew ever more steady. By the time she reached the bottom of the steps leading to the front porch, a fire burned in her chest.

"Let him go," she said. Her voice rang out clear and calm, feeding her growing strength.

"Oh, I will," Gage said. "I don't want anything to get in the way of what I have planned for you."

Goosebumps rippled across Kate's arms. She tried not to think about what he would do next. Gage held his knife near the baby's throat.

"Walk up the steps slowly and stand right in front of me," he ordered.

Kate kept her eyes fixed on the baby's face. He watched her with beautiful, liquid brown eyes. Only when she stepped onto the porch did she allow herself to glance at Gage. His bloodshot eyes held the same hint of madness she remembered from the first day they'd met. Without saying a word, he handed her the baby and then spun her around so both she and the child stood between him and any shot Peter might try to take. Kate's stomach lurched as he coiled a hand around her waist and pulled her close.

"Oh, I have dreamed of this," he said, inhaling deeply behind her head. Kate shuddered, and he laughed.

"What now, Gage?" Peter called from across the yard. He'd moved around to the side of the car and rested the barrel of the rifle on the hood. He had it pointed right at them.

"I wouldn't do that if I were you, detective," Gage warned. "I still have my knife, and I'm faster than you think."

To prove his point, he held it out for Peter to see and then touched the tip to Kate's side. She held as still as she could. Gage took a few steps to his right, dragging her with him. When he stopped, Kate could see the front door behind them out of the corner of her eye.

"Get out here, woman," Gage bellowed.

Kate heard a shuffling sound from the house, and Mrs. Williams inched out the door. Her hunched shoulders and averted eyes suggested the hours she'd spent with Gage had left an indelible mark.

"Take the baby, nice and easy, and go back inside," he said. "Shut the door while you're at it."

The baby reached out his arms and babbled through his tears as his grandmother slid him from Kate's arms. Joy bubbled in her heart, and she tried to smile reassuringly at the woman. No matter what happened next, the child was out of immediate danger. She could at least take comfort in that. But without his warm little body pressed to her chest, fear began to trickle back into her consciousness.

"Now," Gage whispered. "It's just you and me."

Peter shifted his weight and peered through the scope on his rifle. It had taken every ounce of his self-control not to squeeze off a shot at Gage as Kate walked toward him. He knew there was a chance he might hit the baby, but for one long, terrible moment, he didn't care. All he could think about was keeping Kate out of that monster's clutches. But as he watched her go, Kate's words echoed in his mind. *I could never forgive myself.* If anything happened to the child, it would wreck them both.

So he watched her go and tried to tie a tourniquet around his heart.

"What now, Gage?" he yelled again as Mrs. Williams fled back into the house and slammed the door shut behind her.

He kept the gun trained on Gage and Kate, praying he could get enough of an opening to take just one shot. That is all he needed. But Gage held her so close that her body completely blocked every inch of his.

"Now, it's time Kate and I had some privacy," Gage called. "I'm guessing you didn't walk here. Where did you leave your car?"

Dread cascaded through him. If Gage made it to the car, they could effectively disappear. He might not find them again until it was too late.

"Where is it?" Gage demanded again. This time, he pressed the knife into Kate's side and she gasped. Peter felt the prick of the knife as though Gage had pressed it into his own skin.

"Don't!" he roared, standing upright and bringing the gun to his shoulder. His arms shook with rage.

"Careful, detective. It would be a tragedy if you pulled that trigger and killed an innocent woman."

Gage's words burned into his brain. Images from the nightmare of his past crowded his mind. Innocent women and children, gunned down to feed the fire of vengeance. Slowly, he lowered his weapon.

"The car." Gage said.

"Two blocks that way," Peter jerked his head to the left. "If it's not flooded by now."

He couldn't tell how much the water had risen in the last half hour. He prayed it would be enough to scuttle the car.

"Looks like we're all going to take a little walk then," Gage said. "Start moving."

Peter eased away from the Charger, keeping the gun trained on the house. He backed into the street as Gage ordered Kate to march down the steps. Peter searched Kate's face as they got closer. A steely resolve had replaced the fear that gripped her while she crouched in safety. It was like now that her worst fear had come true, her courage had grown to meet the challenge. She met his eye and held his gaze.

"Keep moving," Gage barked. Peter hadn't even realized he'd stopped.

Their slow march up the block felt like it took hours. Peter's back ached with the effort of keeping his gun raised and trying not to trip. The water swirled around his knees and threatened to pull him off balance. Every so often, he glanced over his shoulder to make sure he was still heading down the center of the street. When he spotted the car in the distance, his heart sank. Water lapped at the tires, but it was nowhere near high enough to prevent them from leaving.

His mind jumped from one plan to the next, searching for a solution that would stop Gage from driving off with Kate as his prisoner. When he sensed he was only steps away from the car and he still hadn't come up with a strategy, he began to pray. It took all his will power to keep from falling to his knees in the water and begging God to intervene. Despite his silent pleading, no answer came.

"Where are the keys?" Gage hissed. His voice vibrated with tension. Peter glanced at the knife pointed at Kate's side. Gage gripped the handle so hard his knuckles turned white.

Peter tried to answer, but he couldn't make his voice obey. He knew as soon as he told Gage where to find the keys, Kate would be gone. A sharp pain took root at the top of Peter's rib cage.

"Where—" Gage yelled, but Kate cut him off.

"They're in the console," she said. Her voice sounded faint, almost as if she were already disappearing down the street. The pain in Peter's chest mushroomed. He tried to take a breath and found he could only manage a series of quick gasps. Kate's forehead furrowed with worry.

"Get on the other side of the street," Gage barked.

Peter stumbled backward. The weight of his failure threatened to crush him. His only job was to keep her safe, and he'd delivered her to a madman.

Gage marched Kate around to the passenger side of the car and ordered her to open the door. Peter watched helplessly as Gage forced her to climb over the console into the driver's seat while he slid in beside her. The knife now hovered next to her neck. He saw Kate fumble with the keys, and then the engine roared to life. She risked one glance in his direction before putting the car in gear and stepping on the gas pedal.

Her eyes seemed to scream the words he'd waited a year to hear. Then she was gone.

Peter collapsed to his knees and let out a guttural scream. The pain in his chest was so intense he thought his heart might explode. It took effort to fill his lungs with air.

"Kate!" he screamed into the empty street.

The wind snatched up his cry and carried it to the heavens just as they opened and unleashed a torrent of rain.

Chapter 23

Kate tried not to think about the knife less than an inch from her jugular as she drove down the street. The wind gusts had grown so strong the car rocked like a boat tossed in the waves. Rain, the first band of the approaching storm, cascaded down the windshield, making it hard for her to see where she was going.

"Just keep driving," Gage hissed.

"Downtown is already flooded. We'll have to turn toward the seawall at some point, unless you want to swim."

Kate had spent the last week shrinking from the possibility of seeing Gage again. Her worst nightmares didn't even touch the reality of the terror he stirred in her heart. But once she resolved to give herself up, she'd regained some control over her panic. In a way, she no longer had anything to fear. And with her fear out of the way, anger filled the void.

Gage cackled. "I'm sure you'd love to drive us right to the convention center," he said. He leaned over the console and whispered in her ear. "Nice try."

She flinched away, and he laughed. He reached out his free hand and clasped her behind the neck. Her stomach heaved.

"Get your hand off me unless you want me to drive us into a tree," she said through clenched teeth.

He clicked his tongue in disapproval and squeezed so hard she yelped in pain. He moaned softly.

"This is going to be every bit as good as I imagined," he said, giving her neck one more squeeze. "Keep driving."

Kate gripped the steering wheel and stared straight ahead. She tried not to think about the agony that contorted Peter's face as he watched them drive away. He would come after them. She just had to stay alive long enough for him to find her. The rain came down in sheets, darkening the sky so much the car's headlights clicked on. Maybe, once they stopped, the storm would give her a chance to escape. The water got deeper as they neared downtown. It arced on either side of the car as they went along.

"Turn here," Gage barked.

She eased the car around the corner and drove up the side street. She couldn't make out the street sign as they passed, but they had to be close to 25th Street by now. Peter had surely called dispatch as soon as they drove away. Crossing Broadway might be their best chance of being spotted. She prayed one of the squad cars still on patrol would be waiting in the median.

"Kill the lights," Gage ordered, as though he could read her mind.

The gloom gave them some cover, but they didn't need it. As they rolled up to the intersection, Kate saw no sign of life. They might as well have been the last people out in the storm.

"Turn left and head for 17th Street," he said. Kate could hear the maniacal smile in his voice. "I think we'll go back to the place we first met."

Peter clutched his chest with one hand and fumbled for his radio with the other. The pouring rain made it hard for him to get a good grip on the slippery plastic. When he finally managed to press the button on the handset, nothing happened. He looked down in confusion. Water swirled around his waist, covering the radio. He struggled to stand, twisting the knobs on the top as the radio emerged from the water. But he couldn't coax it back to life.

Despair filled his soul. The longer it took for him to let dispatch know the direction they'd gone, the harder it would be to find them.

"Please, God," he whispered. "Please don't let her die."

He tilted his chin up, letting the rain wash over his face. It mingled with the tears that he could no longer stop. They poured from his eyes as though a deep vat of sorrow had overflowed. He had spent most of his adult life learning to surrender, retaking the test he had failed so miserably as a young man. But nothing since then had mattered as much as this. It felt like his final exam.

"I can't lose her," he yelled at the sky. Another spasm seized his chest, and he gasped at the pain. He doubled over, panting to catch his breath. The rain that caressed his back felt like a gentle hand. A gust of wind knocked him to his knees again, and as it whipped around him, it seemed to form into words.

Let her go.

He struggled to stand again, but the water pinned him down. The wind murmured again in his ear. He stopped flailing in the water and took a deep breath. He had fought so hard to save her, but her future, and his own, was out of his control. Hands over his face, he hung his head. For a moment, everything around him seemed to still. A peace he hadn't felt since he was a child washed over him. The pain in his chest slowly eased. He took a deep breath and raised his head.

Red and blue lights flashed in the distance.

Kate kept her eyes on the road and tried not to think about stepping into Gage's old house again. She knew someone had bought it after the murder and completely remodeled the inside. It probably looked nothing like it had the day Gage forced her into the living room and held her hostage.

She shuddered as she recalled those terrifying hours. Her ordeal ended that day when Peter came crashing through the back door. How ironic that the event marking the start of their relationship sewed the seeds that threatened to end it.

"Perfect," Gage murmured. "Absolutely perfect. I couldn't have done better if I'd planned it this way all along."

"So what's next? Once you kill me, I mean." Kate had the odd sensation that she was talking about someone else.

"Who knows?" Gage let out a whoop that made her jump. The car swerved and the blade of the knife sliced the bottom of her earlobe. Blood spurted out, hitting Gage in the face. He seized the back of her neck and shook her. By some miracle, she managed to keep the car moving forward. Her ear throbbed, and she clenched her teeth to keep from crying out.

"Careful," he hissed, letting go of her neck and wiping his cheek. "I don't want you to lose too much blood before it's time."

He pulled at the hem of his T-shirt and used the knife to make a slit. Then he tore off a strip of fabric, folded it into a pad, and pressed it to her ear.

At 17th Street, Kate turned right. The car now pointed directly into the oncoming wind. It rocked and shuddered, making it hard to steer straight. Kate kept her eyes on the road, searching for any sign of a police car or one of the high-water vehicles. But the flooding on this end of the island wasn't any higher than at the Williams house. Any rescue calls at this point would come from neighborhoods much closer to the water. Most of the houses they drove past had sheets of plywood covering their windows. It looked like everyone here had heeded evacuate orders.

"Here we are," Gage murmured. "Turn right."

Kate peered out the windshield into the gloom. The pouring rain had let up enough she could see halfway down the block. The side street sat lower than the main road, and water covered it from curb to curb. Kate couldn't gauge the depth. She was about to turn anyway when Gage held up his hand.

"Pull over. We can walk from here."

Peter struggled to his feet and waved his arms over his head. He had hoped to see a squad of cars, but as the lights drew nearer, he realized it was just one car. His eyes widened with shock when he made out the man behind the wheel.

"Chief Lugar?"

"What happened?" Lugar barked as he sprang out of the car. He scanned the street, trying to assess the situation. "Where's Gage?"

"He just drove off in my car," Peter said, running around to the passenger side of the chief's cruiser. "He's got Kate."

Lugar jumped back behind the wheel as Peter hurled himself into the passenger seat. Lugar threw the car in gear and headed back the way he had come.

"I have no idea where they're headed," Peter said. Another wave of hopelessness threatened to crash over him.

"He doesn't have a lot of options at this point," Lugar said. "More than half the city's already flooded. Some streets with water are still passable, but it's rising fast. And spreading."

Lugar picked up his radio and relayed their location to dispatch.

"We need to send a high-water rescue crew to the Williams house," Peter said. "And have EMS ready to meet them. Gage used his knife on the baby."

Lugar swore. "Is that how he got Bennett to go with him?"

Peter nodded miserably. "He didn't know she was there. But he wanted someone to bring her to him."

"That when you made the call? I was standing next to the dispatcher when it came in. I knew something wasn't right. But I didn't have any officers available to send."

"Thank you," Peter said.

"Don't thank me yet," Lugar said. "We've still got to find them."

Kate thought about making a break for it when Gage dragged her out of the car. But almost as soon as the thought formed in her brain, Gage extinguished it. He pulled her to her feet and twisted her around in one fluid movement, wrapping one arm around her waist and putting the knife back at her neck.

"Don't try anything stupid," he murmured in her ear. "Now, walk."

They sloshed down the street in what felt to Kate like a bad parody of a sack race. Gage's legs pressed against hers with every step. They made slow progress, giving Kate plenty of time to scan the houses for any signs of potential help. But no door opened. No cry of alarm came from Gage's former neighbors. If any witnessed his triumphal return, they were too afraid to acknowledge it.

The wind swirled around them like an invisible battering ram. More than once, Gage forced her to crouch down to resist an especially powerful gust. But the rising water worried Kate more. It had deepened noticeably in the time it took them to inch their way to the middle of the block. Now it tugged at their knees with a force that reminded Kate of the incoming tide.

Gage swore as he fought to keep slogging ahead. Then he looked up and cackled.

"There it is," he said. "Home sweet home."

The new owners had fixed plywood over all the windows, but Kate could tell it was still as well-kept as it had been when Gage's family lived there. She had avoided driving down the street for the last two and a half years. Seeing it again brought back a deluge of the fear she'd felt the first time she'd met the troubled teen. She closed her eyes and pictured Peter's face as he bent over her that day after crashing through the back door. One moment she thought she was going to die. The next, he was lifting her to her feet and cutting the ties that bound her wrists. His warm eyes and comforting smile still had the power to calm her trembling, even in memory. She whispered a prayer for a repeat performance.

"What are you waiting for? Up!" Gage barked.

Kate opened her eyes and saw the house looming ahead. Gage pushed her from behind, and she stepped from the street onto the sidewalk. She expected him to march her up the front steps onto the porch and out of the water. But instead, he dragged her around to the driveway.

"I bet they didn't cover the window over the kitchen sink," he said. "We never did."

As they made their way around the back of the house, Kate realized with dismay that he was right. The small square of glass glinted darkly from the shadows that enveloped the back porch. Gage forced her up the steps until they were standing right in front of it. He tightened his grip around her waist, spun the knife around in his other hand, and smashed the bottom of the handle into the glass. The sound of it shattering barely even registered against the roar of the wind.

Gage continued to pound at the remaining shards until it was clear enough for someone to climb through.

"You first," Gage sneered in her ear.

Kate gingerly placed her arms through the opening, feeling for a spot that would give her some leverage. Behind her, Gage shifted his weight and then heaved her into the air. She rolled through the window, barely missing the sink filled with pieces of the broken window, and tumbled over the counter and onto the floor. Shards of glass crunched as she landed. Her left arm crumpled awkwardly under her chest, and she whimpered as pain shot through her elbow. She didn't even have time to scramble to her feet before Gage wiggled his way through the opening and pounced on top of her. She gritted her teeth to keep from crying out as he grabbed her other arm and hauled her to her feet. He pulled her so close she could smell the sour stench of cigarettes on his breath.

"Well, now, isn't this cozy?" A wicked smile spread across his face.

Peter gripped the door handle as Lugar careened around a corner and headed for Broadway.

"Unless he ditched the car, they didn't head downtown," the chief said. "The East End is about the only part of the island above water."

"But that's still more than we can cover quickly," Peter said. "They could be anywhere."

"Do you think he might head back to the orphanage? It's not a bad place to ride out the storm."

"I don't know." Desperation clawed its way up Peter's chest. "I just don't know."

Lugar glanced at him as the car bounced over Broadway. Peter sensed something he never expected to get from his boss: sympathy.

"It's as good a place as any to start," Lugar said. "It's not your fault, you know. Sometimes, no matter what we do, things go sideways. I know you believe nothing happens by chance. Hang on to that."

Peter nodded. "Thanks," he whispered. It was all he could manage through the tightening in his throat.

"Bennett's tough. She won't go down without a fight."

Peter thought about Kate's strength and her determination to be self-sufficient. She met every challenge head-on, barreling through obstacles. But eventually, she would hit a wall she couldn't bring down on her own. If this was it, he prayed she'd finally seek help from the only one who could save her now.

They made erratic progress down Broadway, dodging palm fronds and other flying debris. Lugar picked up his radio and called dispatch.

"It's time to call everyone in," he said. "The wind's getting pretty bad. If we stay out any longer, someone's going to get hurt."

Peter's stomach twisted. If they didn't find Kate soon, Hurricane Julio might pose just as much threat to her as Gage.

Block by block, they charged east, abruptly turning right at 21st Street. The farther they got from Broadway and the closer they got to the seawall, the more the water receded. Lugar slowed as they neared the orphanage. Peter peered out the window, looking for any sign of his car. But the street was empty.

The chief pulled around the back of the building, and Peter jumped out of the car. He had to struggle against the wind just to walk the few steps to the wrought-iron fence so he could look into the backyard. The door to the shed where they had found Bill Presley's body stood open. But he saw no sign anyone had been there since the crime scene crew left.

"They're not here," he said, climbing back into the car.

"Any other ideas?" Lugar asked.

Peter closed his eyes and prayed for guidance as Lugar eased the car back into the street. Peter opened his eyes just as they passed under a street sign. Something about the name caught his attention. Then the answer snapped into place.

"This isn't far from his old house, where we caught him the first time," Peter said, his heart thudding at the memory. "That must be where he took her."

Chapter 24

Kate cradled her wounded arm against her chest as Gage pushed her into the living room. The new family's decor had changed its external appearance, but not enough to erase her memory of what had happened there. A heavy stillness filled the room. With the window boarded up, the only light filtered in from the broken kitchen window.

"Sit," Gage barked, pushing her toward the couch. "And don't move a muscle."

He felt along the opposite wall for the light switch. Kate heard it click, but no light cut through the gloom. Gage swore.

"They must have cut the power when they left," he muttered, swearing again. Then he sauntered back toward Kate, hands on his hips. "That's fine. I like the dark better, anyway."

Kate shuddered. She tried to hide it, but Gage saw. He giggled almost like a little boy. As terrifying as the sound was, it gave her an idea.

"What was it like growing up here?" she blurted. "Your parents must have been monsters."

"Monsters?" Gage cocked his head to the side and narrowed his eyes. "They weren't monsters, at least not at first."

"So what happened?"

"They never let me grow up. Never let me alone," he sneered. "All I wanted was my freedom, but they wouldn't let me go."

Freedom. Gage's words hit Kate like a slap in the face. She had said almost the same thing to Peter during their big fight. She never met Tommy Gage's parents, but she knew exactly why they wouldn't let him have his own way.

"They loved you," she whispered. "That's why they couldn't let you go."

Gage bellowed a curse so loud Kate cringed into the couch cushions.

"Love is worthless," he growled. "I wanted what I wanted."

"And they just got in your way?"

"That's right," he said. "Just like you."

Gage took his eyes off her face long enough to glance around the room. He huffed a mirthless laugh. He turned to face the window, as though he could see through the plywood covering.

"This is almost exactly where I was standing when I spotted you talking to our nosey neighbor. I could tell by the way you were looking at the house that you planned to walk right up to the door. I couldn't risk you seeing dear old Mom, lying there in the kitchen."

Kate remembered how the teen had burst out of the house and urged her to come inside. He'd had a wild look in his eyes, and every instinct told her to run. But it was her first day on the job. She wanted to impress her new boss by getting an exclusive interview with Mrs. Gage, whose husband had fallen out the window of an abandoned hotel a few hours earlier. Everyone thought his death was a suicide.

Gage took a few steps to his right, closer to the front door.

"And this is where I was standing when your boyfriend came charging through the back door and shot me." He rubbed his shoulder and glared at her. "It still hurts sometimes."

He started pacing in front of the boarded window, just like he had that night.

"I was five minutes from being ready to drive away," he said, his voice rising with every step. "Five minutes! If you had just stopped for gas on your way over here, I would have been long gone."

Kate blinked back tears as she thought about what a difference that would have made. Those five minutes had changed her life's trajectory. When Peter came crashing through that door, he did more than save her. It took a long time for her to recognize it, but their paths had become inextricably intertwined. As time went by, that connection drew them closer together. Without it, she might never have considered him as anything more than another source. Scenes from the past two years whirled through her mind as if carried by Julio's winds. Five minutes would have cost her all that. If she could go back and change it, she wouldn't. No matter what happened next.

Gage rubbed his hands over his tightly cropped hair.

"Now I've got another chance," he murmured. "Another chance to get away."

Kate shook her head in disbelief. "Where are you going to go? The causeway's closed."

"Once this storm blows through, it'll be complete chaos. They'll have their hands full with the damage. No one's going to be worried about me."

"Peter will," Kate said, with all the defiance she could muster.

Silence filled the room, and then Gage exploded with laughter. He laughed so hard he doubled over to catch his breath. Kate shifted uncomfortably on the couch.

"Good," Gage said, wiping his eyes with the back of his hand. "I hope he does."

Before Kate could respond, Gage jumped over the coffee table and seized the front of the bulletproof vest she still wore. He hauled her to her feet and pulled her to the center of the room. Kate gasped as pain shot through the arm she still had cradled to her chest.

"He thought this would protect you," Gage sneered, tugging on the vest. "Nothing can protect you now. Not even him."

He pulled her against his body, pinning her arms between them. He leaned toward the top of her head and inhaled deeply. Kate fought against her rising panic and worked to wiggle her good arm free.

"Just like I dreamed it would be," Gage murmured.

He was so lost in his murderous fantasy that he didn't notice when Kate finally worked her arm loose. Or that she held a long shard of glass from the broken window.

She drew her hand back, and with all the force she could gather, she plunged it into his side.

Gage gasped and staggered back. Kate shoved him in the center of his chest, knocking him to the ground.

Then she ran.

His scream split the air as she fumbled with the locks on the back door. It only took her a few moments to wrench it open, but already she could hear him struggling to his feet behind her. She jumped down the steps, splashing into the floodwater. It had risen significantly in the past hour and now covered the front yard. Kate veered to her right and bolted down the street, trying to keep close to the houses where the water was the most shallow. Rain streamed down her face.

She was halfway to the next intersection when she heard Gage screaming her name.

"There it is!" Peter yelled, relief and hope coursing through him as Lugar's headlights swept across the back of his car. Water lapped about halfway up the tires.

"Is that the street?" Lugar asked as he pulled to a stop about twenty yards away.

"Yes," Peter gasped as he wrenched open the door and rushed into the wind and rain.

"Johnson, wait!" Lugar yelled.

He was about to turn around when another sound cut through the storm. Gage. He was screaming Kate's name.

A surge of adrenaline propelled Peter forward. He couldn't see anything at first when he turned the corner onto Gage's old street. He floundered as the water rose nearly to his waist. Just as he got his footing, another guttural shriek cut through the wind. He peered into the gloom and spotted a figure about halfway down the street.

"Gage!" Peter roared. He struggled out of the street toward the houses. In the shallow water, he started to gain ground.

Gage turned and saw him. He let out a howl of fury and struggled toward the end of the street.

That's when Peter spotted Kate. His heart leapt with joy. She didn't look hurt, and she had a good head start on Gage. But just as she reached the intersection, she stumbled and fell.

Kate gasped as the water swirled around her shoulders. Her arms flailed, and she kicked her legs frantically, trying to regain her footing. In her desperation to get away from Gage, she'd forgotten to expect the curb.

The current pulled her away from the sidewalk toward the middle of the street. Something slammed into her back as it washed by, leaving her momentarily stunned. Disoriented, she tried to turn around so she could get her bearings. The heavy vest threatened to drag her under, and she struggled to keep her head above water. Just as her feet found solid ground, she heard a massive splash. Gage burst out of the water in front of her and grabbed her by the shoulders.

Before she realized what was happening, he plunged her under the surface.

Kate thrashed and twisted, trying to loosen his grip. She clawed at his hands, but they held her fast.

She opened her eyes, but the murky water made it hard to see anything but a faint smudge of darkness looming over her. Terror gripped her heart, and she fought back a scream that would empty her lungs of air but do her no good. She closed her eyes to shut out Gage's hazy image. Her mind raced with panic as her lungs started to burn, but a stillness washed over her soul.

Fear no evil.

She could hear the words almost as though Peter were standing next to her, whispering in her ear.

For you are with me.

She had read those words half a dozen times, but always as though they applied to someone else. Finally she understood. They were meant for her, too.

Kate stopped struggling against Gage's grip. Her arms and legs relaxed, and she felt the tug of the current as the water washed over her. It carried away the last of her resistance to a reality she could no longer deny.

Suddenly, the weight pressing her down lifted. Her heart thudded once, twice, before she realized she was free. Swinging her arms, she thrust herself up. When her face broke the surface, she gasped, filling her lungs with air.

The first thing she heard was Peter's voice calling her name.

Peter threw himself into the water just as Kate's head broke the surface.

"Kate!" he shouted, relief piercing the sob building in his throat. "Thank God you're alive."

In seconds, the current pulled him to her, and he wrapped his arms under hers, keeping her head above the water as she coughed and gasped for breath. He held her tightly to his chest.

"What happened?" she rasped.

He shook his head. "I don't know. It was almost as if someone picked him up and tossed him down the street."

"Is he gone?"

Peter looked in the direction he'd last seen Gage before the water whisked him away.

"I think so."

Kate shuddered in his arms. "I thought I would never see you again."

"I know," he whispered.

He closed his eyes and tried not to think of his own dark thoughts during the last hour. He never expected to get another chance. Keeping one arm wrapped around Kate, Peter lay back and used his other arm to guide them toward higher ground. He waited to plant his feet until he was sure the water was shallow enough not to pull them down again. Kate staggered under the weight of the bulletproof vest he'd forced her to wear. He shook his head in amazement. Every plan he'd made to protect her had only put her in more danger. And yet she'd still survived.

"Is she alright?" Lugar's voice made Peter jump. He'd completely forgotten they weren't alone.

"Yes," Peter said as he turned toward where the chief stood panting in knee-deep water. "But only by a miracle."

"What happened to Gage?" Lugar asked as he bent over to catch his breath.

"I'm not sure. Something knocked him into the water. That's when he let go of Kate. The last I saw, he was headed east. Then he went under."

"He was hurt," Kate said, her voice so low Peter could barely hear her above the wind. "I stabbed him."

Peter stared at her in amazement. "With what?"

"A piece of glass from the window he broke to get into his old house. That's how I got away."

The chief grunted and stood. "I bet he never saw that coming. Maybe he just finally lost enough blood that he collapsed. Hopefully that's the last we'll see of him."

A gust of wind raked over them, making the chief stagger. A loud cracking noise nearby signaled a tree had just given up its fight against Julio.

"We need to get back to the cars," he said, dragging Kate from the water and half carrying her back the way they came.

They made slow progress, occasionally pausing to huddle against a house when a powerful gust of wind screamed by. Lugar spent the time on his radio, relaying their location and status to dispatch. Peter only half listened.

"Are you okay," he murmured in Kate's ear. "Did he hurt you?"

She shook her head. "Just my elbow. When he pushed me through the window."

The familiar anger flared in Peter's chest. If only he'd gotten to Gage before the current did. He tightened his grip around her waist.

"It's crazy," she said, a small smile tugging at the corners of her mouth. "But if I hadn't fallen the way I did, I never could have picked up that piece of glass. A broken elbow seems like a small price to pay."

Peter's anger fizzled, and his revenge fantasy turned to ashes. He couldn't argue with a providential wounding.

The water around the cars had risen, but not by much. Peter whispered a prayer of thanksgiving when he opened the door and saw the keys sitting in the seat. Before helping Kate in, he unstrapped the vest from around her chest. Lugar sloshed up next to him just as he was easing Kate into the passenger seat.

"Dispatch said to head toward the seawall. That part of the island is just about the only land still above water."

Peter nodded. "Chief, I don't know what I would have done if you hadn't shown up. I never would have found her. Thank you."

Lugar wiped the rain out of his eyes and looked at Peter for a long moment. He could tell the older man wanted to say something, but he only nodded before turning toward his own car.

Peter took a deep breath and opened his door. Kate lay back against the seat, her arm cradled against her chest. She opened her eyes a crack and gave him a weary smile.

"I don't think I've ever been this tired," she whispered as a shiver racked her body.

Peter fished around in the backseat for the towels and tucked one around her.

"Try to stay awake, okay? I'll get you to the convention center as soon as possible. Just hang on."

Fear slithered through his mind. If she was going into shock, she needed medical attention right away. He slid the key into the ignition and cranked the engine. It roared to life. Behind him, the chief's headlights gleamed in the rain.

With Lugar leading the way, they eased down the street. The cars rocked in the wind, and Peter had to keep the windshield wipers on full speed to clear the driving rain. After a few blocks, the water receded. But the closer they got to the seawall, the more debris littered the streets. The parts of the island spared Julio's flooding now suffered the brunt of the storm's full fury.

Peter drove carefully, glancing often at Kate to make sure she was still conscious. Lugar pulled ahead. Peter reached out and put his hand on Kate's forehead. He turned back to the road just in time to see a board flying at the windshield. He swerved hard to the right, and it glanced off, leaving a divot in the glass. Kate yelped in surprise and sat up. Peter gripped the wheel with both hands and focused his full attention on the road.

Several more boards sailed through the air above them. Peter watched in the rearview mirror as they cartwheeled down the road. He swerved again to miss another projectile and plowed over a pile of debris mounded at the side of the road. The car lurched and wobbled.

"What was that?" Kate asked. Her voice trembled just slightly.

"I think we just popped a tire. I would get out and look, but I'm afraid I'd get pummeled by all this debris."

Peter reached for the radio and hailed Lugar.

"Where are you?" the chief barked. "I'm almost back to the convention center."

"We got hit by some debris and I think we've lost a tire."

Lugar swore. "It's getting worse out here every minute. This storm is about to come barreling over us."

"I know. I just wanted to let you know where we were. If we can't make it back, we'll just find somewhere to hunker down."

Before Lugar could reply, the glint of something metallic caught Peter's eye. A giant metal sign sailed toward them like an enormous frisbee. He hit the brakes, but not in time. Kate let out a piercing scream as the windshield splintered into a glittering spiderweb of cracks.

Chapter 25

Peter put a reassuring hand on Kate's shoulder, but his heart pounded hard against his ribs.

"I thought that was going to come straight through," Kate said, the tremble in her voice no longer small.

"Thank God it didn't," Peter said, reaching out to touch the shattered glass gingerly. The windshield bowed just slightly as he pushed. It would hold together for now, but the slightest blow would send it crashing in on them.

"We've got to get out of this debris field," he said, glancing at Kate. She sat wide-eyed and perfectly still, her face pale. "I'm going to head back toward Broadway and try another cross street. Even if we have to drive through some water, it would be better than getting hammered by whatever Julio has already torn apart."

"Do you think we can make it back to the convention center?"

He looked into her worried eyes, and his chest tightened. "I don't know, but if we can't, we'll find somewhere to ride it out."

Kate said nothing as he eased the car toward the next intersection. Small debris continued to rain down around them. It thudded on the roof and bounced as it hit the street. Peter gave up trying to avoid driving over anything. The car now pulled hard to the right, and he could feel the shreds of the tire thumping against the wheel well. He gunned the engine anyway. Between the pouring rain and the splintered glass in front of him, he could hardly see where he was going. But after a few minutes, the falling debris lessened.

After another block, they hit water. Peter let the car roll to a stop.

"Where are we?" Kate mumbled, squinting at the windshield.

Peter looked at her, alarmed.

"I mean, what cross streets? I'm just trying to think of anywhere we might find shelter."

"I thought you were getting delirious. We're on 20th Street, coming up on Avenue N."

Kate gasped. "That's just blocks from the old orphanage."

Peter peered out his window. The water was already over the curb.

"I don't think we can drive any farther," he said. He turned to look out the back window. Toward the seawall, large chunks of wood still careened past at an alarming rate. And with Julio getting closer to land, the wind and what it carried would only get worse.

"We can't go back either, can we?" Kate turned to follow his gaze and gasped.

He shook his head slowly while his mind raced for another option. He'd failed to keep her safe once today. He wouldn't make that mistake again.

"Then we have to go forward," she whispered.

Peter looked out his window. Every instinct fought against wading out into the storm again. But he didn't see any other choice.

Kate clamped her teeth together as another bolt of pain shot up her arm. She didn't want Peter to know how much it hurt, but every movement made her want to scream. The creases of worry at the corners of his eyes told her she wasn't fooling him.

Without saying a word, he twisted around in his seat and rummaged in his backpack, pulling out a bottle of water and a long-sleeved T-shirt. Then he fished a container of ibuprofen from the car's console.

"Take a few of these," he said, handing her the water and pills. "I'm going to make you a sling out of this."

Moments later, it was ready. Kate held her breath as he slipped it over her head and gently worked it around her arm. She managed to limit her reaction to a few small whimpers.

"Thanks," she croaked when he was done, blinking back tears the pain brought to her eyes.

Peter put his hand on her cheek. "I'm so sorry."

"It's not your fault. I just need more practice jumping through windows."

He shook his head and smiled. But she could almost hear the recriminations running through his mind. Before she could say anything else, he turned to the backseat and grabbed both their backpacks.

"We'd better get going before it gets any worse," he said.

He took a deep breath as if to steel himself against the onslaught and pushed open the door. The wind screamed as it tore at his hair and clothes. He staggered around to her side of the car and wrenched open her door. Grasping his hand, she struggled to her feet. It took all her strength just to stay upright.

"We need to hurry," he yelled, his voice barely audible over the wind.

Hand in hand, they lurched up the street. The rain stung Kate's face and made it hard to see more than a few feet ahead. But she could only bear to look down for a few moments at a time. The water swirling around their legs seemed to rise with every step. The current pulled so hard she thought it would drag her down. But Peter's grip never slacked.

She clung to his hand and prayed for mercy. She had surrendered to whatever the future held just an hour before, but now her heart longed for the second chance she thought she'd lost.

Suddenly, Peter's grip tightened on her hand. She had just enough time to look ahead and see a section of fence wobbling before Peter yanked her down into the water. A panel of pickets tore out of the ground and sailed over their heads. Peter slid his arm around her back and yanked her up, practically dragging her forward. Fear etched his face into a grimace.

"Move!" he barked, jerking her to the left as the frame of a lawn chair, its tattered cover trailing behind it like a kite's tail, flew past.

Kate gasped as she slipped into the water again, this time up to her shoulders. Planting her feet firmly on the ground, she pushed herself up.

"I see it!" she yelled, pointing ahead. The hazy outline of the orphanage loomed, barely distinguishable through the rain.

Peter lunged ahead, pulling her with him. She stumbled over something in the water she couldn't see, and he lifted her off her feet, carrying her the last dozen yards.

The building's front windows looked untouched, but debris clung to the porch railing. Thanks to the storm's angle, the wind swirled right through the spot they had hoped to take shelter.

"Around back!" Peter yelled, pulling her along.

They staggered past the building and around the side. The crime scene tape that had cordoned off the backyard around the shed whipped back and forth. But as they ran up the path toward the building, the wind lost some of its power. Peter took the back staircase two steps at a time. Kate followed more slowly, gasping for breath by the time she reached the top.

Peter grabbed the handle to the back door and heaved. It didn't budge.

"Come on!" he yelled, pounding on it in frustration.

Kate made for the corner and huddled down behind the half wall that circled the porch. Thanks to the roof overhang, it was completely dry. Peter pounded on the door again. When he turned and saw her on the floor, his face crumpled.

"I don't think we're going to get in," he said, dropping down beside her.

"I don't think we need to. I can hardly feel the wind down here at all."

He stilled, as though her words had finally broken through his internal hurricane. He peered out over the wall.

"You're right. The building is sheltering us from the worst of the storm."

He laughed and shook his head.

"What's so funny?"

"Just that everything I've done today has been wrong. Everything I've done to keep you safe has failed. But every time I think it's all over, God has made a way."

Still shaking his head, Peter shrugged off both backpacks and scooted up against her. He pulled a sweatshirt from his bag and helped her put it on. Then he wrapped his arm around her and rested his cheek on the top of her head. After a few minutes, she stopped shivering. The wind continued to howl around them, but Julio no longer felt like a terrifying monster.

"I can't believe how many times today I thought I'd lost you," he murmured. "I never thought I'd see you again after you drove away with Gage."

"I knew you wouldn't stop looking," she whispered.

"Then, when I found you by some miracle, I thought I was going to have to watch Gage drown you." His arm tightened around her. "I still don't know how you escaped."

Kate closed her eyes and imagined the water washing over her again.

"I didn't escape. I surrendered." Peter sucked in a breath, and she turned to look at him. "I've been running my whole life, and I finally decided to stop."

Tears filled his eyes. He squeezed them shut and leaned his head back against the wall. When he opened them again, they glittered with joy.

"I've waited so long to hear you say that."

She smiled. "I know, and I'm sorry. I guess I had to get to the end of everything before I could finally give up."

He shook his head again. "The very thing I tried so hard to prevent turned out to be your lifeline."

She closed her eyes and imagined the water pulling at her lifeless limbs.

"I can't explain it, but as soon as I surrendered, it felt like I was floating." She opened her eyes and looked at him. "That's when I realized Gage had let go."

Peter looked at her, wonder filling his face. Her breath caught in her throat.

"There's something else," she whispered. "Something I need to tell you."

He reached for her hand and squeezed it in his. She took a deep breath.

"It's about my mom," she said. The familiar urge to run and hide wrestled with her determination to tell him everything. She forced herself to go on. "My mom had schizophrenia. She hung herself when I was twelve."

Kate stopped and cleared her throat. She could only remember saying the words out loud a handful of times. Every syllable burned with the fire of anguish and shame she'd carried her whole life. Peter said nothing, but the gentle pressure of his fingers around hers pulled her on.

"It's hereditary, you know. Not always. But sometimes. Every day I wake up and wonder if it will be the day my genes finally catch up with me."

Her voice broke, and she wrenched her hand from his, covering her face with it. Tears streamed from her eyes and the blood rushing through her veins roared in her ears. She felt as though she were standing on the seawall, facing down Julio's full fury. Even that would be less terrifying than ripping the cover off her deepest wound.

Peter leaned his head against hers and cupped his hand to her cheek. Gently, he turned her head toward him and tugged at the hand covering her face. His eyes met hers, and she saw no trace of the fear or hesitation she'd dreaded.

"I love you," he said. "You can't scare me off that easily."

Tears filled her eyes again. "I love you, too," she whispered. Her heart pounded so hard she thought it would burst.

"I know," he said, a mischievous spark lighting his eyes. "I was just waiting for you to admit it to yourself."

He leaned forward and gently touched his lips to hers. Cracks splintered the last of the walls she'd built around her heart. She pulled him close, and for several moments, everything around them disappeared. When he finally pulled back, they were both breathless. He touched his forehead to hers.

"You have no idea how long I've wanted to do that," he said, his throaty chuckle sending shockwaves through every nerve in her body.

He rested his cheek on the top of her head again and wrapped his arms around her. They sat like that for so long, Kate felt herself slipping into dreams.

Peter listened as Kate's breathing slowed and deepened. He felt her body relax in his arms. His mind whirled with everything that had happened in the last 24 hours. But his soul resonated with joy. All his striving, his self-doubt and fear, had blown away on Julio's winds. He had never had the power to fix anyone or save anyone. Not Kate. Not Danjumo. Not the village, or his family. All of them were out of his control. The only thing he could do was lay them at his Savior's feet. It's what he'd wanted to do all along.

Kate stirred in his arms. "Peter," she murmured. "I can't hear the wind anymore. Am I asleep?"

He raised his head and looked toward the top of the wall. Night had come on, and a heavy silence surrounded them.

"You're not asleep," he said, carefully lifting his arm from her shoulders and pushing himself to his feet. "It must be the eye of the storm."

He turned back and pulled her up to stand next to him. The rain had stopped, and the trees stood completely still.

"It's like Julio is taking a breath," she said. "How long have we been here?"

He glanced at his watch. "A couple hours."

"Do you think we should make a run for the convention center?"

He looked down the steps to the yard. Water now covered some of the bottom steps, although he couldn't tell how many.

"It's too risky. The water's even higher now than it was when we got here. I think we're stuck for now."

She moved to the top of the stairs and then headed down, stopping about half way. After peering into the darkness for several long moments, she retreated to the porch and sat down.

"There's so much water already," she said, a hint of despair in her voice. "And Julio's not even done yet. The whole island must be covered by now."

He sat down beside her and thought about everywhere they'd been during the day.

"Not the whole island, but a lot of it," he admitted.

A single tear trickled down her cheek. She didn't bother to brush it away.

"I never realized how much I loved this place," she said.

"It's still going to be here in the morning, I promise," he said. "This city has survived worse than Julio. It might be a bit of a mess for a while, but nothing a little elbow grease can't fix. It's going to make for a great story."

She smiled and rested her head on his shoulder. A few minutes passed in silence.

"What's going to happen when this is all over?" She lifted her head and look at him with renewed worry. "I mean, to us."

He sighed. He'd hoped she wouldn't ask that question yet.

"Don't worry about it. I'm not."

She drew back and frowned. "How can you not be worried? The chief's been breathing down your neck for weeks. I doubt he's just going to forget about it."

"Do you trust me?" He laced his fingers through hers and held her gaze.

After a few heartbeats, she nodded. "You know I do. It's just—"

He held up his hand. "Don't worry about it. I promise you it's going to be okay."

Before she could reply, a smattering of rain fell around them. Scrambling up, they retreated to the corner of the porch just in time to avoid the downpour that followed. With no other warning, Julio returned at full strength. The wind tore through the trees in a rushing cacophony. It howled as loudly as before, but the tone had changed. Now that the eye had moved inland, Julio pummeled them from a different angle.

Peter tried not to think about how vulnerable they were as he pulled another dry shirt from his bag and rolled it up to put behind Kate's head. Then he scooted against her and murmured a prayer for their protection. With his back against the wall, he could feel the building reverberating in the gale like a giant guitar string.

Chapter 26

The faint light of an ashen dawn greeted Kate as she slowly opened her eyes. The wind that had lashed their shelter mercilessly all the night had finally blown itself out. Steady gusts still stirred the tops of the trees she could see, but the worst was over.

Next to her, Peter stirred and groaned. He reached up a hand to massage his neck, then opened his eyes.

"We made it," Kate rasped, her voice as rough as sandpaper.

A grin split his weary face. "I never doubted we would."

Kate rolled her eyes. She had drifted in and out of sleep during the second half of Julio's wrath, but she had awakened several times to hear Peter praying over them. She craned her neck to peer over the wall. Now that the danger had passed, she was anxious to see the fallout.

"Do you think it's safe to venture out?"

"I hope so," he said, rolling to his knees and stretching as he stood.

The movement jostled Kate's arm, sending spikes of fire radiating from her elbow. She gasped at the pain. Peter crouched next to her, worry clouding his eyes.

"Safe or not, we need to get you out of here."

He helped her stand, and they moved to the top of the steps. The water had receded, but big puddles still dotted the grass. Peter returned to their bags and shook two more ibuprofen from the bottle he'd stashed in the front pocket. Kate took them gratefully while he rounded up the rest of their things and slung the packs over his shoulder. As they trudged down the steps, she looked back at the corner that had sheltered them from the storm. Debris covered the ground, but the century-old building had endured unscathed.

Kate grimaced when she spotted water still covering the street in front of them. Her clothes hadn't fully dried from the night before, and she could hardly stand the thought of getting wet again. Peter pulled his cell phone from his backpack and held it up as it powered on.

"I thought I might call for a ride," he said with a wink. "But it looks like the cell towers are down."

"I've got that satellite phone Mattingly gave me," Kate exclaimed, kicking herself for not remembering it sooner. "Try using that."

Peter rummaged around in her bag until he found the bulky handset. Kate's hopes rose as he dialed the number for dispatch. A moment later, she groaned as a steady beeping emanated from the speaker.

"The landlines must be down, too," Peter said. "We'll have to make it to the car so I can try the radio. It's not far."

Kate eased one foot after the other into the water. Once they waded to the middle of the street, she could see the car about a block away. It felt like they'd run the length of three football fields the night before, but it hadn't been that far at all. After sloshing for about a block, Kate heard the rumble of a big engine close by.

"Someone sent out a search party," Peter said, grinning from ear to ear.

Moments later, the cab of a high water rescue vehicle eased into view. The driver stopped in the intersection, and Kate could see him looking at Peter's car. Then he spotted them. Three sharp blasts on the horn rang out, followed by an excited whoop. When the truck lumbered toward them, Kate finally made out the driver's face.

"It's Eddie Vasquez!" She waved her good arm, unable to contain her excitement.

The truck chugged to a stop and the city's public works director jumped down from the cab.

"Man, am I glad to see the two of you!" he called. He attempted to jog toward them but succeeded only in sending up sprays of water. "We've been wondering all night whether you survived."

Peter laughed. "We survived, just barely. I think we'll both be happy to get somewhere dry. And Kate needs to see the paramedics right away."

Vasquez shot Kate a worried frown. "Let's get you back to the convention center. I already radioed to let them know I found you."

"How did you get assigned to search?" Kate asked.

"Chief Lugar asked me to go, and I was happy to do it. The water's still too high for the police cruisers to leave the parking lot. But it's going down pretty fast. I told the mayor I was going to see how much dry ground we had."

Peter laughed. "Just like Noah's dove."

Vasquez chuckled. "That was just my cover mission," he said as he put the lumbering vehicle in reverse and backed up slowly before turning around. "My real assignment was to find the two of you. Lugar was pretty upset last night when he realized you wouldn't make it back."

Kate knew Lugar had taken a risk to help Peter find her, but she felt sure his main concern from the previous night had been for Peter. The chief held his lead detective in high regard. But that didn't mean he would suddenly change his mind about her. Kate sighed before she could stop herself.

"Are you alright?" Peter asked, putting his hand on her back.

"Yeah, just taking it all in," she said quickly, sweeping her good arm in an arc that encompassed the scene before them.

Tattered lumber, tree limbs, and the flotsam and jetsam of the homes Julio had torn apart rose in piles up and down the street. The debris field grew the closer they got to the gulf.

"Just wait until we get moving," Vasquez said, shaking his head. "I've never seen it this bad. Julio was one for the record books."

Peter gave Kate a boost into the truck's cab and hauled himself up after her. Vasquez vaulted into the driver's seat and the truck growled to life. Instead of turning right to head back to the convention center, Vasquez pointed the vehicle toward the seawall. He maneuvered around the debris he could and carefully drove over what he couldn't avoid. As they rolled up the slight slope to Seawall Boulevard, Kate's heart pounded. She gasped when they crested the rise.

The remains of buildings and piers stretched as far as she could see. An entire wasteland of shattered structures. Angry waves still chewed at the beach, giving them a glimpse of the destructive power the sea had wielded during the night.

"Most of that's the fishing pier," Vasquez said. "Or maybe a couple of fishing piers. No one's ventured west yet to see if the ones out that way are still standing. But I doubt it."

He backed down the street for several blocks and then turned right.

"These houses don't look like they have that much damage," Kate said, gazing out the window.

"They probably don't. The flooding didn't come up this far."

"But that doesn't make any sense," Kate said. "They're so close to the seawall."

"That's what saved them, at least from Julio's frontal assault. Most of the water came from the back side of the island. Julio pushed it ashore as he rolled on by."

"We know the cell towers are down, and the landlines don't seem to be working," Peter said. "What else is out?"

Vasquez snorted. "Power and water. The flooding submerged everything. As soon as I can get my crews out, we'll get to work. But I can tell you right now, it's going to take a while. We have a generator at the convention center, but it's only powering the essentials."

They rode the rest of the way in a heavy silence. When they rolled into the convention center parking lot, Kate counted a dozen news vans with their satellite towers already stretching into the air. She suppressed the urge to swear. Television stations definitely had an advantage over newspapers in the aftermath of a natural disaster. A half circle of cameras flanked the back entrance to the building. In the middle, Kate spotted Mayor Matthew Hanes, Stephen Rush, and Lugar.

She cringed when Vasquez honked the horn as they drove up. The cameras swung toward them.

"You've got to be kidding me," Kate muttered, hunching down in the seat. She hadn't given a thought to how she must look until she faced the prospect of appearing on the morning news.

"I promised my son you'd give him an exclusive interview," Vasquez said with a wink.

Kate glared in response, too mortified to say anything. The cameras clustered around the cab when Peter opened the door. The reporters' questions began immediately.

"What was it like to ride out the storm on your own?"

"Where did you find shelter?"

"We heard you got captured by the escaped prisoner. What happened? Where is he now?"

Peter hopped down from the truck and reached back up for her. Before she could protest, he pulled her down, scooped her off her feet, and turned toward the building.

"We need a paramedic!" he called.

The cameras parted, and Peter strode through the door. Kate's face burned, but she was grateful her televised humiliation hadn't lasted long. As she disappeared through the doorway, she spotted Doug Cowel and Ben Denison at the edge of the crowd of reporters. Ben had his satellite phone pressed to his ear.

Two paramedics met them halfway down the hall and waved Peter into one of the conference rooms. He set her gently on a waiting chair.

"I need to check in with the chief," he said. "I'll be back."

Peter hadn't gone very far down the hall when he heard someone calling his name. He turned to see Dylan Conner trotting toward him.

"I heard you made it back," the young officer said. "That will probably be the best news we get all day. How's your girl?"

Peter couldn't help but smile at the thought of what Kate would say to that.

"She may have a broken elbow, but nothing more serious," he said. "I'm grateful."

A genuinely happy grin lit Conner's face. "That's great. We were all pretty worried. Several of us volunteered to go out at first light."

Peter clapped the young officer on the shoulder, momentarily unable to say anything.

"Thanks," he finally managed. "I appreciate it."

"Have you talked to the chief yet? He was angrier than I've ever seen him when he lost contact with you last night. Reminded me of my dad when I wrecked his car two weeks after getting my license."

Peter laughed. "I'm headed to find him now. Looked like he was handing out assignments when we got here."

Conner nodded, then offered a snappy salute. "I'm headed toward the West End. I'll catch up with you later."

Peter waved and pushed through the back door. The mob of television reporters had scattered to their trucks. Several of them looked like they were getting ready to broadcast a live update. He ducked his head and hoped they wouldn't notice him. But he didn't make it more than a few steps before one of the reporters pointed in his direction. Peter cringed as she shot toward him like an arrow, quickly followed by most of the others.

He held up his hands before the barrage of questions could start.

"I haven't had a chance to check in with the chief yet," he said. "Give me a few minutes to do that and then I'll answer your questions."

That seemed to mollify them temporarily, and they trudged back to their cameras.

When Peter turned, he found the chief watching him. Peter smiled and walked to where Lugar and several of the lieutenants were talking. The other men shook Peter's hand and clapped him on the back. Lugar watched from under scrunched brows.

"Give us a minute," he growled after the rush of greetings subsided. Lugar crossed his arms as the other men moved away, and Peter steeled himself for another tongue-lashing. The chief took his time before speaking.

"How's Bennett?" he asked.

Peter let out a small sigh of relief. "The paramedics are checking her out now. I think she might have broken her elbow, but other than that, she seems okay."

"Good. I was worried about what Gage might have done to her."

Lugar's words transported Peter back to those awful hours when the same dark speculation filled his own mind. He shuddered.

"I know the top priority now is canvassing the island and looking for storm survivors, but we need to think about looking for any sign of Gage," Peter said. "I'd feel much better if we had a body."

Lugar nodded. "That's what I want you to focus on this morning. Take several men with you, just in case."

"Yes, sir." Peter hesitated and then glanced at the reporters. "What have you told the media so far?"

Lugar sighed. "With everyone packed into the convention center like sardines last night, it was impossible to keep anything a secret. The rescue team dispatched to the Williams house brought the women and baby back here, so they've already told their story. I added the basics of how you and I found Bennett and Gage. All that's missing is what happened last night."

"There's not much to tell about that." At least not that anyone else needs to know, he thought. "I can fill in the gaps and hopefully that will satisfy them until they can head out to inspect all the damage."

"Just don't tell them you're going on a hunt for Gage's body, or you'll have a train of TV vans following you around."

"If anyone asks, I'll tell them we're just heading out to get my car."

Lugar grunted his agreement, and Peter turned to walk away.

"Johnson," Lugar called. "I'm glad you made it back. You had us all worried."

Peter nodded his thanks but said nothing. He owed Lugar more than that, but it would have to wait.

Chapter 27

It took Kate much longer than she would have expected to convince the paramedics not to give her a dose of the heavy painkillers they said she needed. She had no intention of sitting around the convention center in an opioid-induced fog. She'd gladly deal with a few twinges of pain if it meant she could stay clear-headed enough to file a story or two.

"If you change your mind, you know where to find us," the young woman said as she wrapped a bandage tightly around Kate's arm. "Maybe if you stay in one place, it won't give you too much trouble."

Kate's answering smirk turned into a grimace as the woman finished securing the wrap.

"As soon as you can, you need to head to the hospital to get an x-ray," she continued. "I'm pretty sure it's just a fracture, but you need to make sure it's healing properly."

"I will, thanks," Kate said, wondering when the hospital would even open to treat minor injuries.

When the paramedics stood to leave, Kate spotted Ben Denison standing by the conference room door.

"Now that you're all patched up, Mattingly wants you to call him on his satellite phone," Ben said as he sidled over to where she sat. "But I wouldn't do that until you're ready to get an earful. Sounds like he must have downed at least two bottles of Maalox yesterday after I told him you were missing. Now he's just as mad that you're back but hurt. He wanted to know if it was your right arm or your left."

Kate laughed and wiggled the fingers of her left hand, now pinned to her chest in a sling. "Tell him I'm in too much pain to talk, but I plan to head out as soon as I can find my notebook."

Ben raised his eyebrows. "Are you sure? I was just joking about Mattingly. I don't think he expects you to get back out there right away. In fact, he mentioned trying to get Delilah onto the island as soon as they reopen the causeway."

"I'm sure," Kate said, trying not to flinch as an ache reverberated from her bandaged arm.

"Well then, I guess we'd better figure out where we're both going, so you don't get in my way," Ben said with a wink.

After ten minutes of wrangling over territory, Ben headed for the door. Before he and Cowel walked out, Ben turned back.

"I'm glad you're okay," he said. "It wouldn't be nearly as much fun around here without you."

Kate smiled at her co-worker's retreating back. Ben's rare moments of sincerity offered a glimpse behind his crusty exterior. He wasn't such a bad guy after all.

With a sigh, she heaved her backpack from the floor. Even a short time in a marginally comfortable chair had allowed a wave of exhaustion to come dangerously close to cresting over her head. Stifling a yawn, she wondered whether coffee fell into the category of "essentials" covered by the generator. She debated calling Mattingly, but decided to wait until she had a story to file. She didn't feel like answering his inevitable questions about her ordeal with Gage.

She was about to heft the bag over her shoulder and head out to find someone to talk to when an unexpected noise made her stop to listen. The babbling of a baby echoed down the hall, growing louder as it neared the door to the conference room. A moment later, a woman's turban-wrapped head peeked through the door. After she took a quick glance around the room, the rest of her followed.

In her arms, she held the baby Kate had given herself up to save. He held a truck in one hand and a half-eaten banana in the other. Small bandages covered his chunky thighs.

"They told me you was done with the paramedics," the woman said. "I hope you don't mind."

"Of course not," Kate said, setting down her backpack. "I've been wondering how the baby was doing."

Kate walked toward them hesitantly, not sure how he would react. When he turned to look at her, his face broke into a wide smile. He waved the banana at her and babbled something unintelligible.

"He's good," the woman said. "He had to have a few stitches, but he's gonna be just fine."

Kate reached out and put her hand on the child's back. She hadn't spent a lot of time around children. Mostly, they scared her. But she felt drawn to this little life connected forever to her own.

"What's his name?"

"Jamal. And I'm Lashonta Williams, his grandmother."

"I'm Kate Bennett, with the *Galveston Gazette*."

Mrs. Williams nodded. "The woman who saved Jamal's life."

Blood rushed to Kate's cheeks, and she lowered her eyes.

"I came to say thank you," Lashonta continued. "I don't know what I would have done if that monster had killed him."

Kate shook her head. "It was me he wanted."

"And I know it wasn't easy to give yourself up, seeing as what he'd already done. That was real brave."

Kate patted the baby's back as she tried to think of a response. "It wasn't brave," she finally whispered. "I was scared to death."

"But you survived. And now you're free."

Kate met the woman's steady gaze. Her deep brown eyes held a comforting calm.

"I am," Kate said. "For the first time in my life, I'm free."

After giving the assembled reporters a brief account of the previous night's events, Peter headed back inside to check on Kate. He stopped short as soon as he walked into the conference room. She sat on the floor, playing with a chubby-cheeked baby he instantly recognized as Rudy Williams' son.

"Detective Johnson," the child's grandmother said, rising from the chair where she'd been sitting. "I was hoping to find you next."

Peter stretched out his hand, and the older woman took it. But instead of shaking it, she pulled him toward her and into a tight hug.

"Thank you for coming for us," she said, letting him go after a few moments. "We would all be dead if you hadn't shown up when you did."

A twinge of guilt pinched Peter's conscience when he thought about how long it had taken him to get there.

"I'm just glad you're okay," he said, crouching down next to Kate. The baby waved his toy truck at Peter and laughed.

"We'll be fine," the woman replied. "We'll be just fine."

He watched the baby play happily for a few more minutes before turning his attention to Kate.

"I need to head out for a bit, but I'll be back as soon as I can."

She smiled serenely. "No problem. I'm planning to head out myself as soon as I can find a ride. I'm hoping Eddie Vasquez will let me tag along with him."

A spasm of panic gripped Peter's heart. He took a deep breath and let it out slowly, reminding himself that he'd committed to trusting God to take care of her.

"Just be careful," he said.

Kate put her good hand to her heart in mock indignation. "Aren't I always?"

Lashonta Williams' throaty chuckle rolled over them as he shook his head and stood to go.

"Sounds like y'all gonna be just fine, too," she said.

Peter smiled to himself as he headed down the hall.

Fifteen minutes later, Peter climbed into a police cruiser with an officer named Chad Hendrix behind the wheel. Two more officers followed in another car. They headed toward the center of the island, away from the seawall and the worst of the debris field. They drove all the way to Broadway, which had already emerged from the flood. But just a block further north, closer to the port, the murky water still lingered.

Peter directed Hendrix to turn right, and they drove east until they hit 17th Street. A few minutes later, they pulled up outside Tommy Gage's old home.

"If he survived, he would have come back somewhere he knew he could take shelter," Peter said. "We'll clear the house first."

They crept around back with their guns drawn. When they rounded the back of the house, the smashed window caught Peter's eye first. He imagined Gage forcing Kate through, and his pulse quickened. The back door stood open.

Peter led the three officers inside. Glass crunched under their feet as they moved across the kitchen floor. Peter spotted drops of dried blood that got bigger and closer together as they neared the living room. In front of the couch, a larger pool of blood had seeped into the area rug and darkened the wood floor.

He waved the officers toward the hall leading to the rest of the house while he scanned the room until he found what he was looking for. Under the boarded up picture window lay a long shard of glass, covered in blood. He drew a pair of latex gloves from his pocket and used one of them to pick it up. His hand trembled at the thought of Kate clutching that to her chest the whole time Gage ranted and raved, waiting for her opportunity to use it.

"All clear, sir," Hendrix said as he and the other two officers returned to the living room. "The rest of the house doesn't look like it's been touched."

Peter stood and nodded. "Let's head out to where we last saw him and see what we can find."

The water that once covered the intersection where Kate nearly drowned had fled back to the bay, leaving a slimy brown film in its wake. Peter's heart thudded as he relived the horror of watching Gage plunge her below the surface.

"The water was flowing south when he went under, but it changed direction during the night after the storm passed over. Let's split up and head in opposite directions."

Hendrix followed him north, along the path of the retreating flood. They'd walked a full block before shouts from the other two officers called them back.

"Detective Johnson! I think we found him."

Peter ran as fast as he dared across the slippery mire, his heart pounding painfully against his ribs. The two officers stood around a pile of fence pickets against the side of a house. Next to it sat the grimy shell of a deep freeze carried by the floodwater off someone's back porch. One officer drew back while the other pointed toward the bottom of the pile. Peter could just make out the outline of a bloated hand.

He and Hendrix carefully removed board after board until they had a clear view of the body. Tommy Gage's sightless eyes stared back at them. A mask of rage and surprise contorted his face. For a moment, Peter could hear nothing but the whooshing of his own blood in his ears.

"That's him, right?" Hendrix asked as he pulled his phone out of his pocket to snap several photos.

"That's him," Peter said. "Radio dispatch and tell them to let the chief know."

Four hours later, Kate slumped against the convention center's back wall. Her arm throbbed, her head ached, and exhaustion threatened to drag her to the ground. Vasquez had taken her all over the island for a tour of the destruction. The extent of the damage weighed heavy on her heart. She knew houses could be rebuilt and roads repaired, but the extent of the work seemed almost insurmountable. She wondered bleakly if the island would ever be the same again.

She flipped through her notebook and tried to collect her thoughts before calling Mattingly. With no easy way to send a story electronically, the editor had ordered them to phone in their reports. Just like they did during Watergate, he'd added. Kate composed her first few paragraphs, then picked up the bulky satellite phone and dialed Mattingly's number.

"How ya holding up?" he asked as soon as he answered.

"Great. I'm great," she said, trying to inject as much energy into her voice as she could muster.

"You're about to drop where you stand. Ben said you looked like you'd been run over by a truck."

Anger flushed Kate's cheeks. "Well, maybe so, but as long as you don't mess it up, I'll still be filing a better story than he will."

Mattingly chuckled. "That's my girl. I'm ready when you are."

For the next twenty minutes, Kate dictated her story, pausing every few sentences to compose the next batch in her head as she scanned her notebook to verify details. Once she was done, she felt like she had used up every word her brain could produce.

"Good story." Those two words would have been tepid praise from anyone else. But from Mattingly, they amounted to a Pulitzer prize. "Now, go and get some rest. Maybe by tomorrow you and Ben can come back to the office. Right now, the water's still too high."

Kate hung up, closed her eyes, and leaned her head back against the wall. She wasn't sure she could move, even if she wanted to.

"Long day?" Peter's voice sounded close to her ear, and Kate smiled without opening her eyes.

"Long week," she said, taking a deep breath and straightening up to look at him. He'd put on clean clothes, and a Galveston Police Department cap covered hair she knew needed washing as much as hers did. She frowned, suddenly embarrassed by her own filthy clothes and matted hair.

"Say the word and I'll go get your bag," he said, as though he could read her mind. "I figured you'd want to clean up once you got done filing your story."

She smiled and shook her head. "I don't suppose you found a portable shower on your excursion."

"No, but I just ran into Vasquez, and he says he thinks they'll have water restored to this part of the island by tomorrow.

Kate groaned. "Sounds like I'll have to make do with wet wipes."

She pushed herself off the wall, then paused. She looked up at him, the question she couldn't bring herself to ask filling her eyes.

"We found him," Peter said softly. "It's over."

Relief flooded through her. A dread she hadn't realized she still carried lifted like the remnants of Hurricane Julio blowing over the horizon. She threw her good arm around Peter and buried her face in his chest. She didn't care who might be looking.

Galveston residents emerge to muddy mess

Julio's flooding crippled utilities, inundated most of the island | By Kate Bennett

Less than twenty-four hours after Hurricane Julio washed over Galveston, Annette Wilkins sat on the steps of Ball High School, smoking a cigarette. Her tousled grey hair and bloodshot eyes testified to the harrowing night she passed in the city's makeshift shelter.

"It was terrifying," said Wilkins, 68. "I've lived here all my life and I've never experienced anything like that. We thought the building would collapse on top of us."

Wilkins took shelter in the school's cafeteria with about 300 other island residents, who chose not to leave their homes until it was too late to escape across the causeway. Many of them lived in neighborhoods near the bay, where the floodwaters rose the fastest and the highest. Wilkins is still waiting to see what's left of the home she's lived in for the last 30 years.

"I've heard the water might have gotten as high as the roof," she said. "If that's true, I've got nothing to go back to."

Hurricane Julio's floodwaters submerged thousands of homes and businesses when they washed over Galveston.

At the storm's height, water covered about three-quarters of the island. At least five people are missing. Three others are confirmed dead, although officials have yet to publicly identify them.

"This is a disaster of historic proportions, but it could have been much worse," said Stephen Rush, Galveston's emergency management director. "Thankfully, most residents evacuated, and the ones who didn't found shelter before the water got too high."

One victim drowned in his car. Two others died in their homes. Before the phone lines went down, police dispatchers fielded dozens of calls from residents forced to flee into their attics.

The water remains too high in many places to search for survivors, but Police Chief Sam Lugar said his officers will go house-to-house as soon as they can. Lugar expects troops with the Texas National Guard to arrive tomorrow to help with search and rescue efforts.

The flooding also incapacitated the city's utilities. Officials say it could take weeks for them to restore basic services like power and water. Teams from power companies across the southeast are headed to Galveston to make repairs. City crews are working to get water treatment plants back online.

Until then, Mayor Matthew Hanes said he would not allow residents to come home.

"I know people are anxious to check on their houses, but for now, it's just not safe," he said.

Hanes strongly encouraged anyone still on the island to leave, but he stopped short of trying to force them to board the buses arriving tomorrow.

Annette Wilkins at first said she would not go until she had a chance to see her house. But she changed her mind when she learned it could take days for the water to recede. She vowed to return as soon as she could to start cleaning up and making repairs.

"I know it looks bad now," she said, waving a hand at the mud soaked and litter strewn landscape outside the high school. "But we'll get this island put back together before you know it. No storm's ever beaten us. Surviving is in our DNA."

Chapter 28

Peter stood in the door of the police chief's office and watched as Lugar pored over a copy of the *Gazette* spread out on his desk. He could tell from the section that his boss was reading Kate's story. Lugar looked up reluctantly when Peter knocked on the open door.

"What can I do for you, Detective Johnson?"

Lugar looked slightly less annoyed than usual. Peter almost hated to ruin his good mood.

"I figured it was time we had that talk, sir," he said, easing into a chair in front of the chief's desk.

Lugar sighed and sat back. He squinted at Peter for several long moments before responding.

"Before the storm, I hoped you might change your mind," he said. "But after everything that happened, I knew you wouldn't."

Peter assumed Lugar had come to that conclusion. He'd only waited to bring it up until the initial flurry of storm recovery had passed because he didn't want to make Lugar's job any more difficult than it already was. But now that four weeks had passed, he didn't see a need to put it off any longer.

"I love her," he said simply. "Nothing's going to change that."

Lugar scowled and stabbed at the newspaper with his stubby finger. "She's a good reporter, I'll give you that. Isn't it about time she moved on to the *Houston Chronicle*? Then there'd be no need for us to have this conversation."

Peter smiled. "That would be great, but I can't control when she gets a job offer. And this is only partly about her."

Lugar narrowed his eyes. "If you're going to work for another agency, it had better be outside Galveston County."

"I'm getting out of police work altogether."

Lugar exhaled a heavy sigh. "I would try to talk you out of it, but I suppose I'd just be wasting my time."

"I'm afraid so."

The chief leaned over the desk and crossed his arms. "You're a great detective. I hate to lose you. I hope Ms. Bennett appreciates your sacrifice."

Peter smiled. Kate knew nothing about his plans, but she would before the night was over. He'd find out then whether he'd made the right choice.

Julio's stench still hung in the air, a mixture of mildew, dead fish, and decay. It permeated everything. Kate had almost gotten used to it. But as she drove down Bayou Shore Drive, the stench grew so intense it made her eyes water. Immediately after the storm, a layer of slime coated every surface Julio's floodwaters had touched. It dried weeks ago and now crunched under her tires as she rolled slowly past forlorn houses.

Piles of soggy furniture, carpet, and drywall filled every front yard. Kate pulled up next to one of the tallest piles and stepped out of her car. Carl Neal waved to her from his front porch.

"You'll have to move that if the dump truck makes a pass," he called, pointing at her car.

"I thought they were supposed to come by here yesterday." Kate trudged up the steps until she was face-to-face with the man she'd helped Peter rescue.

"They were," he grumbled. "That stuff's been sitting out there for days. Be sure to put that in your story."

Kate followed him inside. The week before, a volunteer group from a church on the mainland had helped the couple tear out drywall and rip up ruined flooring. The house now had the feel of a boxy skeleton. Box fans pushed the heavy air across the exposed studs.

"At least this cool front should help to dry everything out," Kate said.

Julio had moved north, dragging a wet blanket behind him. The last four weeks had passed in muggy misery. But the first breath of a cool breeze had blown over the island overnight, with the promise of fall temperatures by evening. She stepped out the back door and waved to Gigi, who was scrubbing what looked like a set of ornamental vases in a tub full of soapy water. Gigi waved back but kept scrubbing.

The tent where the couple had slept for the last two weeks filled the back corner of the small yard.

"I don't know how much longer the city's going to let you stay here," Kate said, turning back to where Carl stood in his empty living room. "They've started talking about enforcing the 'no camping' ordinances."

"They should stop flapping their jaws and start issuing permits. I'm ready to put this place back together as soon as they give us the green light."

"So you're just going to rebuild? What about raising the house?"

"The city says we don't have to."

"But if we get another storm like Julio, you'll have to do this all over again."

Carl waved his hand dismissively. "That was a 100-year storm. None of us will ever see anything like Julio again."

Kate pressed her lips together to contain her reply. She knew better than to argue. Most people shared his perspective about the likelihood of future storm damage. That was partly why city officials opted not to require elevation for most houses. Homeowners simply needed a permit to start rehanging drywall.

"Did you find someone to do the work?" she asked.

"Nah, I'm going to do it myself," he said. "It's not that hard. And Gigi can help. We make a pretty good team."

Kate grinned. She couldn't argue with that. The couple had faced Julio's devastation and the long slog of recovery with a single-minded resolve.

"What's your secret?"

Carl shrugged. "I have no idea. I just know I couldn't do anything without her."

A cool breeze blew Kate's hair away from her face as she sat on her favorite window sill. It felt like a tall glass of ice water after an afternoon at the beach. Long shadows sliced across the street below her. It was as eerily quiet as the day Julio made landfall. All the downtown businesses remained shuttered, and only a handful of residents had returned to their apartments.

After living for two weeks at the newspaper office, Kate had welcomed the chance to come back home, even though she had no hot water and no refrigerator. The lingering stench of rotting food had left an indelible mark on its insides, and she'd persuaded the landlord to throw it out. But it was taking longer than she expected to get a new one. She'd survived thanks to a cooler borrowed from Peter.

They'd spent almost every evening of the last two weeks together. The undercurrent of tension that permeated their relationship before the storm had given way to an easy camaraderie. It had taken Kate several days to put a name to a feeling she'd never experienced: contentment. She tried to take every day as an unexpected gift and not look beyond the next sunrise. That's when her newfound sea of tranquility got choppy. They hadn't talked about the future since the night Julio made landfall. But Kate knew they'd have to face reality soon.

At Peter's soft knock, she hopped down from her perch and trotted to the door. She flung it open, and the unmistakable scent of garlic and butter wafted over her.

"Is that dinner?" she gasped, her eyes flitting from Peter's grinning face to the bulging plastic bags hanging from each of his hands.

"Gino's is back in business," he said. "Well, not officially, but they're offering takeout for first responders for the next few days while they get their kitchen back in shape."

"I guess having friends in high places has its benefits," Kate said with a smirk as she took a bag and ushered him inside.

He dropped a quick kiss on her forehead as he passed, sending goosebumps cascading down her arms.

"I know we're still enjoying the novelty of electricity, but tonight calls for something special," he said, pulling two tall pillar candles, a tablecloth, and a bottle of wine from his bag.

Suspicion crackled at the edges of Kate's mind. "What's the occasion?"

"If you pepper me with questions, your shrimp Alfredo will get cold," he said with a wink.

Squelching the urge to demand an answer, she gathered silverware and glasses while he spread the cloth on her small kitchen table and lit the candles. They ate slowly, savoring the culinary comfort only heavy doses of butter and cream can provide. Kate told him about her visit with the Neals, and he recounted the latest developments in several cases of price gouging the chief had assigned him to investigate.

When she couldn't eat another bite, she set down her fork and pushed away her plate.

"Alright," she said. "You've kept me waiting long enough."

Peter's eyes widened, and he burst out laughing. Heat flushed Kate's cheeks. She tried not to smile.

"You know what I mean," she said, lobbing her wadded up napkin across the table at his chest. "What's the big secret?"

Still chuckling, Peter wiped at the corners of his eyes. Then he reached across the table and grasped both her hands in his. He took a deep breath.

"I gave Lugar my resignation today."

Kate sucked in a breath. She tried to pull her hands back, but he held them tight.

"You can't do that," she stammered. "I would never ask you to do that."

"I know. That's why I didn't tell you until now. I've actually been thinking about this for months."

His words acted as an emergency brake to her spinning thoughts. For months? She stared at him, speechless.

"My job was an obstacle, but only as long as I let it be," he said.

"But you love your job," she said, unable to hide the tremble in her voice.

"No, you love your job," he murmured. "And I would never ask you to give it up. Especially not when I had a much better plan."

Kate swallowed against the lump in her throat. "What are you going to do?"

"I'm going to the mission field."

His words felt like a slap in the face. "Overseas?" she finally squeaked.

He chuckled and squeezed her hands. "Only for quick trips, and probably not that often. I'm going to serve as a security consultant for missionary sending agencies."

"What does that mean?"

"I'll assess potential threats, train teams heading to new assignments, and step in if anyone gets in trouble."

"What kind of trouble?"

He shrugged, then grinned. "Nothing too dangerous. I'm sure I'll mostly be bored to tears."

She frowned. "That sounds terrible."

Peter's fingers tightened around hers. "Bored to tears, but happy. Deliriously happy."

Kate's breath caught in her throat. Her eyes filled with tears, and she jumped to her feet. Before she could take a step, Peter stood and pulled her to him. She wrapped her arms around his neck and pressed her cheek to his.

After several moments, she whispered the only thing she could think to say. "Me, too."

Afterthoughts

From the moment I began writing Kate and Peter's story, I wanted to give them a hurricane to live through. No narrative based in Galveston would be complete without one. My encounter with Hurricane Ike was a formative experience for me, both personally and professionally. Of course, I didn't have a vengeful murderer hunting me, but many other events in this story are based on things I saw and reported on. Students of hurricane history will even notice that the track and effects of the fictitious Hurricane Julio are strikingly similar to Ike.

That storm made landfall directly over Galveston as a Category 3 storm on September 13, 2008. For about a year, it felt like the island would never be the same. But by the two-year anniversary, few signs of the devastation remained. Ike taught me that humans are remarkably resilient. And it echoed the spiritual renewal we experience when we're "washed by the water."

Fans of Needtobreathe will recognize that phrase as the title of their hit song by the same name. It came out in 2007 and became a number one hit just a few months before Ike spun to life off the coast of Africa. It perfectly captured the message of death and rebirth I wanted this story to convey.

Thank you to my beta readers, who helped polish the story before I unleashed it on the world.

Thanks to my family for helping me keep my weekly writing night date, and for cheering me on!

And thanks be to God, without whom nothing is possible.

About the Author

Leigh Jones started her writing career in elementary school with a story about an enterprising hamster making a bid to take over the world. But after college, she set all dreams of fiction writing aside to chase the daily adrenaline rush of seeing her byline in print. She covered school board meetings, city council intrigue, and the occasional heart-warming feature for several daily newspapers in Texas. She even covered a few murders and one very big hurricane.

She never considered returning to fiction until she became an editor and no longer got to see her byline on the front page. Facing serious adrenaline withdrawals, she began plotting her first novel. Eight years later, it finally hit the virtual store shelves as *Look The Other Way*, book one in the Galveston Crime Scene series. *Adverse Events*, the second book in the series, came out a year later.

When she's not writing fiction, Leigh works as the executive features editor at WORLD News Group, a national Christian media outlet that practices biblically objective journalism. There she shepherds long-form story projects for print and podcast.

She lives with her husband and daughter near Houston.